The Goddess of Undo

A Novel

Kat Drennan

KC Publications

The Goddess of Undo

ISBN 9780999671405 (paperback)

KCPublications
Ojai, California

More Books by Kat Drennan

A Classic Car Romance - Romantic Suspense
Book One - Mint Condition
Book Two - One of a Kind
Book Three – Hotrod Lincoln
Book Four – Five Window Pickup Coming Soon

Love on the Faultline Collection
Book 1 in Love on the Faultline Series: Borrego Moon
Love on the Faultline Historical:
Lies In White Satin
Love on the Faultline Standalone novel:
High Tide

Serpent's Coil Historical Time-Travel
The Cloisonné Brooch
Lesidi's Coin
The Serpent's Coil

Speculative Women's Fiction - Fantasy
MONARCH – FIRST MIGRATION

Award-Winning Women's Fiction
The Goddess of Undo

DEDICATION

To daughter/caregivers everywhere.
Stay strong and know you were loved.

Contents

ACKNOWLEDGMENTS

ACCORDING TO MENTAL HEALTH EXPERTS and the Centers for Disease Control, about 4 to 5 million people in the United States have some degree of dementia, including Alzheimer's and other forms of mental decline. When we consider their husbands, wives, children, brothers, sisters, and friends, nearly everyone in the country is affected in some way.

When my mother slipped into dementia, she was already caring for a husband with Korsakoff syndrome, yet another form of mental illness. Much like Betty and Evie in *The Goddess of Undo*, we performed a dance of denial and heartbreak until we reached out to resources in our community and found relief. A heartfelt thank you goes out to the manager and caregivers at Casa Blanca Alzheimer's care (now Autumn Years) in Ojai, California, for their loving support during the end phase of her life. They are angels on earth. (And no, they did not let her get out during a fire!)

I would also like to thank my editor, Mayo Morley, and the members of the Ojai Novel Writers Group (aka, The Blockheads) Nancy Decker, Sharon Hall, Roslyn Hammer, John Hannah, John Myhre, Theresa Rooney, and Terry Talent who helped me craft a novel that I hope will resonate with anyone who has had to care for someone with dementia.

And finally, sincere thanks go to Catherine Ann Jones for her workshop and book: The Way of Story, which was an invaluable help in creating Evie's character and journey.

1 Implosion

"911. Is this an emergency?"
Betty waited for her thoughts to start.
"Hello? Is someone there?"
"I'm hungry and Vern is on the floor."
"What's your name?"
"Betty. All I have is chocolate cake."
"Is Vern conscious?"
"His eyes are open. The blood is dry now."
"Did he fall?"
"Yes…and broke the thing, the darn, the pot."
"When did he fall?"
"Not. I don't…"
"Betty, an officer is on the way. Will you stay on the phone with me?"
"The rug is soggy."
"Is anyone else there with you?"
"No one."
"Okay. Don't worry. Someone is on the way."

Betty let the talk dangle from the yellow box and trailed her fingers along the walls as she made her way from the kitchen to the bedroom, trying to remember when she'd last got out of bed. Was it yesterday, or in another life? Nothing made sense except for the soft *zhumm zhumm* pumping at her neck that kept her going, though she didn't know why.

A book lay open on the nightstand. Yes. She had been reading her favorite book when the words stopped coming. Betty pressed her palm to a page and closed her eyes.

"Betty!"

His voice startled her. She thought he was gone.

"My head hurts," he moaned.

She should go to his room, but she didn't want to see.

She pressed her palm on the book again.

The image of a woman's face surfaced in Betty's mind. Emma. Emma Harte still lived inside the words that Betty could no longer read. She wiped her eyes with the back of her hand. She couldn't get the words, but she knew the story. Betty straightened in the chair, lifted her chin, and rested it lightly on the tops of her knuckles, half a smile playing on her lips.

She gazed at the back of a picture frame on the dresser and the door to her memory opened a little wider. She didn't have to turn the frame around to see Vern as he had been—elegantly tall, wavy hair oiled and combed close to his head, manicured nails, and cufflinks of gold and jade showing just below the sleeve of a silk suit they'd bought in Hong Kong. Five suits, one for each day of the week and *Sansabelts* for the weekend. A fitting match for the executive suite. A fitting match for Compton College's *Glamour Girl*.

Then, like a naughty ghost, another image slid over her husband's face. A younger man in Levi's and a V-necked T-shirt, toasty brown hair curled haphazard across his forehead. His eyes sparkled blue and full of mischief, a pack of Lucky Strikes rolled up in the sleeve at his shoulder. Shoulders she had once clutched against her own. Frank Sinatra had crooned in the background wherever they went. Jimmy had looked just like him. Evie looked just like Jimmy.

Betty's face warmed. Thinking of Jimmy still did that to her.

"Tch." Memories were easy. Images crowded in even when she didn't want them to. Words were a different matter. The more Betty needed a word, the farther it fled down a winding path she could never seem to follow. Naughty children, ringing the doorbell and running away.

Her stomach rumbled, urging her out of her chair. She shuffled back to the kitchen, to the box, *the cold thing*, and opened the door, but it was the same as it had been the last time she looked. Nothing there but a few pickle jars and a half eaten round of chocolate cake. *"Dammit."*

"Betty? Where are you? Who are you talking to?" Vern's voice sounded weaker, dried up, like her own. She should go to him, but there was nothing she could do and she didn't want to see his eyes.

"No one," she said, annoyed more with herself than with him. She should have done something long ago. She should have told the truth. Asked for help. Something Emma Harte would never do, but Emma was just in a book. Betty was in the real world. Most of the time.

She riffled the refrigerator shelves, found a familiar pink carton, and opened it with wobbly fingers. The fuzzy-junked lid fell, face down, on the floor. "Blahhhh!"

Her stomach growled again, pulling into a knot. She was going to have to tell. She *had* told. Someone. She ran her fingers through her tangled hair and then saw it hanging against the wall. She pulled the thing up by its twisty cord.

"Hello?" she asked, hearing nothing on the other end. *Where did that woman go?* Never mind. She pressed the big number one on the touch pad.

The voice that answered should have been her daughter's, but instead it was that man in the machine. Pressure built inside her chest and pushed out a cough that hurt all the way to her ears. She banged the thing back on its hook.

"Ma'am?" A voice boomed inside the house, then two men in big yellow coats with clumpy shoulders shuffled through the front door. Betty pulled her Christmas sweater over her nightgown and stood in her bedroom doorway as they strapped Vern on a cart and took him away.

"Where's Betty?" she heard him ask as the last man out the door turned to her.

"You'll be all right here alone? Is there someone you can call?"

Betty lifted a shoulder. There was only the answer man at Evie's.

"Yessss," she whispered, ending in a wheeze. She would try again, after Vern was safe.

She went back to the cold box and scooped a piece of dry chocolate cake into her hand, grabbed a fork from a pile in the sink and stuck it in her purse, and followed the men outside, licking sweet brown goo off her fingers.

In the passenger seat of the red Cadillac, she fished lipstick out of her purse, pulled the visor down, and ran smooth color over her lips. She flipped the visor back into place, and waited in the quiet. "What is taking you so long?" she asked out loud, and then realized her mistake.

"*Goddammit!*"

She got out and went around to the steering wheel side. She hadn't driven in a long time, and her feet could barely touch the pedals, but the steering wheel felt right in her hands and they knew what to do. At the turn of the key, the engine thrummed up in her ears and the Cadillac took her away, following the big yellow truck.

❧

A woman in a white hat helped Betty sit in a wheelchair and guided her down a hall with a shiny floor. "What's your name, dear?"

She pointed to where the men in yellow coats lifted Vern out of the ambulance. "Betty. That's my Vern down there."

Her voice came out like gravel and tar. She had to push hard to make the words, and her chest burned. The woman wheeled her to a high counter. A yellow-coat man wrote on a clipboard, and then set it on the counter with a clatter.

"That's her, the one I told you about," he said, nodding his head at Betty. "You drove yourself?"

Betty smiled at him with the side of her face that worked. "The Cadillac did it."

She straightened and craned her neck to see a man in green pajamas cover Vern with a thin blanket and wheel him down the hall. The back of Vern's head was crusted brown. He wore nothing but his underwear. Her chest tightened a moment, and then sent her in to a fit of ragged coughing.

"That's him," she said again, pointing. Her face burned hot. "I can't find his pants."

The woman talked to another pajama man over Betty's head. "Don't worry about it. I'll finish checking her in." And then to Betty, she said, "We'll see what we can do. In the meantime, can we call someone for you?"

"Evie."

"Is that your daughter?"

Betty nodded.

"Do you know her number?"

Betty looked into that place in the corner of her forehead where all the thoughts came from. "One."

The nurse stared at her. "One?"

After a moment, she patted Betty's shoulders with both hands then reached for her purse. "Maybe we can find it in here."

Betty stiffened and held tight to her bag, a loud rumble rolled up from her stomach. "I'm starving to death."

The woman stepped back. "Okay. We'll get you something to eat, and then we'll check you out. You seem a little flushed." She leaned into the counter, catching the attention of a lady in a pink apron. "Get me a case worker."

She spoke softly, as if she didn't want Betty to hear, but she could hear quite well. In fact, she heard things nobody else did. It was the talk she had trouble with. She pushed out of the chair until she could see the woman behind the counter too. "And get me a hamburger sandwich."

2 Shipwrecked

I passed a red Cadillac in the parking lot as I headed toward the emergency room. Was that my mother's old golf hat in the window? I backed up, stopped behind the car, and got out. The doors were locked. I pressed my forehead to the tinted glass and peered inside. There were no personal items I could identify, only a large chunk of chocolate cake melting on the dashboard. *What the hell?*

Inside, I bypassed the reception desk and followed the directions the caseworker had given me. When I found 233A, I peered through the half-open door. The room was dark and cool and smelled of strong antiseptic. Vertical slivers of light diffused to bars of gray across two hospital beds, one empty.

My eyes adjusted to the dim light and there he was. My stepdad—finance director, international steel buyer, world traveler, Hong Kong suit wearer, country-club member, lifelong drinker of bitter Manhattans and sweet success.

He lay facing away from me. The green hospital gown gaped open exposing his backside and a blue plastic diaper twisted between his legs. Panic gathered at the back of my throat and I swallowed it down.

At the sound of my footsteps, he turned and those Norwegian blue eyes met mine, widening for a moment before he relaxed and dropped his bruised head to the pillow. He looked like he'd been on the losing end of a street brawl. A bandage swung free from a nostril, exposing the cruel deformity of a recent basil cell surgery. He peered back at me; his expression segued from fear to guilt, a child who had wet his bed. Finally, the light came up in his eyes.

"How'd you know I was here?"

If he didn't know how I knew, he was in no condition to hear the long version: That I'd been calling their number for two days after my mother left a cryptic message: "Mom" on my answering machine. I had already planned to drive to San Diego if I couldn't get through today, but a social worker called during an urgent product meeting at work.

I did my best to get past the initial shock and find a smile, and gave him the short version: "They called me." I tipped my head toward the doorway. "Sorry it took so long."

Vern's brows drew together under a forehead mottled with footprints of years of golf without the protection of a hat. He stretched his arm out to me as far as he could before a restraint tied to the bedrail stopped him. A small can of *7-Up* sat precariously close to the edge of a rolling tray next to the bed. A Flex Straw, bent and bitten, poked up out of the can.

"Want some?" he asked, always the gentleman. His elbow bumped the can into tottering motion. He pulled the sheet up again, eyes wide.

I stopped the can, moved closer, and patted the loose bandage back across his ravaged nose. The fear in his eyes stripped my courage and left my throat aching in its place.

"Maybe later," I said, pushing through for his sake.

"Where's Betty?" His voice came weak, like a child wanting his mother. He fiddled with the bandage until he had it loose again.

"She's nearby. I'm sure she'll be fine." I had no idea. Not yet. But it seemed an appropriate answer for a man in his state. I sat on the edge of the bed and pulled the sheet over his backside as best I could without making a fuss. "I'm going to see her after I visit with you for a while."

"Can I come?" He struggled to sit. "Can you get these off?" He held his tied wrists out to me. "I have to go to the bathroom."

I loosened the straps—*who ties an old man up like a criminal?*—and helped him up, steadying him as he shuffled across the floor, gown gaping open; his bare thighs slick with accidental pee. A zipper-row of black stitches poked out of a purple bruise on the back of his head.

My heart pulled itself into a tight little ball, cold and achy. Forty years ago—*could it have been that long?*—I couldn't wait for the weekend before Christmas when I'd go to Mom and Vern's to open presents—a full week before any of my cousins got theirs. I'd dance on Vern's feet to Tony Bennett and Thelonius Monk, and my mother would show off her latest bauble with her trim, fashionable flair. Now—the weekend before Christmas, year 2000—the dreaded millennium—my world had been Y2K'd. Big time.

Vern appeared in the bathroom doorway holding the diaper in place at his hips. "I want to go home."

Some people said the world was coming to an end in a week. Maybe it was happening right now. I refastened the sticky tabs on the diaper. "Where are your clothes?"

"In there." He pointed an elbow in the direction of the closet, still holding on to the diaper. "There should be six pair of slacks, six dress shirts in there."

This he recited, standing momentarily erect, as if giving direction at a staff meeting. The hospital room closet was empty except for a paper sack tucked into the corner. I pulled out a pair of Velcro-strapped shoes stuffed with dirty socks, a bloodied T-shirt and a raggedy pair of Jockey shorts. He'd been shipwrecked. Abandoned without so much as an extra pair of pants. The weight of the moment hit me hard in the gut. I'd seen this coming a year ago and tried to get my mother to take action. *He shouldn't be drinking. He shouldn't be driving. He shouldn't be left unsupervised.* But she wouldn't have any of it. *He's just an old fart,* she told me. *He only makes right turns.*

Jockey shorts in hand, I guided him back to the bed. "This is all you've got?"

"That's how he came." I jumped nearly out of my skin and turned to see a heavyset woman in flowery hot-pink scrubs that strained over her belly. She dropped a clipboard noisily into a plastic holder on the front of the door, and charged in. "I need him out of here by five p.m. You his daughter?" she asked, barking like a drill sergeant.

"Yes—I—Five p.m.?" It was closing on noon already.

Vern touched my elbow and leaned close to my ear. "Where's my car?" he asked, his voice a rasping whisper.

"He should be in a 24-hour facility, not here."

"Sure. Right. I'll get right on it." *Like I have a clue where to start.* "His wife is here too, somewhere…" The case worker had told me over the phone that my mother might be transferred to the convalescent hospital. I'd yet to find out where that was. My stomach flopped on its back. If it had a tongue, it would be hanging out. It was lunchtime. How was I supposed to get Vern situated before dinner?

"I need at least a day. I don't know what's going on here, let alone how to fix it."

"Five o'clock," she repeated, her chin dimpling under a hardened grin. "And he'll be restrained until you pick him up." She wagged the straps at me. "He wanders."

Vern touched my elbow again. "Where's Betty? Have you seen her? Where's my car?"

The aide slid a clean diaper between his thighs. His eyes shone wet and bright inside drooping, red-lined lids. The bandage swung off his nose again as she wrestled him back into the bed and replaced the straps. She gave me the stink eye, tossed the dirty diaper in a stainless steel waste can, and stalked out of the room.

Vern watched the trashcan lid *wip-wap* back and forth until at last the room was quiet. "Where's my car?" he asked again, softly.

I covered my gaping mouth with my hand and sucked in air through my fingers. "I'm getting it now," I lied, the first of many I would tell him. "I'll be back soon."

"Don't go." The anguish in his words tore at me. How could I leave him in this state? But I had no choice.

"I've got to check up on Betty, and then I'll take you home with me." I had no idea what I was going to do, but it seemed like as reasonable a plan as any.

"*Evie?*" he asked, realizing it was me for the first time.

I went to him, brushed his kinky gray hair back across his head.

"How'd you know I was here?"

I hugged him close. I wanted to crawl into his lap and be rocked and told everything would be all right. At the same time, I had the feeling that's what he wanted from me. The truth was, we had never been that close. But, it was obvious the baton was being been passed, and as far as I could tell, I was the only one in line to grab it. I was sure once I talked to my mother, we could come up with a solution for Vern.

"You be good now. And stay in bed," I told him. "I'll be back soon to take you home."

Except for the sounds of the big woman wrestling someone in the next room, the nurse's station was quiet. No relatives visiting with flowers and presents, no doctors giving instructions. Just old men in wheelchairs, chins on their chests, pushed by orderlies in drab, green outfits. A white-haired man in a wheelchair sat muttering softly to his feet. He'd been kicked to the curb and forgotten.

I promised myself, no matter what else happened, at least *that* would not happen to Vern.

Back at the reception desk I asked about my mother. An ancient survivor in a pink striped apron riffled through papers on a clipboard. "It looks like she's gone."

"Gone? What do you mean, gone?" I was running out of patience with clipboards.

"Checked out," she said, flipping another page. "Wait. Here she is—transferred. To the convalescent hospital." She looked up and responded to my frown. "It's not far from here. Only a few miles."

Miles? She smiled sweetly and handed me a photocopied map. "Right down the road."

As in Yellow Brick.

3 Boomerville

A rumpled version of my mother lay in the hospital bed, covers drawn to her chin, pale cheeked and lopsided bed hair. I barely recognized her.

The bed on the right was occupied by skin-covered bones drawn up into fetal position, shocks of white hair fleeing a blotchy pink scalp. In the only chair in the room, a middle-aged man talked softly into a cell phone.

Yes, he'd be leaving soon. Yes, he'd stop for milk. No, no changes.

In the bed on the right, another woman ate greedily, complaining around the food in her mouth. An orderly ignored her, cleaning the bedside commode.

Don't pay any attention to the people behind the curtains. Just get Mom back home, then figure out what to do with Vern. Not on my to-do list when I crawled out of bed this morning, but as a software test engineer, I was good with broken things.

I added my purse and keys to a pile of clutter on the commode, and sat next to her on the bed. "Hi Mama."

"Hi sweetie." Her words pinged back from a forgotten corridor inside my heart. I sucked in my bottom lip by reflex.

But when she pulled me into her signature awkward hug, I squeezed back, and slid my arm behind her shoulders.

Under a thin hospital gown she wore her heavily decorated Christmas sweater along with a pair of red Isotoner gloves, one of which had her ring and baby finger crammed into the same hole.

"Are you cold?" I adjusted the fingers in the glove and looked into a pair of tired eyes, glossy with fever and something I hadn't seen in them before. She had always been distant. She was practiced at it. But this was different. It reminded me of the time I looked over a stone wall at the back of our property straight into the face of a crouching bobcat. It scared the crap out of both of us, but neither of us moved a muscle. We were frozen, locked in our own fears, until I blinked and the cat bounded away, leaving my heart racing.

My mother broke the connection, making a valiant attempt at recovery with a familiar lift of her chin as she adjusted her posture to *Betty*. "I'm ready to go home," she said, releasing me. She swiped at a tear ready to spill and forced a smile. "You look…tired."

"It's a long drive from Santa Barbara at this time of day." I didn't tell her it took three days for the social worker to find me, or about the deadline at work my boss had to make up for, or about the encounter with road shrapnel on the 405 Freeway coming through Oceanside, the extra hour for tire repair, or the encounter with Vern.

I brushed a matted curl of hair off her forehead, her skin hot and clammy under my fingertips. My mother had been a capable woman, but Vern had always been in charge. I had the sense that life as she knew it had just taken a wrong turn and she had skidded off the high road. She wasn't ready for it. Neither of us were. Instinct told me to take this one step at a time.

I heard a rustle and looked around as a tall woman in a sharply pressed white coat swept confidently into the room. I swallowed the lump jammed in my throat and helped my mother slide to a more upright position, straightening the hospital gown that had bunched up over her sweater. The woman closed the curtains around the bed to give us privacy and stood at the end of the bed. "You must be Betty's daughter."

I nodded, my throat suddenly dry. She moved a silver pen across the pages of a black leather notebook as she spoke, then she turned her full attention to us. "We're so glad we found you, aren't we Betty?"

Mom nodded, pulling the covers back to her chin.

"People in her condition usually have an ID bracelet or something," said the woman, glancing at me as she moved in closer. "We were about to turn her over to Senior Services."

Had the temperature in the room suddenly dropped, or was it my own skin that chilled? What did she mean, *her condition*? I glanced at Mom, who had tightened her grip on the blankets. She lowered her chin and rolled her eyes away from me.

"It's okay, Mom. Everything's going to be all right."

Everything is going to shit.

I looked back at the doctor. "My phone number was in her wallet, right next to her driver's license. Is it so hard to look in a wallet?"

The woman straightened. "*I'm* the staff psychiatrist, I didn't do her intake." She shifted the notebook to her other arm and extended her hand to me, forcing a smile. "Marion Clark."

I took it and stopped, mid shake. "Psychiatrist?"

My mother continued to shrink into her pillow.

"Your mom has pneumonia and she shows some signs of impairment. Sometimes when older patients are ill, they get a little confused. Chances are that when she feels better, it will disappear and she'll be back to normal."

Older? I hadn't thought of my mother as *older*. Seventeen years older than me couldn't be that old, could it? This latest in the successive events of the day broke over me like a wave of suffocating white water, holding me down; my thoughts struggled to find some air.

"Impaired? Like, how?"

"I was just about to administer the MMSE," said Clark. "It's a simple mental evaluation. You'll need to step out in the hall."

My mother eyed the doctor, her expression both apprehensive and curious. I remembered when she had her first angioplasty. She had been fascinated by watching the monitor as the instrument worked its way through her veins and into her heart. She had a pretty good attitude about the whole thing, considering the possible outcome. Despite her confusion, my mom was definitely there somewhere inside the hospital gown, Christmas sweater, and gloves. It was strange. I had only begun to know her in the last few years, during encounters in hospital rooms like this one. She was a victim of bad genes—her mother had died at fifty. Mom had beaten her by twenty years. But this was…*different.*

"Okay," I said, finally. The gravity of the situation sinking into my bones. *Okay.*

I slid my arm from around my mother's shoulders and squeezed her red-gloved hand. "I'll be right outside."

I leaned against the wall in the narrow hallway, holding my breath. I could hear my mother's replies as the psychiatrist asked questions.

"Betty, can you tell me what year it is?"

After a pause, my mother answered, very softly, "19—55?"

My heart sank a little. In 1955 I was a little kid.

"Good," said the doctor. "Do you know the season?"

"Cold."

"Very good. Now, what day of the week is it, Betty?"

I didn't hear an answer.

"That's okay. People don't always know that when they've been in the hospital for a few days."

"I think it's my birthday," Betty said, confidently.

It was December. Her birthday was in March. Same as mine. The doctor went on without commenting. I leaned harder against the wall outside the door, my hand clenched over my mouth.

"Good. Now can you tell me where you are?"

"The hospital. Where's Vern?"

"Vern is fine. He's in another room. Let's just finish up here and then your daughter can come back in, okay?"

"I'm ready to go home."

"Sure. In a few minutes. Now, Betty, I'm going to tell you three objects and I want you to say them back to me when I'm finished. Okay?"

"Okay."

"Cat. Apple. Chair."

"Cat. Apple. Chair," my mother answered, her voice getting

softer.

Whew.

"Very Good. Now I'd like you to count backward from a hundred by threes."

"Threes."

"Right. So, ninety-seven…and … what's next, Betty?"

There was a long pause, during which I held ninety-four in my thoughts as if I could help her through telepathy.

"Where's Evie?" she blurted, finally. She sounded tearful and annoyed.

"Betty, can you remember the three objects we talked about?"

Could I?

"No. My daughter is waiting for me," Betty answered, then what had begun in a sob ended in deep, phlegmy coughing.

Tears welled in my eyes. I looked to the ceiling but they spilled down my cheeks anyway. A woman from the nurse's station closed the distance between us in a couple of gliding steps and put her arm around me like a familiar aunt.

"Are you all right?"

My throat closed off on any words I might have said. I shook my head. She pulled a chair close, slid me into it, and handed me a tissue.

"I'll get you some water." She headed back to the nurse's station, sidestepping a white-haired woman in a wheelchair.

A drink of water. As if…

The wheelchair lady kept coming until the footrests bumped my leg. "Where's my son?" she asked, her voice loud and tinged with anger. "They said he would be here soon."

She was thin and pathetic in her faded nightgown. She clutched a shabby, white patent leather purse in her lap.

"I…I…don't know," I said.

The nurse returned with the water and handed it to me. "Okay Marge, back to the rec room."

She redirected the chair and I watched them navigate the narrow hall between housekeeping carts loaded with bedpans and water bottles. I pulled back inside myself like a snail whose *antlers* had been touched. This was not a place I wanted in my life. My mother definitely did not belong here. Not now, not ever.

"Evie." Mom shouted from her room. "Where did Evie go?"

"She's right outside. I have one more question, and then I'll go get her for you."

"Okay." My mother's voice mimicked the psychiatrist's placating tone. *Good for her.*

"What is this, Betty?"

"That's your time, your—*time.*"

I imagined the doctor was pointing to her wristwatch.

"All right, Betty. That's it. You did just fine."

"I didn't know some of the words." Her tone changed from bewildered to angry. "I know the *thing*, but the right word won't—*find.*"

"Don't worry. You don't have to get all the answers right."

I could hear the doctor's voice closer to the door, and then she stepped through and out into the hall.

She sat in a chair across from me. "Because she is ill," she said, snapping the pen into the clip at the top of her notebook, "I didn't do the whole test. Your mother has significant cognitive impairment. Have you noticed a decline in her mental capacity recently?"

How could I? I rarely saw my mother. She and Vern had a beautiful home, friends, and traveled often. They were in their early seventies, living their retirement dreams. We lived three hours away from each other. Since her angioplasty, I had started touching base each week, making small talk. I got down to see her whenever I could, but, I had to admit, not often enough. My kids were grown and living their own lives. I had lived on a shoestring and paid off every bill and credit card. I had started a new business and a new marriage. Everything was coming together. Finally.

This is not in the plan.

The doctor raised her eyebrows as if she could read my mind. *What? Do I fit the profile of selfish, ungrateful child? If only she knew.* I pinched my nose at my eye sockets, reserving judgment, and focused on the last few days. In phone conversations she did have a little trouble thinking of a certain word. I had joked with her about it.

"Come on, mom, spit it out." She had laughed too and said the doctor told her she may have had a mini stroke, nothing to

worry about, and the skills would come back.

Apparently, they hadn't.

I drew myself up to answer as best I could. "Now that you mention it, I guess I have noticed a change. She told me she never cooked anymore. I thought, 'oh, like, only soup or microwave' not, like, '*never*'."

How had I missed this? Why hadn't I acted? Still in the impact zone, I was drowning in waves of remorse, guilt, and fear.

The doctor stood, smiled a genuine smile, and then offered her hand. "Welcome to *Boomerville*," she said. "Her primary physician will be here soon. I'll give her the report. You know, your mom really may come back up as she recovers. We'll just have to wait and see. For now, she shouldn't be by herself."

My mouth hung open on that thought. Right. *Right.*

A nurse's aide poked her head out the next door down the hall. "Doctor, we're ready."

"Nice meeting you, Eve. Good luck." She turned away and walked into the next room.

Alone again in the hallway, I hesitated, staring at the door. My mother was on the other side waiting for me to rescue her.

My cell phone beeped inside my purse, making me jump.

I flipped it open. Robert. "Hi, babe."

I leaned in to the comforting voice of my husband.

"So what's the story?"

"Double Implosion." I took a deep breath and blew it out through puffed cheeks.

"What?"

"I've been transported to *Boomerville*."

"Come on, Eve, make some sense. Do I have to come down there and get you?" He was joking, of course. Robert tended to view life as a series of amusing challenges. I held my breath, wondering suddenly if he was up to this one.

"You know. Baby Boomers. Children of the World War II-ers? Our parents are imploding, dropping, *en masse*, and now we have to look after them." *Ha ha ha ha ha.*

There was silence on the other end of the line while Robert took this in. Once again, I held my breath. Robert and I had gotten together late in life. I was the one with all the baggage. I'd come into his life on the heels of a divorce that had devastated my bank account and my self-esteem. Since then I'd fought back from zero, and after helping him start a successful business, I felt like I was at least earning my keep. Now *this*.

"Comes with the territory," he said at last. My heart took a little leap. The old regime had taught me to fear, Robert had taught me to trust. He had said the same thing when he inherited my eighteen-year-old daughter, and he'd meant it. Turned out to be a rough road, but we all made it through.

"I'm not sure what this territory means," I said, breathing a little sigh of relief. All he wanted to know was when I was coming home.

"We've got Oxnard tomorrow, you know, the presentation to the Road Department?"

"*You've* got Oxnard. I've got one parental alien tied to a bed until I find a place to put him and the other one thinks it's 1955."

The massive chrome grill of a white '55 Buick grinned at me from a distant memory. Buicks and T-Birds and pearls and highballs—diamonds and luxury cruises and dry martinis—mauve Cadillacs with matching golf carts and crystal chandeliers—my parents had led a fairytale life without me. *Until now.*

"So, you're staying the night?"

"At this point I don't know what I'm doing."

"Okay. I'll handle this end. Just keep me posted. Love you."

I could hear the disappointment in his voice. Since the day we had gotten together four years ago, we'd never slept apart. The distance between us suddenly expanded by lightyears.

"Love you, too." I swallowed hard and ended the call.

My hand lingered on the door handle to my mother's room. My parents really had lived in the sweet spot of the American Dream. This looked like the night sweats and terror spot. If only I could hit the Undo button and roll back time, I would make the ending come out better. *If only...*

My chest swelled up like it would burst. Somewhere deep inside, a little girl keened for her mother to stay. *Big girls don't cry*, the mother answered, and the pressure popped like a balloon. I pushed back at the memories crowding my heart, put on my best smile, and opened the door.

4 Weeping Willow

"Hi Sweetie." Mom pushed herself up and arranged her face into a smile. Before I had a chance to say anything, a nurse's aide came swooping down on us.

"How about a shower, Betty?" She sang the words as if we were in some swanky spa hotel. Her nametag read "Gretta."

Mom glanced at me. Her hair, usually perfectly dyed and styled—at least that's the way I'd remembered—was flattened on one side, dark roots overdue for a touch-up.

"Sure, Mom. Go ahead. You'll probably feel better." I helped her undress and put on a hospital robe, then get settled into a plastic chair on wheels. Gretta rolled my mother down the hall and into the shower room. I realized, as the aide pushed the robe down over my mother's shoulders, that I hadn't seen her naked since I was four, maybe three years old. The memory swept over me, borne on hot steam and the ghost of a mournful song...

Weeping willow tree, weep in sympathy,
send your branches down along the ground and cover me...

I closed my eyes. I could see our old kitchen as clearly as if I were actually there.

I'm on the kitchen table, gouging another finger full of melty butter when she pulls me down into her lap.

"Okay, young lady," she says. "No more butter."

My 'jammas and toys are still in a paper bag next to the back door where she dropped them. She's in a hurry, dragging her scarf off her head and stuffing it into the bag. Her yellow hair falls loose and her cheeks are rosy.

"We have to get you clean before daddy comes home from work." My daddy comes home in the morning instead of the night like other daddies. He sometimes wants her to come to bed with him, just when I'm ready to get up. Sometimes she does and sometimes she doesn't.

I hear his Buick in the driveway and mamma and me go into the bathroom and lock the door. She turns on the water. It's cold and I squeeze past her to the back of the tub as she holds her hand in the warming water stream. Our eyes meet when we hear loud clumping from the kitchen, then louder, down the hall.

"Betty!" He rattles the bathroom door handle, then hits it real hard. "Where've you been? I've been trying to call you since two a.m."

"We're in the shower," she yells back and steps into the water.

Sparkly drops catch in the hair between her legs.

"Pretty," I say and reach for them.

She gets my toy teapot from the corner of the tub and gives it to me. "Here, Evie, play with this."

She turns me around starts sudsing me down, nearly pushing me off my feet. I hear the door rattle again.

"Stop it!" she yells. "I never heard the phone."

She's leaning against the shower wall now, shoulders hunched up and hands holding her elbows. She's shaking even though the water has warmed up.

"Then why're Evie's clothes out here, huh? You were out all night, weren't you?"

I don't like the way he sounds. He's mad at us and I don't know why. I slept at Aunt Jeri's all night, but I don't know how to say this, so I just say, "I love you, Daddy."

Mama stands very still, listening. She fingers the hair on the top of my head. "Shhhh…"

"Screwball!" he yells, and "Bitch!"

I don't know these words but they make her bite her lip and look sad. She turns away from me and pushes her head under the shower. Soapy water runs over her shoulders, down her back and over her bottom. I catch some with my little tin cup. The bubbles are shiny with rainbows all over them.

We stay in the shower for a long time. We can hear him moving in the other rooms of the house.

"Cold," I say and move to the back of the tub again.

"It's okay, sweetie," she says, keeping her voice quiet. "We'll get out in a minute."

She moves out of the cold water too and we stand close until we hear the back door bang shut. The car rumbles down the driveway then roars away.

He never even said hello to me.

Mama rushes us out of the shower and rubs me down with a towel.

I want her to hold me, but she doesn't.

I feel like crying, but I don't.

That was the last time we—my biological father, me, and my mother—were all together. Just a short, confusing vignette, buried somewhere deep in a child's indelible scrapbook of memories.

Reliving it from afar, it wasn't so confusing. I'd done my share of staying too long in the shower or long enough at work to avoid a confrontation. Baggage from my first attempt at marriage.

From behind a thin veil of modest politeness, I watched the water sluice over her back, seeing into my future. Me in seventeen years? Not bad. She had never been overweight. Or tan. In fact, except for some bruisy veins on her legs, she looked a lot like I did now. It didn't seem appropriate, but somehow I couldn't help staring. This was my mother. Naked.

She took the news that she wouldn't be released from the hospital today with a scrunched-up face. Her fever was elevated and pneumonia was not a disease to mess with. With her taken care of for the night, I made an executive decision based entirely on my gut. I called an Alzheimer's care facility a few blocks from my home in Ojai, and was lucky to find a bed available for the time being that could be available permanently, if I wanted. Permanently. As in, once they go in, they never come out.

She took that news with a resigned shoulder lift. I promised her I'd be back in the morning. Another six hours of driving, but I was sleeping in my own bed tonight if it was only for a few hours.

5 *Fly With Me*

Betty woke to a semi-darkened room. Gray curtains were partially pulled around her bed on both sides, leaving the end open. A TV stared blankly at her from its anchor on the ceiling.

New elements of her life fell into place.

The hospital.

Pneumonia.

The medicine must be working because her chest didn't hurt so much and she could take a full breath. Evie would be back soon to take her home. The clock on the wall behind the TV said … said … well, it wasn't morning yet, she knew that much.

Someone snored softly on the other side of the curtain, she could hear a voice rise sharply from some distant room, and then, just, quiet. She was alone with her thoughts.

Her thoughts. *Finally.*

It had seemed like days since she had occupied her own body and her own mind. She had been wandering, dreamlike, knocking on doors that would not open with someone else's hands on the ends of her wrists. Her mind had been circling, rising up to the surface, glimpsing unfamiliar territory, then diving down, down to the safety of the memory anchors of her past. But right now, at least in this moment, she was *here*. Thank *gawd*.

She felt along the fingers of her hands, safely covered in her red gloves. Yes, her rings were there, the Zirconia solitaire she wore on cruises and had taken to wearing all the time, and the aquamarine floating in a nest of filigreed gold sea foam. Yes, her knuckles were gnarled and the tips of some of her fingers turned in. She pulled on the gloves to make them fit snug. They were her hands. But she didn't have to look at them.

She pushed herself up in bed, and smoothed the blanket and sheet neatly over her stomach. She was wearing the nightie Evie had brought her last evening, just before she left. Everything was as she remembered. The new nightie, the new slippers, Evie helping her undress, Evie promising to come back in the morning after she took Vern…*away*. Evie all grown up, in control. She would be all right. Betty closed her eyes again and let the memories take over. She was Betty Laramie. It was 1952.

"Good morning."

"May I help you?"

"Thank you. I'll connect you with Mr. Johnson…with Mr. Jenkins…with Mr. Edwards…with Mr. Salter…"

The switchboard was a tangle of thick cords that slid clackity-back into their holes when you let them go, or buzzed when you touched the rim of a busy connection. All day long, she sat at the reception desk answering calls and greeting guests, except during breaks when she delivered the mail to everyone's office. She didn't mind being stuck there. It was like being at the helm of the entire company. She knew every caller, every department, saw everyone who came in the front door, and they all saw her.

Her nights were never meant to be spent alone waiting for a tired grease monkey to drop his smelly clothes on the kitchen floor and crawl into bed, no matter how handsome he was. Jimmy had been a mistake of exuberant youth, triggered by the end of a war, and those electrifying blue eyes. A regrettable mistake, but repairable. As long as Jimmy agreed that Evie would live with his mother, Betty would give up custody. With this new job she would once again be in control of her own destiny.

She checked her lipstick in her mirror compact, snapped it shut, and slipped it into her pocket, then mounted a rolling stairway that led to the "stern" of the company's newest pipe-laying machine, designed to cast giant concrete sewer pipe right in the ground. Massive wheels towered over her head. Rubber hoses connecting hydraulic systems tangled in and out of steel and followed angular haunches toward the sky. It looked a lot like a giant grasshopper. A sign that read "patent pending" had been hastily taped to one of the giant I-beams supporting the structure. In her full-skirted shirt dress, patent-leather pumps and hair turned neatly under just at her ears, she felt like Doris Day at a movie premier. The company's vice president handed her a quart bottle of 7-Up hastily procured from a local store and wrapped in a cloth napkin from the cafeteria.

"Go ahead, Betty," someone yelled from the crowd. She beamed back at them and gave them her best showgirl wave.

Elbow, elbow, wrist, wrist. Pinkie up.

"On the count of three," the VP said. "One…two…"

Betty took a golf-club-driver grip on the neck of the bottle, lining up her thumbs.

"Three!"

With a hearty swing and cheers from the crowd, she launched the company's future as a leader in constructing the guts of cities. The president, vice-president, and all the managers gathered around the stairway, lighting cigars, shaking hands, and congratulating each other.

Betty stood at the top of the stairs, laughing with the crowd and holding the dripping bottleneck away from her dress. She hadn't felt this alive since they crowned her *Glamour Girl of Compton College*'s class of '47.

Then suddenly, there he was, standing a breath away from her on the scaffolding. Mr. Salter, the company's purchasing manager. The one who stopped by the switchboard every day to say good morning to her. The one who always took a moment away from his work to chat when she made her morning mail rounds. More and more, he had been lingering near the switchboard when she closed it up for the day. Just the thought of him made her feel like she was bouncing along inside a Frank Sinatra song.

> *…You just say the words, and we'll beat the birds down to A-capulco Bay…*

Now, it was as though everyone else had disappeared from the scene and only he remained. He looked so handsome in his brown wool suit, white shirt and striped tie. His eyes flashed up to hers, Las-Vegas-

swimming-pool blue.

He held a bouquet of red roses.

"I'll trade you," he said. He took the dripping remains of the makeshift christening bottle from her hand and gave her the flowers. *"Let's get you out of here."*

Their eyes caught and held. His aftershave smelled crisp and clean, and made her feel warm inside.

"Thank you," she managed to say, out of breath. *"Did I do all right?"*

"Madame," he said, his hand at the small of her back, guiding her down the steps, *"You just launched our future."*

The noon sun glinted off of his wedding band—a point to be taken, she had one too—but not right now. She felt buoyant, inspired, even if just for the moment.

> *It's perfect, for a flying honeymoon, they say*
> *Come fly with me, we'll fly, we'll fly away!*

"C'mon. You can help me set up the bar." Mr. Salter took the lead as they trotted quickly through the crowd, toward the company's Key Conference room.

"But what about the switchboard?"

"Marge is shutting it down now. There won't be any more work around here today."

6 Road Trip

"He's not really peeing," I said to the officer. He had pulled up behind us in the Burger King parking lot. Vern had been telling me he was "going to go" for the last twenty minutes. I had hoped to make it at least to Santa Monica. Instead, I pulled off at an Inglewood exit off the 405 Freeway in search of a bathroom. The officer eyed us as if we were aliens dropped into his perfect world from another planet. I didn't blame him. We were very unlikely traveling companions—a fifty-year-old baby boomer running on coffee and Snicker bars from the hospital lounge, and a seventy-five-year-old man, freshly sprung, cold-turkey, off his regular supply of gin.

I felt like I had been transported through a time warp to my hippie days—the designated driver on a road trip to San Francisco—the only sober person in a vehicle full of crazies, Bob Dylan on the eight-track…

…Look out kid, they keep it all hid…

Vern insisted that he couldn't make it into the bathroom, scrambled out of the car and dropped his sweats to his thighs before I could get out and stop him.

Officer James continued to write on his metal ticket box. "City ordnance. Urinating in public."

The large black man stood a good head and shoulders over me. Putting aside my old hippie *pig-o-phobia* for Vern's sake, I did my best to rise to the occasion.

"But, you *know* that's for bums and derelicts, not just an old man who can't wait!"

I turned to check on Vern, who craned his neck around and scowled at the cop. The sight of him standing next to the car, holding his limp pud in one hand and the edge of the blue diaper in the other sent a stab to my gut.

"It's okay, Vern," I said in my best reassuring voice. It was not okay, but what was I supposed to do? Tell him to go in his pants? I turned back to the officer and leaned closer so Vern wouldn't hear. "See, he's got dementia. Korsakoff , actually—"

The cop stopped writing and looked over at Vern, who continued to concentrate, but so far, hadn't produced any results.

"—See, I told you. He just *thinks* he has to pee," I said, waving my hand in Vern's direction. "He's not actually doing it."

"Indecent exposure," the cop said, and started writing again.

"You're giving me a choice?"

"*Shoulda* gone before he left," said the cop. "This is no place for you people to be getting off the freeway."

"Hey, believe me, I *know*. I mean, ah—well, *naturally*," I said. "We've been driving for two hours. He's wearing a diaper, *see?*"

An oxidized, gray Ford Tempo pulled into the spot next to us. Ignoring the black and white Crown Vic behind me, the occupants gaped and pointed brightly tipped fingers at Vern, who continued, unfazed, to concentrate on his business.

"I'm taking him to an assisted care home," I added, as if it would make a difference.

Then the thought hit me. "Hey, maybe *you* could take him into the men's room for me and then we wouldn't have peeing in public or indecent exposure, would we?" He looked to be a nice guy, about my age. Probably had parents Vern's age.

The pair of black women wearing purple dresses, fancy red

hats, and layers of baubles and beads, had extracted themselves from their car and now stood behind me.

The tallest one squared her shoulders and jumped right in on my side. "Yeah. *Whadaya* doin' harassing this girl? Take the ol' man to the bat'room. Make your mama proud a' you, son."

She bumped my back with her elbow, bracelets jangling.

I took her lead and ran with it. "I bet maybe *you* know somebody old who's having a hard time? Your dad, maybe? Wouldn't you hope someone would help him out of a jam?"

"Yeah, what if that was your papa out there?" the other lady asked, adjusting her hat.

Officer James fixed them with a glare over the top of his glasses. "You ladies move on along. This isn't any of your business."

"*Humph*. No manners, either," said the tall one. The two of them moved off, muttering to each other. The smaller one gave me a little wave and a sympathetic smile before they disappeared into the Burger King.

Suddenly, Vern stumbled forward, whizzer in hand, stopping inches from the cop. He grinned. A weak yellow stream sparkled in the bright parking lot lights.

"Peeee-ing!" he said, and with that triumphant announcement, the stream widened, increased pressure, and pattered all over the officer's boot.

Officer James, pen still poised over his ticket box, jumped out of the way, shook a foot, and cut his eyes back to me.

"Oh. Jeez, I'm s-s-sorry," I said, squashing my bottom lip with my teeth. I held my breath, meeting his glare and then his pen started to move vigorously across the page again, skipping around, checkmarks and periods clacking forcefully against the aluminum box.

When he was finished, his gaze fixed on mine and narrowed as he ripped the ticket off with a flourish and shoved it at me, a department-trained smile stretched across his lips. "It's just a fine, ma'am. You can mail it in."

I snapped the ticket from his hand. "You could have just let it go, couldn't you? You had to make a scene out of a poor old man."

"Just doing my job, miss. Better than having you two out here all alone, right?"

"Oh, like we were going to be mugged by the Red Hat Society?" I stuffed the ticket in my back pocket.

"Still peeing," Vern called out over his shoulder. He had turned the stream toward a herd of snapdragons, targeting a wadded Whopper wrapper.

"It's okay, Vern. You got a ticket to pee."

"I do?"

"Yeah," I said, fixing Officer James with a Betty-*esque* smile.

He shut his ticket box and strode to the front of his prowl car. He opened the door, pulled a red rag from under the seat, and polished off his boot.

"You okay?" I helped Vern pull all of his parts together.

"I hope so," he said, as I rearranged his drawers and helped him back into the car.

"We don't have much further to go," I lied, "So you should be able to make it from here on."

I exhaled heavily as I rounded the back of the car and slipped behind the driver's seat. In five minutes we were on the freeway again, headed north. The time glowed green on the front of my radio: 9:25 p.m. With luck we'd be in Ojai in an hour or so. I turned on the music and forced myself to breathe normally.

"Where's Betty?" Vern asked. His fingers went back to his fly. "I have to go."

I glanced over at him. "You just went."

"I did?" His hands went to his crotch for a moment. He shot me a confused look "Where's Betty?"

"She's still in the hospital, but she's going to be okay."

"In the hospital? I thought she was in the back seat."

I reached across the cup holders and patted his hand. "She's okay. And you're going to be okay too," I said, as much for my own benefit as for his.

He faced the passenger side window, his shoulders sagged as he looked out over the city lights in the distance. "I hope so."

❧

At 10:45 p.m. I rang the bell in the courtyard at Crossroads

Alzheimer's Care with Vern leaning heavily on my arm.

"Can I pee here?" he asked.

"Yeah, I'm pretty sure you can do anything you want." I dropped the paper bag containing Vern's underwear and medical release papers and rang the bell again.

A woman's voice scratched over a speaker somewhere near the door.

"I'll be right there," she said, more cheerful than I felt after an hour of trying to give polite responses to Vern's constant circle of questions. The door opened and a tall woman in a flowered medical office smock let us into a large, open dining room.

"Hello, you must be Vern. I'm Sharlene."

Vern smiled at her, then looked over at me, his brows coming together and his hand going to his pants.

"He needs to go to the bathroom."

Sharlene took him by the elbow. "Oh, sure. I'll take you, Vern."

"You will?"

"Sure. And then we'll have some cookies." Sharlene steered him toward some doors across the room, matching her gait to his.

"Call me in the morning, Eve," she said over her shoulder. "We'll take care of business then." She waved me off discreetly.

Could it really be that easy? Just drop your stepfather off at the gate and wave goodbye?

"Thanks," I said, only now allowing myself the thought of my own bed, just a short ten minutes away. I put the bag of Vern's things on the table and stretched my hands. Sharlene and Vern entered the men's room.

"Where's Betty?" I heard him say. "Seems like we'll be launching pretty soon."

"I'm sure she's around nearby," Sharlene told him without skipping a beat. "We won't leave without her."

"I hope not."

The TV was off and the house was dark when I slipped in my back door. I dropped my purse on the kitchen table next to a stack of binders Robert had prepared—on his own—for the next day's work. Pulling my sweater off over my head, I made it to the back bathroom where I left my Levi's and a bladder full of Diet Coke, coffee, and shaky nerves. A Bob Dylan earworm circled in my head:

…the pump don't work 'cause the vandals took the handle …

When at last I sighed into bed, Robert's arms came around me and pulled me close. His hands slid lazily over my breasts. I turned toward him and nuzzled into his chest. The warmth and the familiar scent of him descended over me like a cloak, but my mind would not be still.

Is this what's waiting for me? For us? Just when you think you've got everything figured out, life gets broken and you don't have the right tools to fix it?

I shuddered. Robert smoothed hair stay wisps of hair off my forehead, his breath close. "You okay?"
"I hope so."

7 Moulin Rouge

"Good morning, Mrs. Salter," sang a nurse's aide, pushing the curtain to the wall. The sun stabbed into the room between a break in dark clouds. Betty opened her eyes reluctantly, still smiling at the memory of her first office party.

"Hi Mama. Feeling better?" She turned her head at the voice. Evie was there, sitting next to the bed.

"Hi, sweetie," she answered, pulling away from her past. "I think so, I think *so.*"

"Seems like you're a little more…awake…today."

"Yes. I was dreaming, but now I'm awake." She pushed herself up again and straightened her shoulders. "I was thinking about Vern. How is he?"

"I took him to a respite care home near my house. I stopped by there at five-thirty this morning on my way here and he was up having breakfast with another gentleman. He'll be safe there until you feel better."

Betty's mind slid off to another memory, more recent. Vern standing on their front porch in the middle of the night, soaking wet in nothing but his skivvies, supported on the arms of two police officers who had picked him up on the steps of the clubhouse golf shop.

"Thank you," she said to Evie. "I wasn't doing enough ... I couldn't control him anymore, I— "

Evie took her hands, ignored the gloves. "I know, Mom. He'll be all right now. Let's get you better. You need all your energy to take care of you. Do you need some help in the bathroom?"

Betty hesitated. No one had helped her do anything for many years. Suddenly, Evie was here, offering. Evie, the daughter with Jimmy's eyes she had given away, here to help. Hot tears stung her eyes and she had to look away. She didn't need any help. She needed to go home.

"No. No, I can do it. I'm just very glad you're here. I thought I was lost." She slipped a leg out of bed, touched down a toe, and stood on her own.

Goddammit! Shit! Aw, gawd!" I heard the water come on full blast. "*Goddamn cocksucker!*"

The blue streak of profanity came from the other side of the bathroom door. "Mom? Are you all right?"

"*I don' thin' so,*" she said, pulling the door open. She held an open bottle of skin lotion in one hand and her toothbrush in the other, drooling white goo. "*Wha's a mattah wit ma mouf?*"

"Other than cussing up a storm? Looks like you brushed your teeth with body lotion." It was hard to suppress a giggle.

My mother scowled at me and then spit the contents of her mouth on the floor. "Bleckeh."

I guided her back to the sink and helped her rinse and then brush her teeth with the toothpaste, then helped her wash her face and apply the skin lotion to her cheeks and arms.

"There. Now all we need is a little lipstick, and you'll be all set."

Her face reddened. She leaned against the sink, short on breath. A nurse's aide appeared in the doorway. Without asking, I supported my mother on one side while the aide supported the other. Together we led her from the bathroom, toothbrush still in her hand.

"Doing okay now?"

Mom nodded and took a deep breath. "*Yes, Goddammit.*"

She shuffled back to the bed and plopped down.

"Seems like she's feeling pretty sparky this morning." The aide emptied handfuls of cups and tissues into the trashcan next to the bed.

"So what do you think," I asked. "Will she go home today?"

"The doctors usually come in for rounds about ten. If her temp is down, then…maybe. That's the way it works. I can't really say for sure."

I checked my watch. It was 9:45.

Mom shivered and pulled at the sheet. I slipped the toothbrush out of her hand and helped her crawl back under the covers. Both hands free now, she pulled the sheet almost up to her nose. Her eyes rolled away from mine, to the TV, to the tent of her toes under the blankets, and then back to me. Her hands shook and her chin hardened, pulling her lips straight.

"It's okay, Mom. No big deal. What clothes do you want from home?"

She stared at the ceiling until her chin relaxed. "My chambray shirt and Levi's with the elastic waist. They're at the very end of my closet, in my bedroom."

"There, see? You're doing' fine. Anyone can grab the wrong stuff in the bathroom."

Her posture returned to *Betty*, chin resting on her knuckles, and she managed a smile. "And my oxford shoes. The new ones."

I gave her a quick hug. "I'll be back before you know it, and we can both get out of this place."

"Lipstick," she said.

"Lipstick?"

"You said 'a little lipstick'."

I wasn't sure I wanted her to do it herself.

"Okay, let's see what I can find." I lifted her purse from under the nightstand and rummaged through it. "How about this?"

I read the bottom: "Pink Lemonade." I tried to sound cheery, but Mom scowled back at me. I rummaged some more. "Okay. Rumba Red?"

Another scowl.

"Mocha Polka," she said.

37

The words hit me like a freight train. Mocha Polka. That had been her color when I was still a young girl. I remembered thinking how amazing she was, having lipstick with a name, not simply red. She put it on me for the one party she was there to send me off to. We did our lips and our nails to match. It had been the most wonderful evening of my life because she had been there at the start.

And then the train went right off the tracks and sent me back to an image fixed in my memory as clear and distinct as though it had just happened.

I was standing in a bedroom in front of a huge dresser, heavily wood-grained in reds and golds. The two side drawer sections supported a huge round mirror between them. The low section in the middle was crowded with perfume bottles. I can almost smell them as the vision deepens: Chanel, Jungle Gardenia, Topaz. The drawer pulls are tortoise-shell discs with beveled-glass balls on antiqued-brass risers. They are loose and some of my favorite playthings.

❧

I'm standing in front of the dresser, spinning a disc one way and the glass ball the other, making gurgle sounds, spit flying on the drawer front and down my chin. I can see my mother's reflection in the mirror. She puts on earrings, pushes at her blonde, pin-curled hair. She runs the lipstick tube back and forth across her lips, then presses them together, leans in, and smiles sweetly. She is so beautiful. I can smell her lipstick on the crinkled tissue when she dabs the spit off my chin.

I hear that song on the Hi Fi, the one she plays over and over.

> *Whenever we kiss, I worry and wonder,*
> *You lips may be near, darling where is your heart?*

The words of the song, and the scene, play out in my head as if I were transported to a past life.

"Muffin Man," I say.

"Shhhh," she says. "Not now, sweetie." She spins away from the dresser, humming with the music. Her skirt twirls and settles around her

calves.

I take a wobbly turn, then go back to spinning dresser knobs.

"Little girls don't spit," she tells me. I bite my lip. At that moment, I notice, on the other side of the dresser, something new. A sugar egg, painted with green and yellow frosting, wrapped in shiny cellophane, and tied with a purple ribbon. One end of the egg has a peep hole. There must be something magical inside a thing so sparkly and perfect. I lift a knee and pull myself up among the lipstick tubes, perfume bottles, and used tissues. I reach for the egg, just as she turns around.

"That's not for you," Mama says. "You stay down now."

She sets me down gently and rearranges the bottles and tubes.

"See, see!" I try again and she pushes me gently back off the dresser.

"Big girls don't whine." She hugs me for second, and kisses me. Her breath is sweet and cool against my cheek. The fragrance of flowers fills my head. I snuggle into her knees, her smell drifts over me like fairy dust. She pushes me gently away again, winds my panda bear and slips it into my arms. I hug it close as the tune tinkles out the "go to sleep" song.

I don't feel all that big. A tear slips out.

"Seeeee…" I insist.

She looks down at me and smiles. "Okay. You can see, but don't touch. It's not for you."

She gets it off the dresser, kneels down, and holds me against her body. I feel her halo of curls touching mine. She puts the peep hole up to my eyes.

I hold my hands obediently at my sides. Her arm, long and fragrant, gently rests across my shoulders. I peer into the egg.

Inside—all sugar, pastels, and sparkle dust—is a tiny world. In front, a rabbit dressed in a soft green jacket sits at the edge of a garden fence. Beyond that are rows of cabbages and carrots. Further inside is a tiny cottage, and next to it, a silvery pond ringed by paving stones is shaded by flowering vines.

Breathless, I grab for the egg. Mama gently removes my hands. "That's enough now, you can look again later, if you're a good girl."

She releases me and places the egg back on the dresser. "Mama has to go now."

She puts my sweater on me and a knitted hat. "Uncle Leo will be here any minute. You go play with Susie."

She opens the back door and I run out. Susie comes to greet me, wagging her tail. She licks my face all over. I run to my favorite corner of the yard and pick a Tulip from Aunt Ruby's garden. Susie runs after me.

39

Around and around, we chase and play. I hear the car in the front driveway. Susie runs to the gate and barks.

"Mama?" I go to the back door screen, push my nose against the rusty metal grid. "Mama!" I call, louder.

No one answers. Susie waits on an old braided rug spread across the raised back porch. She takes a couple of turns, lies down behind me, and gives a big sigh. I sit down next to her. Soft fur rubs against my back as I lean into the curve of her warm stomach. Uncle Leo will be home soon. That is what Mama said. I'm a good girl and I don't whine or do anything naughty. Tree branches move overhead, their purple flowers wave like a pretty fan.

I watch until I can't hold my eyes open any more, but I know the purple flowers are still waving, and then, it is so quiet I can't even hear my own thoughts. I'm inside the sugar egg. A slender white cat sits like a marble statue on the paving stones next to the pond. Slim black moons slide back and forth in her pale blue eyes. A golden fish swims circles just below the surface of the water.

*   *   *

"Mocha Polka." My mother's strident voice startled me back to the present.

Mocha Polka? Oh. Yes.

"Well, let's see…" I pawed through her bag some more, but I could barely see through choked off tears. Left alone with the dog? "Maybe you have some at home—"

I had been a happy child. I could have been wretched. There was that little room that no one could enter, the tiny corner where the images were stored. The frightening and the magical huddled together inside a quiet, private, little sugar egg, a place I was not allowed to go. But the path back to her was there. I could see it, taste it, smell it. We could almost be there…

"Knock, knock." A voice sang at the door of the hospital room.

I turned to see a woman in a light gray, pinstriped suit.

She stepped through the doorway and extended her hand to me. "Hi, I'm Helen DeVant, from social services? We talked on the phone?"

I swallowed hard on the sting in the back of my throat. "Oh.

Yes. Of course. Good to meet you." I turned to my mom. "This is Betty."

Helen shot me a brief puzzled look, no doubt catching the watery eyes. She sent me a smile that said she understood, then she stepped to the bed and addressed my mother directly.

"Well, Betty, you look a lot better than the last time I saw you."

Betty slipped her gloved hands under the covers.

"I understand your husband is in assisted care and you could be released today?"

Mom looked at me for the answer.

"If her temp is down and her lungs are clear, then, yes. She could be released today."

"Well," said Helen, making a production out of handing my mother a brochure. "I just wanted you to know about our LVN program. If you're going home alone, we can have someone check up on you every day until you're better."

Betty brightened and nodded a yes, but all I could see was a little soul waiting on the back porch, alone.

"That...won't be necessary," I said, drawing Helen's attention back to me. "She'll be coming home with me."

8 Boomer's Nightmare

"Normally I'd keep you another day, Betty, just to give you the rest. But since you're going with your daughter, I'll release you right after your physical therapy."

Physical Therapy? Betty lifted her chin and pulled a smile that involved her entire face. That sounded better. She liked physical therapy, it felt like working out and she'd missed that. How long had it been? A year? Not since Vern dropped her off at LA Workout and couldn't find his way back. When the taxi had pulled up in front of their townhouse, Vern was backing their shiny red Cadillac out the driveway. The window slid down on the passenger side and he had shouted, "I'm going to top off the tank," then nearly took off the taxi's back bumper as he bounced the Caddie over the curb and pulled slowly down the street.

Vern never went out without topping off. Then he would drive and drive on a well-worn path, to the grocery store, the liquor store, the bank, and back home in a series of right-hand turns. And then he would start all over again. Betty should have hid the keys, but how could she?

Vern. She missed him. Oh, not the way he was now. Now he was a royal pain in the ass. It was a relief not to be in charge of him. But the way he was then…

Her gaze slipped away from Evie and the nurse. She only

half heard the rest of their conversation—they would see a doctor as soon as they got settled, they would check her meds, they would talk about arrangements and directives, whatever those were.

Betty stared at the pattern in the wallpaper next to the bed. A lattice work, threaded with green and white ivy, floated above the surface, and behind it, an image emerged. It was the old Vern, sitting at his desk in his brown striped suit. In slow motion, he looked up, grinned, and invited her in. *Yes.* Strains of longing wafted through her mind on the words of an old song ...

> *Angel eyes, that old Devil sent, they glow unbearably bright...*

She took a deep breath, drawing in the fragrance of his aftershave and the promise in those eyes...

> *Need I say, that my love's misspent...*

She diffused into the mournful melody, reached out to touch him, but the image went flat and the music stopped.

"Hmm," she mused, bringing her fingertips to her chin. A little rumble in her throat triggered a coughing spell.

"We need to keep an eye on that," the doctor said on her way out the door.

"We will," Evie assured her.

Betty blinked. Where was she? A hospital room had imposed itself on her reality. Evie was in charge. *Evie with Jimmy's eyes, not Vern's.* Evie was talking too fast. Betty couldn't keep up.

"While you're in PT, I'll go to your house and get you some more clothes. I figure we'll just take a few things for now, and see how you feel in about a week. Robert's downstairs. He'll drive your car and we'll store it in the garage...until we see how things go."

Until we see how things go. What things? Certainly some things had gone. Some words, some numbers. But she had herself. She ran her hands over her face, her breasts, her crotch. At least she still had the important parts. And now Evie would help her get back the rest. Her car, her clothes, her life. She would buy a new house. Redecorate. Maybe get a job. Go on another cruise. Not to Alaska though. Someplace warm, like…like… It all depended on how things went. She looked back over at the wallpaper. *Yes.* She would redecorate…

"Mom?"

"Oh," Betty said. She slipped out of the circle of thoughts that held her half in a trance and blinked at her daughter's concerned expression. "Until we see how things go," she said, finally, repeating Evie's words. It was easier than coming up with her own. "And get my pink rose. The one on the patio."

Evie nodded and got Betty's purse from the nightstand and put it in her lap. "I'll need your keys to get in the house."

"You can get them." Betty pushed the purse back to Evie. "I'm not sure which key it is. Vern always drives."

Evie opened the purse tentatively. "What about the security code? I don't want to set off the alarm."

Betty thought for a minute. They didn't use it anymore. "Umm …Vern couldn't remember the code, so…we don't use it."

Another of the things that went.

Evie shrugged. "That's okay, I suppose, as long as I can get in."

She kissed Betty's cheek gently. Betty could feel the tenderness of her touch, the warmth of her skin. She closed her eyes. She'd missed the tender touches. Lately, there'd been precious few. Lately, Vern would barge into her room in the middle of the night, pushing his way into the bed with a limp dick and good intentions. Sweet, but damn annoying. And sad. She had taken to locking her bedroom door. He'd rattle the doorknob a couple of times, then move on to the kitchen and rattle the liquor cabinet, and make himself a highball which he seemed to remember how to do just fine.

Her eyes welled up. It's a good thing we don't see ahead of time, how things go. When she opened her eyes, Evie was still there. She reached out to caress Betty's face and wiped a stray tear away with her thumb.

"We'll figure it all out, Mom. I promise you."

Betty wasn't convinced. Vern was definitely lost, and lately she felt she wasn't far behind. She shook her head, turning away.

"You have to sit tight a little bit longer, Mom. Then we'll

break you out of here."

"Sit tight," said Betty, finally. *What am I going to do? Run the halls in my underwear?* The thought tickled her out of her funk. *Just swing my legs around and run down the hall. Oops, I don't have on any underwear!* She giggled out loud. *Oh Betty, you would never!*

"You going to be okay, then?" Evie studied her face as if she could read her mind. Betty stared back into her daughter's eyes. She had not been okay for a very long time. She wasn't even sure what okay was. But Evie didn't need to know that. She scooted up in bed, smoothed the covers over her stomach, and patted them down. "I'm going to be just *peachy*."

9 Unfamiliar Territory

The trip home was easier than I expected, considering my experience with Vern, but it was still a long time to be in the car. When we pulled in the driveway, Mom agreed she could use a little rest.

I carried the potted rosebush to our front porch where my mother suggested it would get the best sunlight, then brought the rest of the things we'd decided she couldn't live without into our guestroom. She settled herself to recline on the bed and said she was comfortable and insisted that I rest too.

I dragged myself down the hall and plopped down on the edge of my own bed. A bedraggled image in the dresser mirror stared wide-eyed back at me. Two trips to San Diego in as many days had tramped dark circles under the eyes, woven extreme travel hair at the back of my collar, and spawned a sniffling cold. I looked like a homeless woman up from the river bottom.

Robert walked in, dumped his wallet and change on the dresser, and caught my gaze in the mirror, probably thinking the same thing.

"Got a *dollah* for a cup of coffee, *mistah*?"

He laughed. "It's not that bad. Looks more like you could use a little rest."

"I'll be fine." A psychologist friend of mine once told me to act like you want to feel and then you start to feel that way. I hoped he was right. "Let me lie here for a few minutes."

"Take your time. The cats are circling their dishes in the kitchen. I'll go take care of them," he said, and left me to myself.

I flopped back on the bed and stared at the ceiling, searching random patterns in the acoustic cottage cheese for a place to resume normal life.

Normally, I would be at work in Santa Barbara. I needed to call my boss. Normally I'd be stopping by the store on the way home. Did we even have food in the house? I had no clue. Normally, I'd be rushing to finish my Christmas shopping, bake cookies for the neighborhood cookie exchange, and clean bathrooms in preparation for the inevitable holiday drop-ins. My mind jumped from one chore to the next with neurotic precision, but my body didn't respond. It lay there like a rag doll with fixed, button eyes.

Robert held court with a cat in the kitchen, using his special kitty talk. Our clothes dryer thrummed in the garage. Smooth jazz played on the digital box. The other cat padded across the carpet and jumped onto my chest. He purred and pushed his wet nose into my neck, making his kitty dough. The comforting sounds of home would eventually work their magic, but for now, I couldn't take my thoughts off my mother, resting in the next room. After a lifetime of distance, there was only the space of a hallway between us. The little girl inside me wanted to go in there and lay by her side, but the woman in me remembered how that might go. I threw my arm up over my eyes as the memories tumbled in. The more they came, the smaller I felt.

"E-v-e-e-e-i-i-i-e-e! You're mama's here, baby doll." Grandma came around from the kitchen, wiping her hands on a dish towel sewn to the front of her apron. I was already at the window, and she was right! Mama had just pulled up in a shiny new pink T-Bird convertible. Vern's arm stretched across the pink and white seats behind her head as she pulled off a jersey hood. She ran her fingers through short, blonde hair and shook it out. They looked like people from a car ad in Grandpa's Look magazine. I was out the door and off the porch before my mother could get out of the car.

"Hi sweetie." She gave me a short press to her chest. She felt hard and pointy, not soft and warm like my grandma and now she held me at arm's length.

"Be careful." She smoothed my hands down to my sides. "Ladies don't jump on people like little puppies. Now, let's get your things."

If she noticed I'd broken both my new front teeth since I'd last seen her, she didn't let on.

"Are we gonna go swimming? Are we gonna eat tacos?" I asked as I rolled my bathing suit up in a change of clothes on the front porch. "Is Johnny coming?" I shouted to Vern as I skipped out to the car, pulling my mother along by the hand.

"Yes Johnny is coming and we'll probably do everything." He took my spare clothes and laid them in the trunk between golf bags and a red plaid, metal cooler. "Hop in, ladies. We've still got a way to go."

I ran around the side of the car and we slipped into the seat. Our bodies pressed close, just like we belonged together. "Wow, I didn't know you got this car! I've never been in a convertible, and it's pink!"

"That was your mom's choice," Vern said as he shifted into gear.

Mama quickly tied a scarf over her hair and put on a pair of tortoiseshell sunglasses. Then she pulled her jersey hood over my head and got a pair of sunglasses out of the glovebox for me. They were too big and she laughed. "Ready?"

"Yes!" I couldn't believe I was wearing her hood, and sunglasses too, just like Grace Kelly.

The car jumped forward and we pulled away from the curb as Grandma waved to us from her front porch. The engine hummed deep and low and we picked up speed. We zoomed down Garfield Avenue and got on the freeway, then headed toward Fontana through the late, smoggy, Sunday morning. It felt just like Heaven.

"Sharlene says you look like Kim Novak," I said after a while.

"Oh, really?" Mama looked at Vern and raised her eyebrows. He just smiled, only half listening. The baseball game was on the radio.

"And how does Sharlene know about Kim Novak? She's only twelve, isn't she?" Mama lit a cigarette and held it low so the wind didn't blow ashes on us.

The sparkle of her diamond ring caught my eye and I touched it. "Sharlene knows about all the movie stars—Liz Taylor, Rosalind Russell, Marilyn Monroe—she says Kim Novak is the prettiest, and the most racy. She made a movie about a picnic, but Aunt Alta says we can't go see it."

People turned their heads to look at us as we drove past them on the freeway. Mama blew cigarette smoke up so it would stream out behind us. "Well, Aunt Alta's probably right."

"How come everybody's staring at us?"

Vern chuckled, shifted his right hand to the top of the steering wheel, and rested his other arm on the side of the door. "It's the car. Not very many of these on the road yet."

The car might be pink, but I could see that he liked it just fine. The familiar voice of the man who talked about baseball all the time flew out of the radio and into the wind like pennant flags disappearing as we roared along the foothills.

At Johnny's mom's house, Vern left the motor running while he stepped up to the door. I saw Johnny's face disappear from the front window just before the door flung open.

"Bye Mom," he shouted as he and his father came down the steps together. My mother stared straight ahead, smoking her cigarette.

Johnny hopped through the driver's door onto the hump between the seats, clutching his bathing suit in one hand and a deflated pool toy in the other.

"Whew! You two better not get any bigger, we'll have to get a trailer and pull you behind the car." Johnny and I giggled, our heads already together. We saw each other seldom, near Christmas, or maybe a birthday, but each time we did, it was instant camaraderie. Our blonde heads and blue eyes matched so well, people thought we were a real family.

Before long we were at the apartment, wearing ourselves out in the pool. Vern coached us from the deck on our diving technique, positioning our hands, heads, and knees and laughing as, time after time, we jumped in, feet first. Mama sat on the edge of the pool, kicking her feet, her pretty face framed in a pink-petaled bathing cap. Later, I took a picture of her leaning up against the door of the T-Bird in her bathing suit, one hand behind her head. (That was for my cousin, Sharlene.) Johnny and I sat on a plastic tablecloth on the living room floor, and we ate tacos and refried beans while we watched Lassie on TV.

When I finished my grape soda, I ran to the kitchen for more. There, I saw Mama and Vern huddled together, giggling at Herkey, the parakeet, who tasted a drink from a fancy glass. Vern slid his hand off Mama's fanny when he saw me.

Mama smiled at him and then me. "What is it, sweetie?"

I held up my empty glass. "I want what Herkey's drinking."

"He's sipping a martini," Vern said, "You're too young for that."

"How old is Herkey anyway?"

Vern lifted me up on his knee so I could see the parakeet take a drink from the glass through the cage bars. "Oh, he's a lot older than you, in bird years."

"Herkey's a lush." Mama laughed and I loved the sound of it.

"What's a lush?"

"Never you mind," she said, tapping my nose with the tip of her finger. She took my glass and went to the refrigerator.

"Herkey! Herkey," the bird said. We all laughed.

"You like her, don't you?" I asked Vern.

"Herkey's a him, short for Hercules, and yes, I like him. He's a funny little guy."

"No, I mean my mama. You like her." I tilted my head toward Mama.

Vern looked at me for a moment without saying a word, then he put down his glass, stood up, and held me in front of him. I put my arms on each of his shoulders and looked him straight in the eyes.

"I don't like your mom," he said. "I love her, and you know why?"

I shook my head. Mama came over to us with the soda and leaned against the kitchen counter.

"Because she's just as pretty as you." He tickle-pinched me just above my knee till I squirmed and giggled, then he put me down.

"Evie, run on back to the TV, and I'll carry the soda." Mama followed me to the big white plastic tablecloth and waited while I sat down. "Now you guys finish up, we've got to take you home soon."

The top was on the T-Bird for the drive home. By seven I was back at Grandma's, by eight I was in bed with my visions: Mama in the car, her white scarf blowing in the wind, her pink blouse with the collar turned up, her tight black Capri pants and white high-heeled sandals, her pink, pink lipstick and blue, blue eyes, her long, perfect fingernails and her small, perfect fingers, her cigarette poised, just so.

The next day, I had to sit in the corner twice, once for wearing one of my grandmother's silk scarves outside, and once for pretending to smoke with a broken twig.

It would be another long time, maybe until Christmas, before I saw my mother again.

❧

The hum of the dryer and the cat's rhythmic purr blended together and lulled me into a much needed nap. When I awoke, the light had completely faded and I had drooled on the pillow. I was so deep into the memory, I half expected to see the seersucker curtains of my childhood room when I opened my eyes. Instead, it was the new shades of our bedroom and Robert was standing in the doorway. "Your mom and I are having some tea. Would you like to join us?"

"Oh my gosh, was I ever out." I wiped the corner of my mouth with the back of my hand and sat up. "What time is it?"

"About six. Relax. She's doing fine."

"Thanks, Robert. You are wonderful, you know."

"Yes, I know."

"And humble."

He gave me one of his easy grins and escorted me down the

hall, his hand mischievously playful on my backside.

After a quick dinner of soup and salads, Robert headed for the TV room and Mom and I chatted at the kitchen table. She had promised to make Robert some tapioca pudding, and he had promised to give her one of his famous back rubs.

After a few moments of silence, her gaze slanted away.

"Evie, I don't know how to do this." She waved her hand vaguely. "I don't want to be trouble. To you and Robert. I don't want to make a…problem."

A sharp memory of my mother's mother stabbed at my thoughts. Her square-jawed face, the dark circles under her eyes, how she called me her precious child as if I were about to die. My grandma had talked about *that Lola* as if she were the Anti-Christ. As far as I knew, she was only an Episcopalian. I don't recall much about my maternal grandmother living with us, except the dark-cloud feeling that hung over a room whenever she was in it. My mother wasn't anything like her mother. She had always been the brightest light in my life and I wanted her there. I reached across the table and took her hand. "It won't be a problem, Mom."

She squeezed my hand and traced her fingers over mine, the most tender of acknowledgements.

"It's just…I don't know what *this* is," she said. "How much is it, really? How long? I can't think of the right words. Sometimes I can't think at all."

"I know what you mean—"

"No," she insisted, taking a stronger grip. Her steel blue eyes were crazed with a veneer of fear and uncertainty, wet with threatening tears. "I don't think you do."

Her words stopped me cold. Made me think. I had been trying to make light of this situation. For the first time in our lives, my mother was trying to make a real connection with me. It was unfamiliar territory. I had nothing to guide me but what I had learned by living without her.

What if I got it wrong?

I was more frightened than I wanted to admit.

"Tell me how it is." I pulled a chair around next to her and settled in closer.

She straightened in her chair and stared at the table for a long moment. "Sometimes it's okay, then everything shifts and

I don't know what to do."

"We're here with you now. Whatever happens."

"What about Vern? They'll want money, but he writes the money, not me."

"We'll go there tomorrow and see what they need."

"I'm tired of seeing him, how he *is*. Is that bad?"

"Nobody blames you for feeling that way. You took care of him too long by yourself. I should have helped. Or Johnny."

"Ps-s-s-h. Johnny. He hasn't been around for years."

"I'll call him tomorrow. Tell him where his dad is."

"Ps-s-s-h." Betty fiddled with a wadded tissue, shredding it to tiny pieces. She sniffed and stuttered. "Evie, I know I haven't always—haven't always been—"

Words I might have wanted to hear one day, I didn't want to hear now.

"It doesn't matter, Mom. Not anymore." I pulled her into my arms, my heart straining along familiar cracks.

"I'm here for you. Whatever it takes." I held her cheek in my hand the way I always wanted her to do to me, and said the words to her that I always wanted to hear.

She shook her head, took a deep breath, and struggled to regain her classic Betty pose: chin up, one wrist bent just at her shoulder, fingertips touching her collar bone. Her gaze shifted away again to survey the backyard through the sliding glass doors. I imagined the thoughts battling in her head were the mirror image of my own.

"Okay," she said at last, her voice so low, I could barely hear it. She sipped the last of her tea, patted me back into my chair, and sighed. "Let's make tapioca. I could use a good back rub. I feel like I've been rode hard and put in the wet house."

I laughed. "You mean 'put away wet'?"

"Yeah. Put away wet."

"That makes two of us."

10 Reality Check

Betty stood at the shower door looking in, her body distorted in the reflection of the curving chrome faucets. The tiles on the floor looked like raised waffles. She was unsure where to step. She pulled away and rested her hand at her collar bone. *For Chrissakes, get a grip, Bett. You're awake, you're at Evie's, and you smell bad. Let's go.* She breathed deeply through her nose, stepped in, and turned a knob. Cold water came streaming out, drenching her.

"Agh!" She pulled back out again. "Freezing cold, *Goddammit.*"

She wrestled off her wet blouse and dropped it on the bathroom floor.

When she looked up, an old hag in a soaking wet bra scowled at her from the bathroom mirror.

"Oh, go away," she said, opening the mirrored door. She inspected a basket of makeup on the first shelf, and then moved on to an assortment of brushes on the next. Where was *her* stuff? She selected one of the brushes and pulled it gingerly through her hair while the shower ran, hoping this would turn out to be one of her "real" days. It was time she pulled herself together and got on with it.

From the next shelf she pulled down a tube of cream. She patted dots of it on her face and rubbed it in, around her mouth and up along her cheeks in a familiar pattern, keeping the mirrored door open so she wouldn't have to look at the hag. She didn't want anybody to see her right now. Not until she was ready.

Steam billowed over the top of the shower door. Betty opened it again, carefully, then pulled back. "Agh! That's burning up!"

A knock at the door startled her.

"Mom? What are you doing?"

Betty opened the door a crack. "Oh, *goob* morning, *Ebie.*" Her lips felt oddly stiff, like someone was pinching her cheeks back. "Did you *sleeb* well?"

"It's four a.m."

Evie slipped into the tiny half bath with her. She gasped, at first, then covered a laugh. "Looks like you found my Sea Mud."

"Sea mud?" Betty put her hand to her cheek, felt the drying crust, and frantically checked the mirror. The old hag had a dirty green face now, and great big eyes.

"Gawd!" She stared at herself in the mirror, picking at the crust, then looked back at Evie. "Will it come off?"

"Of course, it'll wash." Evie shifted around to where she could open the glass door. "Let me help you with this."

She reached in and turned the knobs. "There. Try that."

She moved out of the way and let Betty stretch her hand into the streams of water.

"That's okay," she said after a moment, then stepped in to the warmth.

"Wait, Mom, your clothes."

Betty looked down. "Oh, my goodness." She slipped a little on the wet floor, stretched out her hand and steadied herself. "Whoops!"

"Oh, Jesus." Evie spread a towel on the shower floor, water steaming into her hair. "Stand on this."

Betty stepped gingerly onto the towel. "That's better."

"Now let me help you get your clothes off." Evie

unsnapped her bra, slipped the straps off her shoulders, and tossed it out onto the floor. "Now, brace yourself for a minute."

Betty did as she was told, suddenly not so confident. Evie undid her slacks and slid them down, along with her panties, and helped Betty step out of them.

The water felt warm and safe. Betty pushed her face into it, rubbed the drying mud off, and then bent her head forward to enjoy the streams of water running down her back.

"Want to wash your hair?"

"Yes, it smells like hospital."

Evie's laugh felt warm and cozy like the water sluicing off her back. Together they scrubbed and rinsed, Evie in her soaked nightgown and Betty in the buff. When they stepped out of the shower, Betty immediately felt the cold. "Your house is cold. I'm freezing."

"Yep, that's Ojai, the land of fire and ice. It's probably near thirty outside. I can hear the orange grove fans going."

Orange grove fans?

Evie covered the toilet seat with a towel. "Sit down here, mom." She pulled more towels off the rack and wrapped them around Betty's head, shoulders and legs. Betty scowled at the pile of wet clothes on the floor. "We've made a mess."

"Oh, it's no big deal." Evie kicked the wet clothes into the corner.

"Morning, ladies." Betty heard Robert's voice at the door. My, he was certainly an early riser.

"Oh, Robert," Evie called out. "Could you get us some more towels?"

"Sure. And I'll make some coffee. Looks like we're up for the day, huh?"

Evie cracked the door open so Robert could hand in some towels from the hall closet. "Looks like it."

A half hour later, Betty and Evie were back at the kitchen table. Evie brought out a mirror and a makeup basket. Betty chanced a look. Evie had blown her hair dry, the ends were turned neatly under. Not exactly the way she would do it, but it looked clean and neat. Betty lifted her chin and turned her head, shifting her eyes sideways. The hag woman was still there, but at least she had cleaned up well.

"I'm sorry Mom. I didn't think about bringing your own

makeup."

Evie wiped off her first attempt at redrawing Betty's eyebrows, which she had to admit, had gone a little off the mark.

"I'm afraid I'll hurt you if I press too hard. You can probably do it better." She handed Betty the red Mabelline pencil.

"That's okay. You keep doing your morning. I'm fine here." Betty dibbed and dabbed at her eyes, her cheeks, her lips, as much by ritual as by any directed skill or desire, while Evie cleared an empty fruit bowl from the table, all the while talking on the phone.

"Barb. Evie. I know I said I'd be back today, but, the situation here is a little more—complicated—than I first thought."

"A little more complicated." Betty repeated the words softly into the mirror.

Evie looked over at her and smiled. "Call me when you get this. Talk to you later. Bye."

"He doesn't say much, does he?" It seemed odd to Betty that Evie didn't let her boss get a word in edgewise.

"She. That was her answering machine. It's only four-thirty, so she's not there yet, but normally, I'd already be on the road. To beat the traffic."

Betty straightened in her chair, remembering the lighted makeup mirror in their Oldsmobile Toronado. It was why they had bought the car. That and front wheel drive. Vern had insisted it was the wave of the future. "Vern and I used to drive to Alhambra every day."

"It's a major traffic jam heading to Santa Barbara."

Betty made another attempt to draw her brows, this time slipping off across her temple, almost to the top of her ear.

"…we've had lots of rain so far this year, so highway 150's been closed, and—"

"Tch." Betty tossed the eyebrow pencil down on the table.

Evie pulled a coffee cup from the cupboard and set it on the counter.

"Uh oh. Let me try it again." Evie dabbed some crème on a tissue and wiped the errant eyebrow off. Betty relaxed into her touch.

"…Anyway, we've got a lot to do. See Vern, get you set up with a local doctor, maybe look at some places for you, and I've got some work to do for Robert."

"You work too much." Betty imitated her daughter's pursed lips. She didn't mean to sound harsh, it was hard keeping up with the conversation. Lately she had mostly ignored Vern's endless questions, and the TV never asked any.

"Yeah, probably, but we've got this new business you know, and I do most of the computer work."

"So you work in Santa Barbara and you work for Robert, and now I'm here." *A pain in the ass, something she swore she would never be.* She held still. Evie lifted her chin with her fingertips and carefully stroked along the imaginary lines of an acceptable eyebrow arch. Betty's eyebrows had never been such an ordeal. Just slip, slap and they were on. Practiced moves, she could do it blindfolded.

But not anymore. This was exactly what she was afraid of. This was exactly why she had to pull herself together.

Evie stood back. "Now. That looks more like you. Here."

She tilted the mirror so Betty could see. "You'll be back to your old self in no time. Meanwhile, we'll just do the best we can."

Betty did her best to pull a smile for her daughter, but the inside of her still frowned. The image of the old hag with the green sea mud on her face laughed at her.

Old self. Would she ever find her old self? The one who knew what came next? Knew what to wear and what to eat? Knew why the coffee thing didn't work anymore. Where was *that* Betty? How long had she been missing? The one in the mirror had only half a smile, she wanted the other half back.

"Tch." She tipped the mirror away from her face, closed her eyes, and climbed out of her pity pot on a purging, ropy sigh. It was no use feeling sorry for herself. Emma Harte would never do that. At least Vern wasn't here fixing her a highball first thing in the morning. That was a good thing.

Vern.

She missed him, and then again, not. Not the falling down. Not the wandering off. Not the endless circle of questions and the driving, driving, driving.

Near the kitchen door one of the cats meowed and circled

as far away from her as it could, and then looped in and out of Evie's legs at the kitchen sink.

"Here kitty." Betty bent down and tried to attract the cat's attention, but it skittered back out of the room. "It doesn't like me."

"She's just persnickety. Want some coffee?"

Betty nodded.

Evie poured two cups. "Take anything in it?"

"Just some of that, uh, powdered white, uh, stuff, not sugar."

"Will a little milk do?"

Betty never drank milk. Never. But then, how would Evie know that? She straightened in her chair and presented her best attempt at a radiant, Emma Harte smile. "Black's good for now."

Evie set the cup in front of her, a swirl of clear bubbles floated on the surface of the rich brown liquid. It smelled wonderful as Betty brought it to her lips. She sipped, sputtered, and almost dropped the cup, spilling some into the makeup basket.

"Hot!" Her voice sounded harsh and out of control. "Get me some ice."

"Oh, Mom, I'm sorry." Evie yanked open the freezer and handed Betty an ice cube. "Here, put this on your lips."

"Cold!" Betty yelled and flicked the ice cube onto the floor. "Damn it."

"Oh, gosh." Evie got another ice cube, hurriedly wrapped it in a paper towel and dabbed at Betty's lips.

"It's all right. Stop. *Stop!*" Betty batted at Evie's hands, batted the ice away and glared at her daughter. Evie backed up. Betty unwrapped the ice cube carefully and dropped it into her coffee cup. Her breath came hard and fast.

"Goddammit, Vern," she said, then shook her head, realizing her mistake. When she glanced up, Evie stood against the cupboards, her hand over her mouth.

"*Tch.* I'm all right. Go. Get yourself dressed."

❧

Back in my bedroom, I leaned against the closed door before I could take a breath. Robert sat up in bed with the newspaper and a cup of coffee.

"What is it?" He dropped the paper into a crinkled pile and shifted up on the pillows.

"She's never been cross with me in her life, and now she's edgy as a ripsaw. I leave her alone and she's in the shower with her clothes on, but if I help, she gets upset. I don't know what I'm doing."

"She's an adult and you're treating her like a baby. That's what you're doing. Maybe you should back off a bit."

I sat on the end of the bed and wiped my face dry with the back of my hand. "I guess you're right, but how much? She can't tell the difference between Cover Girl Summer Beige and a mud pack, which is mostly funny, but, what if she had scalded herself in the shower?"

"She's been managing on her own for a long time, Eve."

"And, managing on her own landed her in the hospital."

There was bumbling in the hallway.

I got up to open the bedroom door.

"Ev-ie." Robert left the second syllable hanging high in the air. He pulled his reading glasses away from his eyes and fixed me in place with a look. "Give her just a little bit of space."

We both listened as we heard movement back down the hall.

I took a deep breath and let it out slowly. In the next moment, the phone rang.

"Oh, Barb. Thanks for calling back." I held the phone between my ear and shoulder as I grabbed a fresh sweater and a pair of jeans from a dresser drawer.

"I was thinking, if I could take one more day, then I could arrange to come in for at least half-days until my mother can fend for herself a little more."

I told my boss about what I'd been through that morning and the last few days.

"Sounds like my husband's dad. He passed away just this last month." She said the words quietly, as if feeling her way. "His father was a high ranking military man, decorated in WWII. Ran a successful investment firm for thirty years. Then, poof, his wife dies and he's wandering around the neighborhood in his underwear."

My stomach lurched suddenly, sending goosebumps up my back. I sat down too hard on the bed. My lips went cold and my face must have gone white. Robert's surprised expression morphed to a look of concern.

Barb went on: "James nearly ended up in the hospital taking care of his dad the last two years. Really tore him apart. It was pretty hard to manage that and fly an airliner. He had to give up a lot of hours." Barb's husband was an airline pilot with a crazy schedule. Not the kind of person you would expect to cave under pressure.

"How is he doing now? James, I mean." I hoped the question didn't sound as selfish as it felt.

"Actually, I think we're better off. It's things like this make you take inventory, you know. Give you a reality check. That's why I'm telling you. Get some help. Don't take this on by yourself." Her tone was gentle but firm. "Listen. You have been a tremendous help here to me. It would be hard to go back to operating without you, but if you need to take some extended time off—"

"Thanks, Barb, I…I'll let you know. But she's doing better already since she's gotten some rest." Surely this was a passing thing. My mother would be back on her own two feet soon.

"I'm not trying to scare you, Eve. It's just that James and I have been down this road, and it doesn't get better. It gets worse." She fell silent, letting the words sink in. "Evie?"

"I hear you." I didn't want to hear, but I did.

She said: "It's almost Christmas, we don't really need you here until after the first."

I heard: "If you can get your act together by then."

I shifted the phone to my other shoulder and jerked on my jeans. "No, no, that's okay. I can come in and pick up my code and finish it off on my laptop."

"Consider it a paid Christmas vacation."

As a fifty-three year old woman in a computer company full of twenty-somethings, the words "unplanned vacation" take on a whole new dimension. Things happen fast in the computer biz. Get caught napping, get left behind. You have to stay focused and you definitely have to stay *there.*

"Eve? You there?"

"Yes…I'm there, ah, here. I…I don't know what to say."

"Say 'Thank you' and 'Merry Christmas' and call me on the third."

"Thank you…and Merry Christmas."

"Tell Robert I said he is to keep you away from here." Her side of the conversation ended with a hollow click.

I looked at the dead phone in my hand, reserving my goodbye. Robert blinked at me again over his glasses, the question in his eyes.

"Looks like I'm off until the third. With pay." *Like severance pay, maybe.*

Robert looked right through to me, then shrugged.

"A gift," he said, turning back to his paper. He'd like nothing better than to see me quit and devote myself full time to our business. The issue had been a tug-o-war between us since we filed for incorporation. I had no choice now but to try it out, for a couple of weeks at least.

When I returned to the kitchen, Betty was at the sink, washing up the cups by hand. Her black suede jacket and red gloves were folded neatly over the back of a kitchen chair and her purse sat on the table.

She turned and saw me standing in the doorway. "Hi, Sweetie. Are you ready to go?"

There was no hint of anger or irritation in her voice. There was a little too much blush on her cheeks, but otherwise, she looked pretty close to the June Allison version of my mother.

"Well, I guess I am. Just let me get my boots."

11 Crossroads

We ventured out, Mom with her eyebrows on straight and me off work on a weekday. To my surprise, there were actually people out on the street—in the health food store, walking their dogs—real people. So this is what *they* do when I'm at my computer testing some piece of software, trying to explain to the programmer why it doesn't work. Something I had a hard time explaining to my husband that I actually loved to do. Something I might never do again unless my mother pulled off a miracle.

I helped her out of her seatbelt, then helped her out of the car and, realizing she was still a little weak, or uncoordinated, or both, I helped her across the sidewalk and into my favorite coffee joint. I ordered my usual non-fat, no-whip mocha while Mom stared at the colorful chalked menu hanging up on the wall behind the counter.

"Smells burnt in here," she said, louder than considered polite by coffee joint standards.

Adele, the shop owner, shrugged it off. "Hi Eve. This must be your mom." *Because she looked like me or because she was ornery?*

Betty sniffed loud and long, and before I knew what she was up to, reached her hand into one of the cookie jars on the counter and came out with a handful of sticky baklava.

I grabbed her wrist. "Hold on. We're going to get you

something."

"Sorry," I said to Adele.

She capped my mocha and pushed it forward. "Don't worry about it."

She didn't charge me for the baklava. I was hoping no one else had seen. Betty pulled me away from the counter, stuffing her mouth with the pastry like a starving orphan.

"She'll have a coconut mocha," I said over my shoulder and angled my mother toward a table. My wish for the idyllic mother/daughter outing had come true, only the characters were reversed. I was the mother and she was daughter. A one-hundred-and-thirty pound, expertly-coiffed-and-eyebrowed, two-year-old daughter.

The adage, be careful what you wish for, took on an amplified meaning. She was there, and not there, depending on your perception. Disappointment stuck in my throat like a rock of air. There was nothing to swallow, but it wouldn't go down. From the candy jar of perfect mothers, I had somehow managed to reach in and pull out the broken one.

I tried to keep her focused on our coffees and one of the tourist magazines, ooh-ing and ahh-ing over the gift shop and art gallery ads, the golf courses and the local scene. I could not remember the last time we had gone anywhere alone together. As she sipped her coffee, I tried to remember the last cogent conversation we'd had. Not that long ago, really, on the phone. She told me she had re-read her favorite novel, *A Woman of Substance*, by Barbara Taylor Bradford. I made a mental note to add browsing the local bookstore to my list of things she might enjoy doing. By nine o'clock, I'd put together a plan. We would check up on Vern, visit the bookstore, and perhaps drive by some places in town that might appeal to her as a place to live—when she was ready.

We had been gifted with another Ojai-warm Christmas season. The air was clear and the sky a striking blue against the chiseled mountains. She managed to drink her coffee without spilling anything down her blouse as we drove ten minutes across the valley to Crossroads Alzheimer's Care. Along the way, I jabbered about Ojai and the Chumash Indians and their folklore. She nodded and clucked and fiddled with her red gloves. I carried on my one-sided conversation, as if invoking the Chumash magic presence might have some kind of healing effect on her.

At the Crossroads main gate, I convinced her to leave the red gloves in her purse while I rang the bell at the office door. A camera mounted just under the eave panned and tilted toward the gate. A disembodied voice scratched out of the speaker inviting us to step inside.

Facing a polished maple desk were two wing-backed chairs upholstered in an elegant mauve floral design. My mother ran her hands over the fabric and smiled her approval. On the wall behind the desk, a Thomas Kinkade giclee in an ornate frame added a touch of bourgeois charm. I patted the chair next to me and my mother perched on the edge. I couldn't help but notice how she had risen to the occasion, despite the fact that she had not initiated one syllable of conversation since we left my house. The color had returned to her cheeks, her eyes shone clear and blue and I told her so.

"Seems like you're feeling a little better today."

She took a deep breath and swallowed hard. "Seems like I'm feeling better today," she said, and settled back into the chair. A moment later, a woman whooshed in to the small office through an inside door, suddenly filling the space with purpose.

"So sorry for the wait." She introduced herself breathlessly as Katherine and handed us each a business card, then sat behind the desk. She was a tall brunette, tastefully dressed in a flowing tunic of wine-colored faux-suede over an ankle-length skirt of the same color. She wore a simple moonstone pendant on a long silver chain and a matching bracelet at her wrist. I could see by the gleam in my mother's eyes that she approved. I was relieved. I suppose I was half expecting someone in a white coat and polished oxfords. Her card proclaimed that she had a doctorate in psychology and a master's degree in public health administration, and that she was the Managing Director of the home.

"And you must be Mrs. Salter." She tipped her head toward my mother.

Mom smiled broadly and extended her hand like royalty. "How do you do."

The hundred and thirty pound two-year-old had

disappeared and my mother sat beaming in her place. Katherine smiled sweetly at us and pulled a folder out of her desk drawer. "You two certainly look alike."

Mom looked over at me as if verifying the fact for herself. "Yes-s-s. We do," she said softly.

"How is Vern doing?" I asked. "I left him here with Sharlene two nights ago on a respite agreement."

"We just love him. He's so polite. So many of our men here are grumpy. And he likes our Christmas cookies."

Betty smiled and nodded. "Yes. He does," she said, her voice barely audible.

She sat erect on the edge of her chair again, holding her purse in her lap with her hands crossed neatly over the clasp. Several fingertips of a red glove stuck out of the closure as if some flat little woman were trapped inside and trying to get out. "May we see him now?"

Katherine's gaze took in the large rings on my mother's fingers and then she replied, "Of course."

Hesitating at the door, Katherine peered into the room through a small window before she gestured for us to get up.

As we crossed the threshold, I got the distinct sensation we were entering a protected, private world, one in which we did not belong.

The space had undergone a transformation since I'd left Vern there only two days before. Despite its linoleum floors and acoustic ceiling, it felt cheery and light. They had decorated for the holidays, a balanced mix of pine garlands and Christmassy bows and the soft blue and white colors of Hanukah. Gene Autry sang *Rudolph the Red Nosed Reindeer* softly over the scene, as if he were suspended somewhere above playing his guitar. The pervasive odor hovered somewhere between snickerdoodle cookie and Lysol.

"This is our social area." Katherine led us to a cheery breakfast room. "We bring everyone here for the day once they're washed and dressed."

Upholstered banquettes were arranged around the room like box seats in a theater, or little human corrals, depending on your point of view. A few residents were gathered in each one, some napping and some eating snacks from paper cups. How had they managed to wash and dress so many people before ten a.m.? It had taken me three hours to do one.

Katherine pointed out video cameras near the front door and the front gate, which we could now see through the window, and in one of the corners of the room. "The cameras are going all the time, so Sharlene, or whoever's on duty, can keep an eye on things from the office."

She showed us a central wall and a bank of tiny lights arranged on a map of the property. "There's a light for each resident's room. Once they've gone to bed, we get a light if there's any movement, both out here and in the office."

At the moment the lights were all dark. What happened when a light went on? Mom moved a little closer to my side and gave me a nervous smile.

"That's good." Her voice had taken on a spindly quality, hiding behind a pair of ever-widening eyes.

"Over here's our dining hall." We passed by a table where a family visited and talked while the apparent resident snoozed in a wheelchair beside them. "And here is our Living Room, where the more active residents hang out and talk or participate in games or exercises."

Here and there quiet souls sat blinking or staring, while others tried to follow a young woman who counted and raised her arms over her head.

"No! That's mine!" A man's voice, stridently frail, pierced the calm. We all looked around to see a woman pulling a blanket from the lap of a gentleman who had sprawled out on one of the larger banquettes.

Betty pointed. "That's not right."

Katherine called out to one of the helpers. "Martina! Did Miss Jenny get her meds this morning?"

A round-faced Hispanic woman with a torso to match hurried over to the pair and returned the blanket to the man, then guided Miss Jenny into the dining area.

"Got her, Katherine," she called to the manager, and then to Miss Jenny she said, "Let's get some juice, okay Miss Jenny?"

Jenny, a tall woman that looked to be no more than fifty, twisted a shock of her tightly frizzed hair. She gazed around in confusion, and then she angled toward the kitchen galley, her expression determined.

My mother's eyes grew wider still, and she fastened herself

securely to my arm as Katherine deftly steered us into another area. Across the room I saw a woman in a flowered smock helping Vern settle into one of the corrals.

"There he is." I pointed him out to my mother.

He looked up as we approached. "Evie? How'd you know we were here?"

I couldn't restrain a giggle, and started to explain, but Mom pushed past me and toward him as he stood up. They embraced awkwardly. She gave him a kiss on the cheek and patted him on his belly.

"I'll just leave you to visit," Katherine said. "Feel free to go out into the garden. Just come back over to my door when you're ready to leave."

I sat down next to Vern, but my mother remained standing, holding tight to her purse. She looked as though she were holding her breath. Another aide passed into our area carrying a tray of paper cups, each filled with bite size pieces of fruit, reminiscent of pre-school snacks.

"It's ten o'clock." Vern pointed to the large clock over the door into the dining room. "They bring around cookies, too. And martinis."

Mother scowled. He patted the seat next to him. "Sit down, Bett. They might think we are leaving." He took two fruit cups from the tray and handed one to his wife. Then he leaned in toward me.

"Did you make a reservation? They have good service here, but this place gets pretty busy." He nodded toward the dining room. "I think that's the captain's table, over there."

"No, I didn't make a reservation, but I think we'll be fine."

Betty snapped at him. " 'S'*not* the captain's table." She held the fruit cup tightly with both hands and sat on the edge of the seat.

I patted Vern's knee. In some ways he was doing much better than my mother. He had kept his manners and sense of presence as one accustomed to travel and dining in fine restaurants. He seemed at home and secure within his five-minute vignettes of memory, while my mother struggled with each new revelation.

Vern smiled back at me. "I'm really glad to see you. How'd you know I was here?"

"I brought you here."

His brow furrowed as he considered what I'd said. Then he looked up startled when an aide pushed a wheelchair past us. The woman in it smiled and waved, a drop of drool slipped onto a towel across her chest. Vern leaned over to me and said quietly, "It must be a special group. There's really a lot of them on this trip. They treat them extra nice, don't they?"

"Yes, they do." What else could I say? Behind us, a woman heaved a long sigh that trailed off like the wail of The Ghost of Christmas Past.

At that, my mother jumped up and started out of the enclosure, the fruit cup spilled a banana slice on the floor, unnoticed.

"Hold on a minute, Mom. We just got here. We can go outside." I gestured toward the windows. Though late December, the patio looked beautiful, and offered a sanctuary from the sights and sounds inside.

"Have breakfast with us?" Vern struggled out of his seat and took her hand.

"Ow!" she yelled, and pulled away. "That's too hard."

She headed for Katherine's door with the little window, only on this side it was a mirror.

"Where is she going?" The loneliness in Vern's voice made my heart ache. "She shouldn't go out there alone. It's dangerous."

"We'll be back in a few minutes." I gave him a quick hug and dashed to catch up with my mother. I had no idea what I was going to do, but it was plain that she couldn't stay another moment in that room.

The woman Katherine had addressed earlier as Martina appeared like an angel out of nowhere. She looped her arm through Vern's and turned him toward the door leading outside to the garden. "It's so lovely outside, Vern. Let's take a walk."

She looked over her shoulder and nodded at me, then hand signaled for me to go ahead and go.

I caught up with Mom just as she reached the door. Katherine opened it, and we scooted back into our seats. My mother took a deep breath, straightened her back, and squared her shoulders, then looked up at Katherine and forced a smile.

"You see? He's adjusting fine, Mrs. Salter. May I call you Betty?"

"Certainly." Her chin came up but her lips quivered and her hands white-knuckled her purse.

Katherine rearranged a notepad and pencil on her desk while we pulled ourselves together. The experience had rattled me too. I honestly wasn't sure if I had done the right thing. Vern seemed so lucid, so calm, while my mother seemed like the one falling apart. How could I possibly leave him here with drooling, vacant-eyed people? He was animated, talkative. He forgot what he'd just said, but otherwise he seemed like a normal person.

I took the deepest breath I could and sighed it away. I'd had trouble enough taking care of one, but who was I to decide what should happen to my mother's husband? To condemn him to live in this place? The weight of the decision, the responsibility, bore down on my heart.

"So. I guess we need to settle up on the respite care and get him ready to go home."

Betty reached across and grabbed my hand. Her eyes filled to the brim. "He should stay."

"Well, I know we had talked about it, but I don't want to force—"

"He should stay," Mom repeated, her jaw set in a way I'd never seen.

Katherine cleared her throat and scooted toward us in her chair. "Evie, has anyone explained his condition to you, I mean, other than this doctor's report?" She tapped her finger on the manila folder on her desk. "Korsakoff's Syndrome is irreversible, and he's *sun-downing*. I just get the feeling you don't know what you're dealing with here."

"P-s-s-h-h." Mom hunched her shoulders up around her ears and twisted the filigreed wedding band on her finger.

"Betty knows, don't you Betty."

Katherine pushed a box of tissue toward my mother and she took one and dabbed at her eyes. She looked over at me and said, "He's gone, Evie. Leave it here. Right now."

She opened her purse and pawed through it, collecting her wallet, a checkbook, and a pen and pushed it into my hands. "We have lots and lots of money."

I flipped open the checkbook cover, glancing up at Katherine as I did. "I can't sign on this account, but I guess I can fill it in," I turned back to my mother, "If that's what you really want."

"Ye-s-s-s," she said quietly, tapping the checkbook cover. "There's plenty. Vern went to the bank every day."

I flipped to the last entry in Vern's spindly but clear handwriting. It had indeed been done on the day before his fall:

Balance $50,970.00

My heart thunked hard in my chest. That seemed like a lot of money to keep in a checking account for two people who had an empty refrigerator and stayed home all the time. I quickly looked backward in the register, the usual entries were logged there—gas bill, homeowners association, house payment, MasterCard, *Reader's Digest*, automatic deposits from investment companies—all dated December and the math correct. Vern could still do the math, he just couldn't remember he'd eaten lunch.

"We have plenty of money," my mother repeated, shifting her gaze to Katherine.

"It all looks fine here." I made out a check to cover Vern's care for the remainder of December and January, then slid the book over to Mom and handed her the pen. She slowly signed her name. It was a little large and ended up running off the page. I recognized the familiar loops and angles of her handwriting from the fifty or so birthday cards I'd received, *i's* dotted with little circles, and high flying T's.

My eyes met Katherine's look of concern. "Just put your initials next to it," she said. "We all agree here what's intended."

I did what she suggested, tore the check out of the book and handed it to her. A sense of relief flowed over me, but I also felt like I had somehow betrayed Vern.

Katherine sensed my discomfort. Before she completed our receipt, she said, "It's really for the best, Eve. For him and for you. Believe me. Your mom has been dealing with him for a long time. She knows it's true."

Mom nodded into her lap, expelling a ragged breath. I offered a silent thanks that she saw the truth in the situation. I wouldn't have wanted to make the decision against her will.

We got up to leave.

"It's been a pleasure meeting you both," Katherine said. "Remember you can call and visit any time."

She slipped her arm across Mom's shoulder and looked directly into her eyes. "Betty, you may want to consider making your daughter a co-signer on your bank account. It might make things *easier.*"

Mother frowned at her for a moment, but their eyes held, and finally she smiled briefly, then said, "Thank you."

12 The Way it Is

My mother kept her gaze out the window as I drove us away from Crossroads and headed back into town. The morning sun cast a halo of light around her blonde hair. Her roots needed doing.

We were halfway back to town, and she hadn't said a word.

"Doing okay?" I asked.

She nodded, but kept her face turned away from me, her hands pressed together tightly between her thighs.

Back off a little, Evie.

I pushed a Sarah McLachlan CD into the player. Her voice was soothing, warm, and resonate as we rode on through the valley, the magic peaks watching over us.

"I like Frank Sinatra. He's in my car."

I'll bet.

"I like him too." That was something we had in common.

Her shoulders relaxed into the seat, her arms open and resting now on the armrests. I mentally added her music CDs to a growing list of reasons we needed to go back to San Diego, and soon.

My mind shifted to questions about their finances as I drove. I knew they had money, but I didn't know exactly where and how much. They would have payments and insurance on a new Cadillac neither of them could drive, and a home they could no longer live in together. Of necessity, I had always been conservative with my money. These expenses felt uncomfortable to me. What could easily be five thousand or more a month in separate care expenses could blow through fifty thousand pretty quick.

Years ago my mother mailed me a safe deposit key with a penciled note saying that I would one day be the executor of their estate. I could see that handwriting in my mind. When they were gone, they wanted their estate split evenly between my stepbrother, John, and me.

But they weren't gone. Not really. There had been no provisions for implosion.

Where did that leave me in terms of making decisions on their behalf? How could I ask my mother about her money without seeming pushy or greedy? We had never discussed anything close to what I needed to know. We would need to set up a living trust, and soon, while we could certify she was mentally competent. From what I'd seen, it could be too late already.

My left eyelid started to twitch as we pulled up in front of our first planned stop, an assisted care home in the town's center. It was a low, stucco building with a gray composite roof set back from the street behind a square patch of dirt coaxed green by the recent rains. A maid's cart blocked the first of four doors, each identical, each separated by a plain, casement window. The entire façade was desperately in need of paint. At the end of the narrow, covered walkway, a wheelchair ramp led to a parking lot. There, an old Cadillac hunkered in a nest of grass and weeds, flanked by two tall Cypress trees, like a monument to the fifties. A sudden thought that the former owners might be buried under there snapped me to attention.

Betty crinkled her nose and straightened in her seat. It was a long way from their exclusive golf resort retirement community. If posture could power a car, we'd be halfway to Bakersfield by the sheer force of her intention.

"My sentiments exactly." I pulled away from the curb as if

avoiding a close brush with a steep cliff.

The next stop, only a few blocks from our home, was a little more inviting: a series of cute cottages arranged in clusters among immaculately kept rose gardens and plush green lawns. Each cottage had the mark of its owner—a porch swing, wicker chairs, a collection of orchids, a birdcage hung out for the morning air. We saw a number of men and women outdoors, some using walkers and some moving easily on their own.

Mom gathered her purse and sweater as we pulled up to the curb. A good sign.

Inside the office, we were greeted by a tall woman, thin and stiff as a fence post. Her clamp-on earrings swung like railroad signs off the ends of her earlobes. She freshened her lipstick quickly and volunteered to show us around.

"We have a few openings coming up, but there's a waiting list," she said over her shoulder as we followed her past the main building to a row of cottages at the back of the complex.

The room was large, intended for the resident to live basically, in one room. The bath was small but clean and there was a breakfast bar with an outlet for a coffee pot and microwave. "Residents gather in the main dining room for their meals," the woman said, her face getting longer as she led us inside.

Betty slipped her purse over her shoulder and leaned in close to me. "Where's the bedroom?"

Right. Who lives in one room?

The woman led us back across the complex to the main building, a restored Craftsman-style mansion with wide steps leading to an expansive porch under generous eaves. Some residents breakfasted outside this morning. A server refreshed their coffees.

"We start serving breakfast at six, lunch is our big meal, and supper is usually light, with a nice dessert."

My mother beamed when we entered the dining room. The large, open hall was well lit, and the high ceiling was sectioned in rich, dark woods. Tables were set with soft pink linens and bone china, crystal water goblets, and fine silverware. Gold sateen napkins tented each plate and the chairs were upholstered in matching pink and gold striped sateen. The walls were hung with attractively-framed copies of art classics—Renoir, Van Gogh, and Monet.

"Assigned seating changes every month so residents can get to know a variety of people."

Betty trailed her fingers along the backs of several of the chairs. "Like on a cruise," she said. "I like that."

I could imagine her sitting with a couple of ladies, sipping tea and swapping tales about their trips to Europe. But after our experience in the bathroom that morning, I had trouble imagining her getting up, dressed, and down here on her own.

"What if it's raining, for meals, I mean, or if someone is sick?" I had to hurry to keep up with our tour guide as we continued through the library, across the porch, and back toward the rental office. I guessed she was in a hurry.

"Oh, they use their raincoats and umbrellas," she said over her shoulder, "and if it's *really* bad, we pick them up in our electric carts. They can have meals delivered occasionally, if they're sick."

She cut her eyes back at Mom, who trailed six feet behind us. "If getting to meals is an issue, you may want to consider our facility across the street. There's more personal help and it's all under one roof." *In other words, a nursing home.*

"Would you like to get on our waiting list then?"

The agent handed Betty a form as we passed back through the office.

"I'd like that," Mom said, imitating the woman's business casual tone. She spread the form out on the surface of a small visitor's desk. She looked at it for a moment, then carefully scrawled "Betty" across the full page of boxes intended for name, address, phone, bank references, former residences, references, nearest relatives, and a short bio. When she was finished, she completely missed crossing the T's, drawing a line across the desk instead, then folded the paper in half and handed it to me.

The agent sent me a curious look.

I bit my upper lip, then tucked the form into my purse. "You know, I think we'll take this home and fill it out there."

I masked my disappointment with a thin smile. The place had fed my dream vision: Mom living a couple of blocks away and having some independence. But her response to the form kicked a hole in the fantasy, and through it I caught a glimpse of her at Crossroads with Vern.

I guided us back to the car and helped her in.

"Well," I said, clearing the knot out of my throat. "That was a little more what I had in mind."

"Um hum. I liked it too. I liked the dining room."

"If you got settled there, we could bring Vern over to visit whenever you want."

Betty looked startled, then scowled at me. "No! No Vern."

"Well, of course. You could go see him." She closed up again and scowled ahead to the street.

Our last stop took us to Cameo Villa, a private home on two acres at the west side of town. Fruit trees flanked a driveway leading to an enclosed deck with a sparkling pool and Jacuzzi. A lovely patio offered views of the valley and surrounding mountains. The house was set behind the pool against an easy incline dotted with young avocado trees. The owner, Theresa Cain, a wide-beamed woman with a smile to match, met us at the front door.

"Hello, you must be Betty," she said and offered her hand. Mom shook it skeptically, apparently still a little miffed at my comment about Vern.

"Is this a working avocado orchard?" I asked, hoping to divert my mother's attention to the present moment.

"Why, yes. We've replaced a lot of old growth with Pixie tangerines though. We've been here since the sixties."

"Then you saw the hippie days, down at Libbey Park?"

"Oh yes. And then some."

Mom perked up at this.

"My daughter was a hippie," she said, as if I wasn't standing there next to her. It came out of the blue like that daughter no longer existed. I supposed that was true enough.

"Weren't we all." Theresa laughed easily and showed us inside to the room that would be available in two weeks. The current occupant would be moving, coincidentally, to Crossroads. It had a private bath, ample room for Mom's things, and a nice view across the valley.

Theresa walked us through the main living areas of the home, which, if not elegant, were comfortable, cheery, and clean. She kept up a dialog as we went.

"Some of our residents enjoy helping with meals, but we have a full-time cook. We all love to play cards here. Betty, do you like to play cards?"

I remembered seeing a deck of cards laid out in the Solitaire pattern on Mom's kitchen table the last time I was there. Mom smiled and nodded graciously. "Um hum."

Three women looked up as we walked into the dining room where the one nearest us was collecting a well-worn deck. "We're just about ready to have lunch. Why don't you join us, Betty, and your daughter can come back later?"

"That sounds nice," I said. Mom lifted her chin and turned her back to me without so much as a look.

Theresa circled the table and pulled out a chair for her. "We all can get to know each other." She introduced my mother to the other ladies at the table. She smiled widely and nodded in her most gracious Betty style.

I stepped toward the door, half expecting her to change her mind, but she slipped into the role easily and when I said I'd be back in an hour, she waved goodbye confidently.

"She'll be fine, just leave me your phone number in case…well…just in case. And," Theresa slipped her hand into her pocket and brought out a card, "Here's my number, too."

"Thanks. This is wonderful," I said, keeping my voice low. "I haven't had an hour to myself in four days."

"This is really the best way to introduce a new resident…before we make any commitments…you understand."

I was a little taken aback and I hoped it didn't show. It had never occurred to me that my mother might not be accepted. *My movie-star mom under scrutiny?* "Well, of course."

Theresa followed me out to the car, her voice lowered to be sure only I could hear. "The lady who's moving out? She's in the hospital now. She was borderline a few months ago when we took her. I knew it was a mistake. Our residents are frail, but they have all their mental faculties. She just didn't fit in here."

"Well, my Mom's doing fine. She's been a little confused since her bout with pneumonia, but she's getting better every day."

Theresa's mouth curled up in a smile, but her eyes looked doubtful.

"She certainly looks well, and she's a lovely woman, I'm sure. I expect she'll be fine." She pushed my car door closed gently, her eyes warm, compassionate, but reflective as they met mine. "We'll talk after lunch."

As I drove back toward town, I had to grip the steering wheel to stop my hands from shaking and my eyelid twitched faster. I had just left my mother with a stranger. My stomach took a roll and I worked to breathe out of a panic. *Just go downtown to the bank, and maybe get a smoothie at the health food store. She'll be fine.*

I sat outside at my usual spot, sipping and watching a young mother unload her daughter from the back seat of an old Toyota. She reminded me of myself in the sixties—poor, a bit raggedy, worried about the rent and the car payment—and so in love with the smell of the top of my baby's head. I went without fancy clothes and nights out on the town so I could stay home with her. As I watched them make their way down the street, another image slipped into my mind: A mother and daughter riding a horse. They look into the camera, their faces shining, their curly hair the same, pale blonde. The baby's hands grip the pommel of the saddle. The mama holds the reins tightly around the baby's sides. My mother and me.

When did she decide to let me go? I straightened in my chair, uncrossed my legs and planted my feet firmly on the ground.

The smooth rumble of a big Lincoln Navigator pulling up behind the Toyota brought me back to the present. I watched the hurried father jump out. A young child was strapped into a kiddie seat in the backseat of the car. The man opened the door and said something to the boy that made him shriek, then shut the door and sprinted into the deli.

Suddenly, I felt small and alone, like the littlest kid on the merry-go-round, unable to slow the spinning or get off by myself.

I put down the smoothie and craned my neck around to see if the father was coming.

Not yet.

I turned away and squeezed my eyes shut. *Mind your own business.*

Robert. I needed to talk to Robert, just hear his voice, something to hold onto that felt right. I checked the time on my cell phone. Eleven o'clock. He would still be in his meeting at the county and he had a doctor appointment after that. I would have to pull *myself* together, the way I always had.

The phone buzzed in my hand and I nearly jumped off my seat. The number on the display was unfamiliar—oh, that would be Theresa.

"Is everything all right?" *Could an hour have passed already?*

"Oh, sure. Your Mom's having a great time. I just want to chat with you a moment, before you pick her up."

I detected a purposeful edge to her tone. *I had dared to hope.* "You know, every once in a while, she can't think of a word, but mostly she's—"

"It's more than that, Eve." She cleared her throat and I could tell she was searching for a way to continue. I pressed the phone to my ear. The kid in the Navigator was screaming now, tears running down his reddened cheeks. His little arms reached suddenly toward the window, and I turned to see his father coming out the door, a coffee in one hand and a bottle of juice in the other.

"Eve? Are you there? Can you talk?"

"Yes." My heart leapt out of my chest. "I'm outside, at Healthberry, downtown. There's a car, just a moment." I gulped air. Holding his juice bottle, a straw poking out of it, the little boy choked back tears. I shifted the phone to my other ear as the Navigator pulled away. "I can hear you now, please, go on."

"I'd be remiss if I didn't give you my…opinion…on this. In my business, Eve, we see the progression, and we *know*. She might never be back where she was. Have you thought about that?"

My arms went rubbery weak, the smoothie suddenly heavy in my hand. "I realize now I've been trying not to."

I looked around me—people across the street, in their cars, in line at the deli, sitting at the next table—their lives seemed to be on even keels. Their truth, at least for the moment, simpler and easier than my own.

"I know this is difficult for you. It's sad to see your mom slipping away."

Slipping away.

"We had a nice conversation about where she was born and where she had traveled, even though she was polite, the other ladies were, well, a little impatient with her. She missed the concept of taking turns at cards, and couldn't get it that we were laying down the same suit or number. When these kinds of things fall away, they don't come back. Six months from now, the picture will be…very different."

My stomach took a roll. I struggled to control my voice. Who was she to tell me what my mother could or couldn't do?

"What am I supposed to do? I can't put her in one of those, those, nursing homes."

A woman sitting in a nearby table moved further down, giving me a disapproving look. "She can't be ready for that," I said, lowering my voice to a whisper. "She's always had the best of everything. She'd be mortified. She'd die!"

I drew in a deep breath, shocked that I had just blurted my innermost fear to a stranger. It was as if I had this one chance before a giant wave rolled into Ojai out of nowhere and sucked me down.

"Oh, Eve, honey. Hang on. There are several homes in the valley like mine that do take people like your Mom. We meet together often. Come get her and do something fun with her this afternoon. I'll call you with some numbers later. I'm so sorry I've upset you."

Mom was quiet again on the way home. At the signal in the middle of town, I reached over and caressed her shoulder.

"I screwed up." She reminded me at that moment of a child with no valentines in the envelope taped to her desk. I wanted to crush her to me, but the light had changed.

"We're not in any hurry. We're doing just fine for now." *Do something fun.* "Let's go get some ice cream."

She gave me a downturned grin. "Rum Raisin. That's mine."

Rum raisin her favorite ice cream? I didn't know that about her.

My mother was helping me make a salad for dinner, breaking lettuce into a bowl when Robert arrived home. "Well, how did you ladies do?"

If only he knew. I summarized our day briefly, more for Mom's benefit than his. We would have to talk later. "Oh, we saw Vern, looked at a few places, and then we went downtown for ice cream. We had some fun, huh Mom."

"We had some fun." She went back to her lettuce, carefully ripping the crisp leaves into bite-sized pieces. "We're not in a hurry."

Robert sent me a puzzled look. I waved him off. "How did your doctor's appointment go?"

Robert had been ignoring an angry rash on his left arm and side and had finally agreed to see someone about it. "It's shingles. The doc said it was left over from having chicken pox when I was a kid."

He dropped his briefcase to the kitchen floor and pulled up his shirt. "Look at that Betty, I got shingles!"

Betty stopped ripping lettuce and turned around.

"The doc said I got 'em because I'm stressed, and I'm old."

Mom snorted out a little laugh as she sidled up to Robert and ran her fingertips gingerly over the angry spots. She lowered his shirt carefully and patted it down over his stomach. "You're not as old as me. I have brain shingles."

13 Three Geishas

Dear Lolette,

I was so sorry to hear about your mom. She was such a wonderful friend and comfort to my mom over the years. I know Betty really appreciated having someone to talk to once Vern started to fade. She and your mother had so much in common, living through the war times and all. My mother took me across the street to see her the last time we were at the house, just before her birthday in March. She played Moonlight Sonata for us just as sweet and beautiful as I've ever heard it played. I would never have guessed she was nearly blind.

Betty is doing well, thanks for asking. It took us a while, but we found a place where she feels at ease and I don't have to worry about her being alone. She seems happy having less to worry about, but insisted on bringing her rose, which I now understand was a gift from your mother.

I had hoped she would have more of a life on her own; but she really doesn't relate well socially anymore. The Rosewood Cottage is lovely, and Reba, the owner, has much loving patience. I don't know what I would have done without her help. We put Betty on a new medication, which has perked her up a little. It's hard to know how *long it will last, I'm told.*

We put her house on the market last week. August is a good month for real estate, I hear, so we're hoping for a quick sale.

I haven't told Betty about your mom's passing. I'm afraid if I told her that her friend was gone, it would surely break her heart. Much love to your family, Evie

❧

Betty puttered in her own kitchen and listened as Evie and their financial advisor, Edward, got to know one another over mocha lattes and her wrought iron and glass dinette. Betty and Evie had gotten up early and driven three hours to San Diego and she was a little tired. Evie had suggested she lie down for a rest, but first she wanted to see Evie's face when Ed showed her the value of what would—maybe sooner than later—be her inheritance. He went through the checkbooks, the investments, pensions, and IRA accounts. Evie was nodding, taking it all in very seriously.

Betty picked up a hinged photo frame from the kitchen counter, she on one side and Vern on the other. She had removed them from their old passports the last time they ordered new ones. The people in the pictures looked so young and smart. She held the frame to her chest and listened to the conversation. Evie and Edward had not yet opened the folder with the San Diego Bank accounts. Ed was thorough, talking Evie through every detail.

Betty had been fond of Eduardo Ortiz from the start. Not long after Vern began talking and driving in circles, Ed had noticed the change in activity in their bank account and called to see if anything was wrong. Since then he had been helping her manage their money, and their investments had grown accordingly. Often he brought his lovely wife and their sweet little daughter to her home. He had agreed to meet Evie immediately when they called him.

"Now this," he was saying, "is a power of attorney form for each of them. You'll need to get the signatures notarized, and..."

Betty craned her neck over the counter to see that Edward

had picked up the blue folder. That was the one. The one that would make Evie believe. "…this is the summary report."

"Oh, my goodness," Evie said, covering her mouth with her hand. Her face paled, then blushed red. "I had no idea."

She cut her eyes over to Betty. Betty breathed a sigh of relief. This is what she had been waiting for.

"See?" Her fingertips resting on the short string of freshwater pearls at her neck. "We have lots and lots. The number is big." And now Evie knew what that number was, even though Betty couldn't make the numbers in her mind.

She felt an odd mix of sadness and relief. A good night's sleep had left her feeling awake and alive, aware of all that was happening to her. This had been a good thing. She had been able to guide Evie to what was important. But the clarity was also a curse. She could see what was coming. She and Vern had always talked about their three-step plan: retiring early, traveling the world, and when they were gone, their kids would split the inheritance. Betty smiled to herself. Step one and two had certainly gone well. But they had clearly missed a step, even with brain shingles, she knew that much.

"We'll need you to sign these too, Mom. They'll let me make decisions when you…if you need me to."

Betty startled alert again. She went to the table and signed where Evie pointed her finger, then squeezed Evie's shoulder. "Thank you, sweetie." She flashed the side of her smile that worked best. "I don't need the numbers anymore."

She turned away, leaving them to their work, ghosting back through the kitchen and down the hall, feeling suddenly light and airy. It was strange being back in her home after all that had happened. Like visiting the home of a close relative— familiar, but not your own.

She stopped at the doorway to the master bedroom where Vern had slept for the last few years, alone. The dressers and nightstands, hand-painted Asian scenes in soft pastels on an ivory background, brass-cornered and hinged, were part of their last big real estate tradeoff: She would give up her big house in Villa Park and move to the smaller, more sensible townhouse if she got to completely redecorate, starting from scratch. It had been fun, but it was just furniture, after all. She would pick out a few favorite pieces, like the jewelry armoire, and Evie could do what she wanted with the rest.

She opened the painted doors of the armoire, pulled out a drawer, and opened a blue velvet box inside. She took off the pearl necklace and placed it in the box, arranging the clasp at the back, face up, then slipped it slowly back into its vault and closed the doors again. How Vern had loved to buy her jewelry and watch her put it on and put it neatly away, each piece in its own gift box, each box in its special drawer inside the armoire.

Now she and Evie had put him neatly away.

She left the master bedroom, closing the door behind her, and went into her own, smaller room—her sanctuary for the last few years.

She lay down on top of the silk duvet. The room embraced her with its odd mix of Asian art and Country French— knockoffs all—bought at Lloyds of Long Beach. It was important then. Now it was garage sale material. Who the hell wants a fake Samurai helmet anyway?

Betty lay on her back holding the picture frame she had brought from the kitchen. She tipped it up onto her chest. The handsome travelers smiled back at her, their images stamped through with an official seal. They had been headed to a Japanese steel manufacturer in Osaka, where Vern and their company were valued suppliers. After business, they would cruise to Tokyo and play golf, teeing off in full view of Mt. Fuji.

❧

"And now, the most beautiful woman in the world." When Vern finished his introduction, Betty glided out of the bathroom and into the sitting area of their stateroom. She wore an elegant, but conservative suit of pale blue satin brocade with blue pumps she had had dyed to match, white satin gloves, a diamond tennis bracelet at her wrist, and the diamond studs Vern had bought her for her birthday. Vern zoomed in with his new movie camera, capturing her smile on film. "And I'm the luckiest man in the world."

She smiled into the lens like a pro, did a little spin, and then sat provocatively on a banquette near the double windows of their luxury cabin. Their exclusive Captain's Circle passage made them part of an elite group who dined at the captain's table each night of the seven-day cruise departing from Hong Kong and stopping in several ports of call between Osaka and Tokyo.

Vern spun the dial on their personal safe, and then removed a silver box tied with a sateen ribbon. "And these are for my most elegant wife-san."

Betty opened it eagerly, expecting a bauble. Instead, the contents confused her.

She looked at him quizzically. "Golf gloves?"

Vern sashayed over to her side and nuzzled her neck. "I have it on good authority that we, that is, both of us, are invited to play golf with the president of the steel company and Japan's Minister of Finance."

"My goodness. Are we going to buy that much steel?"

"Sweetheart, we're going to buy so much steel, it will make their heads spin." Vern pulled the bottle of champagne out of the ice bucket. Betty didn't remember it being there when they arrived. He popped the cork and poured a half-glass into each specially-engraved Captain's Circle flute.

"But won't our US suppliers be hurt?" She took one of the flutes into her gloved hand.

"Not as much as our buyers when you beat the pants off of them on their own golf course, so you won't be doing that, will you?"

Betty laughed and shrugged her shoulders. "You never know."

"Besides, we're contributing to Japan's economic recovery. And we're helping to build a huge infrastructure there. There'll be Japanese workers, but also Americans. Everybody wins. And I'll be getting a big fat bonus for saving our company millions of dollars."

He clinked his glass with hers.

"Well, I'll drink to that!" Betty emptied her glass. "I'm ready for new bedroom furniture."

"Whatever's necessary."

Vern kissed her on the cheek, careful not to mess up her lipstick, then spun her around to the windows and they looked out over the bright lights of Hong Kong as the great ship began its slow exit from the harbor.

When they arrived at the Captain's table, all eyes were on Betty as they took the last two seats. She rewarded them with her elegant smile as Vern pulled out her chair. Compton College's Glamour Girl had arrived. This certainly beats the hell out of Compton.

The schmoozing began the moment they debarked the ship in Osaka Harbor. The Japanese company's limousine met them at the dock and transported them directly to their hotel where they rested and changed for a pre-arranged dinner at one of Osaka's foremost teahouses.

As soon as they arrived, they were whisked to a private room where they were greeted by two geishas who escorted them to their places at a low table. Though their makeup was flawless, and their kimonos stunning, Betty could see that they were not the young girls they once were. The tallest was maybe near her own age—thirty-ish—but the shorter, rounder one was clearly older, and the wide sash around her torso looked like it was too tight for her to breathe. But Betty admired their graceful postures and the dance-like way they moved their hands.

Vern squirmed uncomfortably in the low seats, obviously designed for people of smaller stature, but Betty was captivated by the elegant décor in the room. Silk paintings graced the walls and low, black-lacquered tables held porcelain vases and graceful fresh flower arrangements. A bonsaied elm stood on a flower table in one corner. A pair of sliding panels opened at one end of the room onto a private patio, where a stone pagoda arched above a koi pond. Small lanterns lit the scene from the edge of the deck. Betty watched in awe as a golden koi fish broke the surface with his searching mouth as if it were an air-breathing creature that could step up onto the deck if it wanted to. She had to pull her eyes away from the sight to join the introductions.

Once everyone was seated, the younger geisha knelt between Betty and Vern, and the other between the two Japanese who had invited them. Betty couldn't help but capture the moment in her mind. It was an event she could never have imagined, yet here they were. At six-foot-two with his striking blue eyes, Vern was as much a contrast to the shorter, dark-eyed Japanese as Betty, with her tightly-coiffed champagne beige hair and face tanned from years of California golf, was to the geishas.

At the center of the table were two boxes wrapped in thin rice paper that looked like patterned silk, each tied with a red cord.

"Mr. and Mrs. Salter, please accept these humble gifts. It is our great pleasure to present them to you for coming all this way to join us."

One of the geishas passed a box to Betty, and the other to Vern. Inside Betty's box was an exquisite brooch of pearls resting on a fern leaf of fine gold. Vern's gift was a set of jade cufflinks, in the center of each rested a calligraphic character, one represented Luck, the geisha told him, and the other Prosperity. Betty was speechless. As suppliers to many corporations in the states, they had been gifted many times, but never anything so extravagant and beautiful. Vern smiled in approval of her silence and then bowed to the men. "Thank you gentlemen, you are too kind."

They were well into their third bottle of sake before the conversation turned to steel and logistics and the practicality of the projects they had in mind. Betty didn't remember much of this conversation. She was captivated by the geishas, who seemed to her like automated dolls, not the kind that would later take the men off for personal pleasure, but there for the sole purpose of responding to their every need.

As the dinner progressed to a close, the two geishas flowed around the table serving yet another round of sake. It was the first time Betty had ever tasted the warm liquor. She didn't much care for the flavor, but it relaxed her and she let herself slip into her glamour girl persona. This did not go unnoticed by the geishas, who mimicked her poses and giggled. Betty quickly picked up on the game and began to exaggerate her moves. They rested their fingertips at their necklines, lifted their chins and smiled broadly at the men who visibly strained to ignore them. Then Betty poured sake for Vern and rolled her eyes away from his puzzled glance. Even the two Japanese men allowed a reserved chuckle, but in the next moment, the room fell silent. The geishas, and Betty, had, by their sheer presence in the room and their contrasting beauty and elegance, succeeded in bringing the business talk to a total standstill.

The two Japanese stood and addressed Vern: "Mr. Salter-san, I think these women are having a better time entertaining your wife than they are us. Shall we take our meeting elsewhere and let them have their fun?"

Vern had bowed deeply, "Whatever's necessary," he said, and winked at Betty.

At first she was a little concerned, but as the men left, the geishas began to giggle again and they poured three more sakes and held theirs aloft. Betty picked hers up and they clinked them together.

"Cheers." Betty drank in one quick gulp and twaked the tiny cup back on the table.

"Cheehs." The two geishas chimed in, and did the same.

"Well, it looks like it's just us chickens."

The geishas looked at her, their white faces cracking quizzical smiles. "Chickens?"

"Girls. Just us girls?"

The two geishas clinked their sakes together once more and chanted: "Jus us gurls," and laughed, their hair ornaments dancing.

Betty rose and went to the silk paintings to get a closer look. Their graceful beauty nearly took her breath away. And the stone lantern in the garden—she would love to have one of those at home.

The room suddenly became very warm and her mouth was as dry as her mother's biscuits. There was a pitcher of water in the center of the table, but the servers had already removed the dirty dishes including all the *glasses. Oh, but she needed a drink of it. She went to the table, knelt down and picked up the pitcher in both hands. The geishas stopped their giggling and stared at her as she tipped it up and drank until she felt the ice cold water cool her insides and settle the room from spinning. Betty passed the pitcher to the older geisha, then wiped her chin with the back of her hand. They each took a turn at the pitcher.*

The young geisha took out a hair ornament and scratched deep into her scalp with it in several places. "You have children, Betty-san?"

"Yes, a daughter."

"She must be very beautiful, like her mother," she said. "What is her age?"

"She'll be twelve, next month." She was beautiful. And at almost twelve, Betty saw Jimmy's face every time she looked at her. She needed to remember to call Evie's grandmother as soon as they get home to arrange a birthday visit.

"An auspicious year for a girl," the geisha said, and stuck the hair ornament back into its place.

The older geisha spoke now, her eyes averted.

"My daughter would be twenty-one now." She dragged her gaze low across the table and away from Betty's.

"Sagi-san, now is not the time...there were many losses, not only our own." The younger geisha slipped her eyes toward Betty as if to suggest she might have lost someone too. "Sagi's daughter was killed in Nagasaki."

Under the spell of the orient and the majestic beauty of their surroundings, it was easy to forget the conflict that had ended only a few years earlier. For Betty, the war had been a short period of waiting glossed over by Glenn Miller and Frank Sinatra tunes, and homecomings at the Coconut Grove. Many US soldiers had been lost, but the majority of US women and children had been spared the true horrors of war.

"I'm sorry, Sagi," Betty said. She wasn't much on politics, so she stuck to Vern's advice and said no more on the subject.

She supposed for all the differences, they were very much alike. They all had their hair done in elaborate buns and swirls, they all wore expensive silk, they were welcome when it was time to look beautiful and wait on their male counterparts; but when it came to make the big decisions, the ones that drew blood, they were forgotten. Betty pushed the thoughts away. Angry thoughts made wrinkles. She put Sagi's daughter and her own out of her mind.

The doors slid open and the men motioned the geishas out. Vern stepped past them and Betty waved to them as he guided her out by the elbow. She thought mischievously about winning at least a few holes at golf tomorrow, just to show them she could.

❧

Betty let her gaze rest on the Samurai helmet. How many years had it sat on its silk pillow in the corner of her bedroom? She closed her eyes, suddenly very tired, and her head ached. She curled up on her side and let herself slip into a catnap.

When she awoke, the light in her room had dimmed, and she heard voices outside the window.

"Vern! There's someone outside! Vern!" She went to the window and peeked out between the curtains, but saw no one.

"Mom?"

Betty turned to see Evie standing in her bedroom doorway. Strange of her to show up without calling first.

"Edward is leaving. Did you want to say goodbye?"

Edward? Oh. Yes. "Sure, I do."

She put her hand in her daughter's and allowed herself to be led to the front door.

14 Auspicious Twelve

Frank Sinatra and friends like Ella Fitzgerald and Lena Horne sang us back up the coast, all the way across Orange County, through the San Gabriel Valley and down the Conejo grade toward home. My mother had fallen into a peaceful sleep somewhere around Westwood, her head leaning against the passenger window, her mouth open. Good. She needed the rest. I knew she had been pushing herself for my sake.

And then it hit me, that face—the slack expression. For a moment, I felt like I was twelve again.

"You know, when you turn twelve," my cousin Sharlene had said, "you can decide which parent you want to live with."

At fifteen Sharlene's worldly knowledge impressed me. I ate up every word. She would later work as a paralegal in San Francisco, and I would learn that most of the decisions that would affect my young life would be made over the top of my head, not inside.

The first one—that my broken front teeth, the result of a pogo stick accident, had not matured enough for caps—was made by a cold dentist and my dad's feeble bank account. I would enter junior high the following year on the social "B" list.

The cosmic decisions were made by Grandma—we were Christian Scientists. We—meaning my grandparents and me;

and the Nathaniels, my aunt and uncle and my cousins, Sharlene and Nick who lived close by—went to church on Sunday mornings and Wednesday evenings. Every week. We read Bible lessons every day before school. I'm the only baby boomer I know without a polio vaccine scar tattooed on my shoulder. We did not smoke, drink, or have sex out of wedlock, and we did not divorce. (My parents did all of those things, but at twelve, I had no choice but to accept it as one of the mysteries.)

We loved the entire universe and the entire universe loved us. In Grandma's house, love was spelled with a capital "L" and could be substituted for God. All other four letter words were banned, unless you twirled up her Irish ire. Then, her tirades could peel the wallpaper. During these times, I followed my grandpa into the dim red light of his darkroom and helped him develop photos he took wherever we went on our Sunday afternoon drives.

Secretly, I had issues with God. Apparently *he* had decided I would be a late bloomer. It was bad enough that he gave me divorced parents and a rip-saw smile, but he had also decided that I would be skinny and flat-chested. The rest of the girls in my Sunday school class, and many of the girls in the sixth grade were sporting at least the beginnings of breasts inside training bras and I had not even the suggestion that mine would sprout, let alone grow into a real bra like Sharlene's. Grandma decided I would wear the training bra anyway. I was in humiliation training.

Two weeks before my twelfth birthday, my father decided that it was time he took responsibility for raising his daughter, brought home a woman he met while job-shopping in Texas, and dragged me like an aching tooth from my grandparents' home in the middle of an orange grove in Anaheim to an apartment building off Hawthorne Boulevard in Torrance, a town that despite being right on California's coast, smelled perpetually of oil, sulfur, and auto exhaust.

The apartment building was rundown tropical—tiki torches out front of a colorless cellblock, two tall palms marking the entry. Sharlene said Fay Wray could be tied screaming between those palms one day when I got home from school. Visions of King Kong staggering down the boulevard had me using the side entrance. From my bedroom window in the corner apartment, I could see the bobbing horses heads of oil pumps by day and the lights dotting the hillsides of Palos Verdes by night.

I would learn that Ruth—an open-mic honky-tonk singer and barmaid from St. Charles, Louisiana who wore deep red lipstick and nail polish, and halter-top trumpet dresses on Saturday night—would be making a lot of decisions for me from then on, usually while squinting around smoke from a cigarette stuck to her bottom lip.

My mother decided to postpone our birthday visit until the weekend after the actual event so that she could recuperate from the exhaustion of her cruise through the Orient and two weeks of furniture shopping for her new home.

In light of recent events, and because I was *officially* twelve, I had made *my own* decision. The time was right to let my mother in on my plan. Though I have forgiven her for all transgressions since becoming a mother myself, my twelfth birthday stands out in my memory as a turning point in our relationship.

❧

"What are you doing still in bed, Evie? Shouldn't you be getting ready to go to your mother's?"

I lifted my head off the pillow to see Ruth's reflection in the mirror across from the bed, my stomach clamped in a painful knot. I groaned and dropped my head back down with a thud. This week, her hair was frizzy black, it matched the black and white tuxedo halter top and short black-skirted barhop outfit she wore at the Golden Gables Bowl where she worked. She swaggered over to the window next to the bed and lifted the shade, her black high heels sharp enough to tenderize meat. Not the image I was used to on Sunday morning.

She spotted the blood-stained pajama bottoms I had thrown on the dirty clothes basket, stubbed out her cigarette in the ashtray on my father's drafting table which shared my room and blew smoke hard out of her lungs.

"You come sick?" She came over to the side of the bed,

smiling as if I had just been nominated Miss Teen Torrance.

"I guess so." It was not the term they used in the facts of life class at school, but I got the meaning. Basically, the facts were that God had made yet another terrible mistake. "My stomach hurts."

I rolled away from her and brought my knees up to my chest against the gnarling pain.

Ruth skipped out of the room. "Jim, guess what? Evie got her per-i-od!"

I rolled back over and gripped my guts. She came back a minute later with a glass of water in one hand and boxes of paraphernalia in the other. I indulged a deep, self-loathing sigh, and swung my legs over the side of the bed. She reached into her tuxedo apron pocket and handed me a little bottle of pills.

"What's this?" I took the bottle and opened it.

"Aspirin. Take two. You'll feel better in a jiffy." She handed me the glass.

I hesitated, the aspirin at my lips. At my grandparent's house, I was the human clicker. Each time the aspirin commercial came on TV—the one with the hammer and anvil clanging inside the guy's head—it was my job to jump up and turn off the sound so we would not be mesmerized by the suggestion of a headache. I felt like Eve with a capital "E," about to partake in "the first delusion."

"Well? Go on, they won't kill ya."

Right then I was more than mesmerized. My guts felt like they were literally twisting themselves into knots. I took the glass from her and downed the first two aspirin of my life. *Sorry Grandma.*

"Here, take this stuff too." She shoved the boxes into my hands and turned me toward the bathroom. "Your mother will be here in half an hour. Oh, and don't forget to put an extra pad in your purse."

When I was ready I sat on the second-hand couch Ruth had scrounged from her sister in Calimesa while she spit-curled down the mistake she'd made cutting my bangs the night before. I got my hand smacked away from picking the colored wax of the Chianti bottle on the equally scroungy coffee table.

"Leave that alone! It's just starting to look good!"

"Sorry."

Ruth beat me to the door when my mom arrived. Silence cold as glass hung in the doorway for a fraction of a second as the two woman took their first look at each other. Mom wore a crisp pair of pink golf shorts with the Tail logo embroidered on the leg, a matching jersey, a spotless pair of tennis shoes and pink anklets with little pom poms at the heel. And Ruth, well, as I said before, she was ready to go to work.

"Oh, … hello," my mother said, as if she thought she might be at the wrong door. Then she saw me standing with my purse on one arm and a party dress on a hanger in the other. "Hi sweetie."

She gave me a brief hug and took the dress in one hand and extended her other. "You must be Ruth."

"Yeah, come on in. Jim's still in bed." She gestured inside, holding her cigarette straight up to keep an inch of ash from falling on the floor. "We had a *lulu* of a night last night, let me tell you—"

If my mother was offended, it didn't show. "Oh, no thank you."

She reached an arm around my shoulder and scooped me out the door. "Vern's waiting downstairs and we've got a bit of a drive."

Ruth stepped onto the landing as we started down the stone and wrought iron stairway.

"*Bye!*" she said in her lilting, country singer drawl. "See you at nine, Evie. School tomorrow."

She stepped back through the door, and then popped back out. "Oh, I almost forgot. Evie got her period today. First time."

"Bye," I said. *Yell it out to the whole compound why don't you.* As uncomfortable as I felt in my new paraphernalia, the cramps had subsided.

It was a miracle with a capital M.

My mother and I crossed the open courtyard, passed by the pool and then out between Fay Wray's trees. My cramps felt better but my stomach still felt tipsy and turny. I was wearing a blouse with a sweater over it, a jacket over that, a pair of Capri pants, huge underwear, thick socks and Keds, but I felt like I'd been caught naked on the stage of a school play: *Look, she's wearing a training bra, and she got her per-i-od.*

I looped both arms through my purse and let it dangle low in front of my stomach. "You won't tell Vern, will you?"

My mother stopped a few steps from a brand new Oldsmobile convertible I had never seen before. "Tell him what, sweetie?"

"That I got…you know."

"Oh. I wouldn't think of it." She laughed softly and I relaxed into the grace of her.

We spent the afternoon at the nursery. Mama and I picked out pansies and marigolds to plant in their new front yard and Vern bought dichondra food. When we got to their home, she took me on a tour; the eaves of their new gingerbread house framed the front windows, and slanted nearly low enough to jump up and walk to the top. It was mostly empty, but she told me where each new piece of furniture would go. There were three bedrooms: a master, and den, and a guestroom.

One of those could be mine.

We puttered in the yard, planting the flowers in tilled soil in front of a low, split-rail fence, while Vern fed the dichondra, their little round heads poking lush and dark green out of thick planter mix. The devil grass crabbing around Fay Wray's palm trees at our apartment seemed crass and uncivilized by comparison.

A next-door neighbor, Margaret, popped over to chat and my mother introduced me.

"I didn't realize you had children," cooed Margaret, patting me on the head. "You look about my daughter's age. How old are you, sweetie? Nine? Ten? You sure look just like your mom."

"I'm twelve. A couple of weeks ago." I mimicked my mother's indulgent smile.

My mother got up from the sidewalk and brushed her hands on her work apron. "We're going to celebrate tonight. A nice dinner out." She gave me a hand up. "In fact, we'd better go in and start getting cleaned up. Nice to see you Maggie."

I watched Maggie thread her way through plastic toys on the trampled dirt of their front yard, past a faded station wagon in the driveway.

"Never mind her." Mom hustled me through the garage. "She stays home with her kids all day, she never thinks about anything else."

Inside, she gave me two boxes wrapped in pink flowered paper and tied with elaborate bows. They reminded me of the samples on the wall at the gift wrap counter at the May Company. "If these fit, you can wear them this evening."

Inside the biggest box were a soft yellow wool pleated skirt and a flowered blouse and sweater. In a smaller gift box was a matching leather belt. Mama had a glass of white wine as I tried them on. They were a size bigger than I usually wore, but I made them fit by cinching the belt up tight.

"There. They make you look like the young lady you are."

I stood a little taller as we put the finishing touches on our hair and waited for Vern in the kitchen.

"Ah, me birthday beauties," Vern said like a pirate. He hooked his thumbs behind the lapels of his silk suit. "Had it made while we were in Hong Kong. Like it?"

I told him he looked all polished and shiny, which he always did.

"Bett, I thought we'd go to Sam's Seafood, in Long Beach, then it will be only a short hop back to Evie's. What do you think? Do you like fish, Evie?"

"I suppose so. I've only had tuna sandwiches but I like them."

Vern held the door for us. "You'll love it. We'd better get going. I made reservations for seven so we could get you home on time. I hear they have something special for birthday girls," he said, ushering us out to the car.

I'd never been anywhere that you needed reservations. My spirits had lifted a mile high, I got past the cramps, and started to enjoy the visit.

It was a fancy restaurant, dark and rich looking, with black and red lanterns hanging from lacquered beams. The hostess showed us to our table the minute we arrived and Vern ordered a liter of wine. All around us, people were dressed in their Sunday clothes—women in high heels and men in suits and ties. My mother looked beautiful as always in an angora sweater set off with a pearl pin fastened near her shoulder. Even I felt fancy sitting there with them in my new birthday clothes. The waitress brought the wine and Vern whispered something to her that I couldn't hear, then he filled their glasses, and the waitress came back with a fizzy red drink for me.

Vern lifted his glass. "To my birthday girls. May you have the best year ever."

We clinked our glasses and sipped together.

Vern poured my mother another glass of wine and filled his again as well. The waitress asked for our orders and Vern ordered for me.

"I got you lobster, with won-tons and an egg roll. You'll like the sweet sauce that comes with it. And some green tea."

Our dinners were served with a flourish.

"Wow, lobster!" I turned, excited, to my mother; she was looking at me funny.

"I *luff* you sweetie. Scoot *ofer* here by me." She lifted her arm to let me move in closer.

I scooted until her arm came across my shoulders. She drank her wine with her other hand. We ate our dinner side-by-side.

The waitress brought a small teapot and cup and set it in front of me. My mother scooted me away a little.

"Go ahead, *sweathy*, you can pour your own."

I tried not to frown, but her words sounded funny, and it made me feel scared, on shaky ground.

"So, when did you *moofe* to your father's?" She drank more wine and gave me half a smile.

"Bett…" Vern's voice held a hint of warning.

"No, I just want to know," she said to Vern. "I agreed Evie would stay with her grandmother until she was *twelf*, and he didn't waste a second, did he? The minute I was out of the country, *swoooosh*, gone."

Until then, I couldn't remember ever having heard my mother complaining about anything. Tears backed up in my eyes. I struggled to pour some tea in my cup without shaking.

"I'm sorry. I didn't know either, until they came for my stuff." I knew it was now or never and worked up my courage. "I was going to ask you tonight, I wanted to choose you guys, honest."

A tear snuck out and I wiped it quick. "But they just came and got me. I had to move schools and everything, and the new school doesn't have an orchestra, or instruments, or—"

"Oh, honey. Don't cry. I *luff* you, sweetie." Her arm came

back around my shoulder, but it felt awkward, forced. I didn't want to hurt her feelings, but I couldn't stop myself from leaning uncomfortably away.

She held her glass out to Vern. "Pour me some more, sweetheart, would you?"

"You know, Bett, I think you've probably had—"

"Just a *liddle* more, I have my daughter here, *an* it's her birthday. *Isn'* she *beau-ful?*"

Her slurred words just didn't go with her beautiful face, her pretty mouth had a little sag to it, and it made me feel bad to look at her. She went on talking as if she hadn't heard a word I'd said. I pushed ahead with my plan, but I already felt defeated.

"Sharlene said I could choose when I was twelve, and I wanted to ask, maybe I could live with you guys now."

There. I'd said it. My heart slammed into my throat.

"Oh honey, you know that just *wouldn* work. You know, we *trafel sooo* much and we have golf on Saturdays and—" She drained the rest of her glass. "*Fern*, how 'bout a Manhattan or something?"

Vern signaled the waitress like he was writing a note.

Travel and golf? I couldn't believe my ears. Travel and golf sounded like an excuse not to have a dog. "But I thought—"

"*Cm* on, sweetie, scoot *ofer* here by me. You are *sooo prettieh* tonight."

I couldn't hold back any longer. "If you don't want me, why don't you just put a pink bow in my hair and put me out on the back porch?"

The lady in the next booth fish-eyed over at us and then back, shaking her head.

I don't know if it was the look on that woman's face, or the way my mother slurred her words, or the way I'd worried about asking all day, but suddenly I felt like I was sitting at a table with strangers.

"*Effie*, what's got into you?" My mother drew back, her eyes suddenly dark and shiny. My words had hit somewhere deep. I wished I could take them back, but it was too late. Instead I just threw down my napkin and ran.

Definitely a Scarlett O'Hara move. Sharlene would have loved it.

I swung into the ladies room and leaned against the door, gasping for breath. A woman was at the sink, washing her daughter's hands inside her own. I pulled away from the door and staggered into one of the stalls, my throat in a tight knot. I don't know how long I was in there. The mother and daughter left, and another lady used a stall and left. I had no idea what to do. I couldn't go back. Everyone must have seen me run out like a spoiled brat.

Then I heard someone call into the bathroom: "Hello, is there an Evie in here? Your father is looking for you."

My father? Oh. Vern.

What was I doing? I had to go out, but I was so embarrassed, for me, for my mother, and for Vern. And I was hurt and angry. How could she spoil my birthday? How could I spoil hers? I gulped air back into my lungs and came out of the stall. The waitress stood near the sink. I saw her stuff a five dollar bill into her pocket. She turned and wet a paper towel under the spigot.

"Here," she said. "Wipe your face. There. You're okay, now. Your father is waiting just outside the door. Go on now. Be a good girl." She reminded me of my Grandma, a little plump with huge breasts and short cropped, steel-gray hair. I wished it were Grandma waiting outside that bathroom door, but instead, it was Vern.

He sat on a bench near the restaurant entrance. He looked pretty silly, his big hands holding a small folded paper box by its tiny wire handle. "We better get you home, you're starting to turn into a pumpkin around the ears."

I wasn't in much of a mood to laugh. "Where's my Mom?"

"She's in the car waiting for us."

"I think she's drunk. I don't like it."

Vern studied me for a minute, then sat us back down on the bench. "Adults drink, sometimes too much. But your mother loves you, Eve—"

"I don't think so. Not really. It's not fair."

Vern looked back at me with eyes so piercing blue they seemed to see right into my thoughts. "You're right, a lot of things in life aren't fair. And none of us do the right thing all the time. We just have to try our best."

I could hardly swallow around the knot in my throat.

"The waitress said she'd sing happy birthday to you in the bathroom, but I didn't think it would be a good idea."

He handed me the box. "I guess you can eat this cake later."

He offered a thin smile. I had to hand it to him, not being a full-time dad. He had tried *his* best. I considered throwing the box away at the hostess stand, but I didn't want to take that away from him. Through the glass doors of the lobby, I could see my mother sitting in the front seat of their big white convertible. Her head lay back against the headrest, her eyes closed, her mouth slack.

"I wish I hadn't seen her this way."

Vern got up and gave me his hand. "Come on. We'll see you again soon and I'll make sure she's...that this doesn't happen again."

I swallowed hard and straightened up the best I could. "No. It's not your problem, and it's not your fault. It's a woman thing, you know. I think it's best if you just take me home now."

Vern smiled wider and held the lobby door open as I walked out. "Whatever's necessary," he said.

When I got home, Ruth was snoring on the couch in one of my dad's T-shirts and a pair of panties with "Sunday" embroidered inside a lacy heart above the crotch. I tried to be quiet on my way to the kitchen, but she snorted awake and cut her eyes up to the clock. "Nine ten. Good enough."

I put the little box on the counter and turned around. There was another empty Chianti bottle on the kitchen table. The ashtray was half full of my dad's L&M butts. I guessed he'd gone to bed after another lulu, whatever that was. I dried my eyes on the sleeve of my new blouse.

Ruth came into the kitchen and opened the little paper box. "M-m-m-m."

She looked over at me and folded her arms, her *Lou'siana* eyes speculating. "Tough night, chickie?"

"Kinda."

She looked me up and down. "Nice outfit. A little big."

I looked down at my skirt and the belt. I'd almost forgotten I was wearing them. "Thanks, my mom picked it out. For my birthday."

I gulped down a dry ball of air.

Ruth circled my shoulder with her arm and nodded back over toward the kitchen. "You gonna eat that cake?"

The little paper box waited on the counter.

None of us does the right thing all the time.

I could break down into tears, but what would be the point? Despite the evening's disaster, I actually felt pretty good. I had become a woman. I had a new outfit. And I had cake.

"Yeah. I'm going to eat it." I opened the little box, slid the cake onto a chipped saucer, and pulled two forks out of the drawer.

❧

Ruth had since died of emphysema, and Sharlene had moved to Savanna to be near her children, leaving her mom in a nursing home in northern California. And finally, my mother and I were together. *Mama.*

I looked over at her again as we made the curve away from the Ventura coast toward Ojai, her features peaceful now. I forgot the painful moments, thinking instead of a photo I'd seen of her as a child, twelve years old, on a small cattle ranch in Oregon. Leaning on a rail fence, a stand of pine in the background, her two younger siblings in tow, she held a long stick at the nose of a hog that dwarfed the three of them. She was shoeless, in ragged overalls, and wore a look that haunted. Who could blame her for feeling stuck when she got pregnant? For wanting something better? Certainly not I.

15 Hot Dog Man

Daylight slashed across the wall and Betty squinted. That something pounded inside her head—*zhumm-zhumm, zhumm-zhumm, zhumm-zhumm*—that dull throb that wouldn't go away.

She pulled the covers up to her chin and looked around. What in the world had happened to her room? The door was on the wrong wall and the windows too. And her closet had moved far away from the bed. Her arms tingled. There was that feeling again. That feeling that she was living in someone else's skin. That feeling that once, a long time ago, everything was okay; and now, it wasn't, quite.

She pushed back the covers and swung her feet stiffly to the floor.

Zhumm, zhumm, zhumm.

There was something wrong about that closet. That red thing, that coat. That wasn't hers.

Betty pushed herself off the bed and shuffled to the closet. That coat. That coat. Someone else's ugly red thing. She grabbed it down off the hangar and dragged it back across the room. Not her coat. *Not her coat!* Why was someone else's coat in her closet?

Betty heard voices coming from down the hall. She dropped the coat to the floor next to the bed and kicked her heels at it until she could no longer see the red material sticking out. And then there was someone at the door, flitting across the room, pulling up shades and opening curtains. Now that was Grace. Her Grace; the lady who stayed all day. Betty relaxed. Oh. Yes. She was at Reba's. She was okay.

"Good morning, Betty. Are you ready to get up? Evie's here waiting for you."

Betty looked over at the time thing on her night table. *Time to get up.*

"My head hurts."

Grace helped her into her robe. "I'm sorry. I'll get you something for it, and then we'll get your bath."

Bath? Yes, that was how it started. The feeling better. The warm. And then there would be tea in the kitchen and something to eat. And it would be like this tomorrow and the next day. Until she was…better.

Evie twisted Betty's hair up into a knot, fastened it with a sparkly comb, and pulled some curls down at her forehead. Betty watched Evie's hands move in the mirror, confidently clipping pieces of her into place; the last touch brought a smile to the face of the old woman in the mirror and a string of familiar words to her mouth. "That's nice, Sweetie."

"I mailed your letter to Lolette today. She'll probably get it tomorrow." Evie squeezed Betty's shoulders and helped her up.

"I hope she brings Emily. I miss her." Betty turned her face up to the light at the urging of Evie's fingertips on her chin.

"Yes, I know you do."

Her daughter was smiling, but Betty thought she looked a little sad, or maybe, she was just a little tired. She worked too much. She worked all the time.

"So," Evie said, blotting her eyes on her sleeve. "I thought we'd meet Robert down at the beach today. He's surfing at the Point. I got you that chair we talked about so you won't have too walk far."

Betty's heart lurched a little. Yes they had talked about the chair. She had said *no*. She would never, ever, go anywhere in a wheelchair, like somebody's baggage. But lately, her legs never went where she wanted them to. Evie wouldn't like that. Wouldn't like it at all. Maybe she could use the chair. Just this once. Just to see.

"Does it match my golf cart?" At least we could match, couldn't we?

Evie and Grace exchanged amused glances. "Gosh, Mom. I'm sorry. They only come in one color—blue."

Betty watched Evie shift clothes back and forth on the rod in the closet. "Grace, have you seen the new windbreaker I got for Mom? I was sure I hung it up in here yesterday."

Grace shook her head.

"We should take your windbreaker, Mom. Have you seen it?"

Betty cut her eyes over to the bed. "That's not my coat. Anyway, it's burning hot."

Evie raised her eyebrows and went to look under the bed like she could read her mind.

Betty started off down the hall toward the front door. "Don't have a red coat." She stopped near the door. "Don't need a red coat."

She should have something though. You have things when you go out. You have *things*.

Betty *huffy-shuffled* back down the hall to Grace. "I have a scarf. A blue one."

Evie and Grace looked at each other like they had never heard of a scarf. *What was the matter with them?*

Grace slipped her arm inside Betty's and headed her back to the room. "I don't remember any scarves, but we can look."

"We can look." There *was* a blue scarf. She had worn it to work just yesterday. Blue with yellow—flowers—and white. She rummaged through her chest of drawers throwing panties, bras, shorts and tops out onto the floor.

"I just don't see anything, Mom." Evie gathered up her purse and folded the red coat over her arm. "Why don't we go before you throw out all your—"

"Blue, *blue!*" *Why wouldn't they listen?* And then it was there, in the back of the drawer. A piece of silky blue fabric, dotted with yellow and white. "Here!"

She pulled it out of the drawer, triumphant, and waved it at them as she pushed her feet through the pile of clothes and shuffled through the bedroom door.

Grace and Evie followed her down the hall.

"But Mom, that's a blouse."

Evie and Grace looked at her with their mouths open.

"Scarf," Betty declared emphatically, and squared her shoulders. What was wrong with them? "It matches."

Betty fussed with the silky material tied to the whippy flagpole on the back of her wheelchair and smiled. It didn't exactly match, but it fluffed and billowed well enough, like a scarf should. And it matched the wheelchair, parked next to her now, close by, so the bums wouldn't take it. Betty had seen a bum earlier, wheeling a wheelchair across the street in front of their car with a bag of shiny cans in the seat. A scruffy, friendless thing. The sight of him had given her the chills.

"There's Robert, Mom. The one with the cap pulled down over his ears."

Betty looked out into the surf where Evie pointed. From the bench where they sat, the surfers all looked the same—black seals with legs. She got up and leaned into the railing in front of them as the remains of a big wave rushed in. The sound of it nearly took her breath away. "Y-e-e-e-a-a-ah!"

Salt spray tickled the back of her throat. Another wave came battering up the rocks. *If she could just touch it, just now.* She got down on one knee and pushed her arms through the railing, but the water wasn't as near as it looked. "Y-e-e-e-a-a-h!"

"Careful, Mom." Evie stooped next to her and slipped her arm around her waist. *Ooh, there goes another man-seal sliding past. Shiny skin. Shiny skin. Shiny, shiny skin.*

"Hey you guys, you made it down!" Robert stood behind them now, still wet, the big board under one arm, his black skin pealed down off his arms to his waist. Betty shuffled a couple of steps and looked up at him. Evie's man was handsome, and his chest was nice, like a, a, she couldn't think of a what, but it made her heart open up big as a beach umbrella.

She put both hands on his chest and held them there on the firm bumps. His skin was wet, but warm under her fingers. "I…like…that," she said and beamed over her shoulder at

Evie.

Evie smiled and scooped her up in her wheelchair. "Yeah. Me too. Let's go get a hot dog before you two get involved here."

Betty let Evie tuck her hair back under a sun hat and pat the red jacket over her lap. She felt like a queen in her new chair. She couldn't remember the last time she had been to the ocean. It smelled like Sunday, and the sounds reached all the way inside her head, drowning out the thrumming.

She reached over her shoulder and squeezed Evie's hand there. Evie squeezed back. Betty closed her eyes, let her head rest back against the chair and breathed deeply, the fragrance of the ocean calling a vision of another day on the beach. She and Vern, on a blanket in the sand, the sunset blazing, little Evie playing next to them. The feeling was wonderful and right, but their timing had been all wrong. The words of a song stole into her mind and carried her up into the memory of his kiss on that night, then let her down softly…

"…*like the tide, at its ebb, I'm at peace in the web of your heart.*"

When she opened her eyes, she was back in the now, rumbling along in her queen chair, next to the seawall. Beyond it was a pier and then breakers frosting the edges of the shore as far as she could see. Her heart soared. Life was out here, she could feel it. In fact, she might even be smiling with both sides of her mouth. Pigeons fluttered off the railings, dogs led their people on leashes. A woman roller skated toward them behind a stroller with a big front wheel. The little baby in the stroller waved her arms and slapped her knees. She stuck her fist in her mouth and looked right into Betty's eyes as they passed. Betty couldn't help but watch them until she had to turn her head back around. "We could do *that!*"

Evie laughed. The warm notes of it filled the open places in Betty's heart.

They wheeled through more wet seal men, people riding bicycles, kids running, squealing with delight as they scared the pigeons off the railing, sending them slipping this way and that in the wind.

"Phew!" She tried her hand at scaring up some pigeons of her own. "Phew! Phew!"

Then Evie tapped her on the shoulder and she turned to

find herself in front of the hot dog stand. A man in a Hawaiian shirt, red faced and potbellied, handed her a hot dog with onions and sauerkraut and everything on it. Her mouth juiced up at the sight of it.

Oh, it can be like this. I will be okay like this.

Evie sat next to her on a stone wall and ate her hot dog. She was smiling, but her eyes were shiny and she looked sad. Why wasn't Evie happy at the beach?

"It's going to be okay, Sweetie," Betty assured her.

"Hum?" Evie gave her a puzzled look, bent down to hear better.

Betty looked into Evie's eyes. "This is *good.*"

She so wanted to have the words forming in her head actually come out of her mouth. She wanted Evie to understand. "We can *have* this. We can *have* this."

"Yeah, Mama. Go ahead. Nothing like a good kosher hot dog at the beach."

Evie didn't understand. But the hot dog *was* good. Maybe that was good enough.

&

Betty was tired when Evie dropped her off. She went to bed early, under protest from Reba.

"It's not even 4:30, Betty. Don't you want to have some dessert? Some melon maybe?"

Melon? What did melon have to do with anything? She wanted sleep, before the low hum of the voices in her head turned into the pounding.

Zhumm, zhumm, zhumm.

The humming, the throbbing, returned the moment Evie dropped her off from their trip to the ocean. It hurt her head like a brainstorm. Sleep was the only thing that helped. In her room, she crawled under the covers with her clothes on. Didn't matter. They weren't her clothes. Her clothes were gone. Gone in the old place in her old life in her old skin. The thoughts made her heart ache.

"Go away!" she said out loud, and tried to think of the ocean. The ocean and the sand and Vern, a long time ago. Tuna sandwiches in waxed paper and cans of beer. She could almost smell the sunset. The thoughts slowly faded as she drifted off.

When she awoke, it was dark. Not even the slightest shade of pink showed through the drapes.

"Who is that?" The voices were at the French doors now. Louder than before.

Zhumm, zhumm, zhumm.

She might as well get up. But then she remembered. Reba had said don't. Don't get up until the drapes are pink. She looked at the velvet curtains that hung over the French doors leading to her patio. They were still as gray as, as gray as... *empty.* Another gray, empty, empty.

Betty slid out of bed as quietly as she could so she wouldn't wake Maria, the lady who stayed all night. She shuffled slowly, her legs stiff as they always were in the morning, trailing her fingers along the bed. She felt drunk and off balance all the time now and she hadn't had a drink since, since, she didn't know when except that it had been way too long.

Zhumm, zhumm, zhumm.

She would go out. That's what she would do. Who were they to tell her when to get up and what to do? She knew how to get to town.

She wanted to go into the bathroom, but her legs wouldn't go. She reached down and moved first one foot and then the other and that got them started. She made it to the bathroom with much effort, then stopped and took a breath.

Just peachy.

Her legs didn't work right. That was going to be a problem. She propped herself against the cabinet and riffled through the drawers next to the sink. Some aspirin, maybe that would do the trick, and then she would make up a little.

Where was that pink, the lip, that *Pink.* "Ah!"

Oooh. Quiet.

She opened the shiny metal tube and screwed out the pink as far as it would go, pursed her lips and rubbed it on. But when she glanced at the result in the mirror, she was horrified. Someone had scrubbed pink all through her hair.

"Oh no. No! Goddamn you, leave me alone!"

She pulled another tube from the drawer and squirted the blue stuff in her hands then rubbed it in her hair. Now her face was covered with it. It burned! She pulled a washcloth from the rack and ran it under the faucet but nothing came.

Nothing!

"Arg-g-gh! It hurts! It's freezing cold!"

"Betty, *Betty!*" Maria was with her now, her arms folding around her. "Oh Betty, what have you done?"

Hot tears stung Betty's cheeks. "That woman," she said, pointing at the mirror. "That woman hurt me, she pinked. *Pinked!* I hate her. *Hate her.*"

"Turn around, Betty. Don't look at her." Maria held Betty's face between her hands and looked straight into her eyes. "*Mire aquí.*"

Betty didn't understand the words but they felt soft and soothing. Maria's hand caressed her cheek until she looked into her face. Dark eyes, dark skin, dark hair. Maria's smile descended over her like a calm, warm blanket and Betty melted into those brown, brown eyes.

"Let's get you cleaned up," Maria crooned in her funny accent, brushing a stray straggle of hair off Betty's forehead. She made the water come, wet the cloth, and gently wiped Betty's face. *"Madré de Dios!"*

"I can't stay here anymore. That woman. She took my face away." Betty shook her fist at the mirror.

"Sh-h-h-h, sh-h-h-h. *Bien, bien, mi hermana.*"

"Everything's changed." Betty pushed her fist into the pain throbbing in her head. "This is not the way it's supposed to be."

"I know, I know, *mi hermana.* But you will be okay, my sister."

"There was someone at the door last night. They woke me up."

"Sh-h-h-h. Let's go back over and sit on the bed." Maria led her out of the bathroom, one step at a time. "*Siéntese a me lado.*"

Betty sat down.

Where were they? This wasn't her room. Maria put her arm around Betty's shoulders. They began to rock slowly. "I'll call your daughter as soon as it's light."

Betty leaned into the woman's ample body and closed her eyes. It was quiet outside now. Maria had chased the voices away. "Thank you."

"*De nada.* You rest now. I'll sing you a song, *sí?*
Jou arrre my e-sun-chine,
my only e-sun-chine,
She sang the words sweet and slow, like a lullaby. "You know this one, eh Betty?"
Jou make me 'appy
When skies arrre gray."

The words came into Betty's head without thinking about them. "You'll never know dear, how much I love you…" but the throbbing returned like a relentless engine inside her skull.

Zhumm, zhumm, zhumm, zhumm, zhumm, zhumm, zhumm, zhumm, zhumm.

16 Pink Moment Plateau

"I think your mom was horny yesterday." Robert slid his arm under my neck and pulled me into his warmth.

I smoothed my hand over his chest like my mother had done at the beach the day before. "Can't blame her for that. God. Wasn't she a kick? She didn't want to ride in the wheelchair, but I think she liked it. Made it easier for me."

Robert pressed his hand against the small of my back and pulled me closer. "It was good to have *you* there. It's been awhile."

"I know. I'm sorry." I slid my leg over his and nuzzled into the crook of his arm until I could just see Chief's Peak through our bedroom window. The morning sunlight was a breath away from warming the tip of chief's nose. "She's doing so much better now. Adjusting. Reba's parents are here from London, and you'd think the queen was visiting. She loves them. They took her to tea. She's safe, she's—"

"Time for you to back off a little, don't you think? Let her deal with her reality, so we can get back to ours."

Robert captured my hand and slid it down to a happy

morning *woodie*. I curled my hand around him, caressing slow. He moved, impatient, against my grip. He was such a morning person.

Since December, my mother's needs had run our life. He had been patient, more patient than anyone should expect. And he was right, of course. It was time I put him back in the driver's seat. He was good at it, and I was so tired of trying to manage my parent's lives as well as our own. And he was so, so affectionately accommodating. It was why we were together, what I thought about when I watched him work with his hands or in front of a crowd. I remembered the only question my mother had asked when I told her we would marry: Is he good in bed? And I had answered: The best.

I would be late to work if I washed my hair, so I decided not to. "I guess I can wear my baseball cap."

"Hmmm?"

I rolled up onto his chest and slid down over him like soapy hands on Sunday morning.

"So. You *have* been thinkin' about me."

"S-h-h-h-h."

I was still thinking about him and our business and everything else as I drove the winding road from Ojai to Carpinteria and on to Santa Barbara for work. My thoughts ran an endless circle around what had to be done. My full time job, setting up our own new accounts and presentations, satisfying our new business partner's requests—Mother and Vern's taxes, our own—and Robert's *expert* attention.

It was true that our lives had really changed. No more surf check on Sunday morning. I had to take my mother so Reba could go to church. If we left town for a weekend, the cell phone rang: Betty was agitated, wouldn't take her prescription, wouldn't eat, had to talk to me, wanted me home. How dare I leave her? I stopped for an hour every day on the way home from work, brought her home three nights a week for dinner. I gave up our Master's Swim team and gained ten pounds. To make her life "normal," our life had suffered. My grown kids avoided us, their grandmother was just too hard to take. Our routine—our crazy, demanding, exciting routine—had been severely impacted. Robert was more than ready to have it back.

And he deserved it.

My mother was in a good place now, despite her complaints. I'd be cranky too if my life had imploded and there was nothing I could do about it. Maybe it was as good as it could get for her.

I swiped my magnetic card through the reader at the front door of my office building and heard the opening click. With my mom settled in a private home, I was finally back on the job. While it wasn't routine, it was working. Mostly. And I was grateful for that. The lights were on in the foyer. I smelled coffee brewing.

"Hey, Eve." Barbara gave me a nod from her office as I rounded the corner for my own.

"Hey. You're here early." I certainly hadn't expected to see her there. She usually showed up around nine with a *Vente* vanilla latte in one hand and her laptop in the other.

"Got some important business to take care of. You?"

"I've been coming in early. Beats the traffic." I dumped my purse and laptop on my work table. The message light on my answering machine was flashing away.

Barbara walked over slowly, steam drifting up from her coffee cup, nodded her head at my phone. "It's been ringing every ten minutes or so."

She fingered a dried leaf on the *dieffenbachia* next to my desk.

"Oh. Gosh. I'm sorry." I sank into my office chair and huffed out some frustration. "You know, she does this in the morning. Usually, there's no one—"

"I know. Look Eve." She put her cup on my desk and stopped me mid thought with a serious look over the top of her reading glasses. "I'll admit, you look a little better this morning for some reason, but you've been looking tired. No, I take that back. Exhausted. This whole thing with your mom has got you—"

I glared at her and started to get up. People tended to get close in a startup company, it was easy to know each other's business. But this was a little too—

"Eve. Sit down." She pulled my visitor's chair up to the desk and sat forward, her hands gripping her cup. I grew more uncomfortable. She seemed to be struggling for the right expression, the right tone. Finally, she began.

"You're trying to be everything to everybody. You just can't do it. I hope we're friends enough for me to say this."

I settled back into my chair, my eyes drifted to the insistent blink on my phone. "You came in early just to talk to me then?"

"Had to. Drew the long straw."

"What? You mean everybody's talking about me?"

"You think we don't see how stressed out you are from behind this stupid plant? Hell, we're *all* choked up around here, watching you."

I sucked in a breath. I had no idea anyone paid attention to me, other than a quick hello and 'Where's my Help file?'.

"My work's okay though, right? I'm doing my job."

Barbara sat back a little. "Well…"

"Oh, jeez." My ego shrank to the size of a fancy pea. My face burned.

"Eve. I'm not talking about your work right now. I'm talking about *you*. Where's that exercise freak making us all feel guilty about sitting on our asses around here all day? And have you seen your hair? When's the last time you had your roots done?"

"My roots?" My hand shot to the top of my head. The burning spread down my neck and across my chest. Next she would offer me a stick of deodorant.

"Eve, we're all sorry about your mom. It's tough, but kind of normal on the scale of things, you know. My parents are both gone, my husband's dad went through this last year."

"So I guess I'm not handling it well."

"Too much. You're handling it too much. You've got her in a private home. She's got three people looking after her. You go there every day after work. You have her on the weekend. What's left for you?"

I scooted back up to my desk, rested my chin in my hands, and stared at the computer desktop.

"She's on her path to the end. That's got to hurt, but it's a fact. Do you think she expects you to go with her?"

I had never really thought about what she had expected of me. The notion hit me low in the gut, had me staring at my hands until my eyes went dry. Finally I blinked.

"I thought I could fix it. I thought once I got her near me,

I could have a normal conversation. Like, hit the Undo button and everything goes back the way it was before you screwed it all up."

My boss sat back in the chair, crossed her arms, and raised her brows at me. "The Undo button?"

Saying it out loud did make it sound absurd. "It's a kind of techwriter religious experience. Forgiveness of sorts."

Barbara shook her head. "Look, Eve. You didn't screw this all up and you can't undo this. You've got to start thinking about you again. Get yourself back on track, even if it means taking a time out."

A time out? Read: get a grip or you're fired?

My stomach went into freefall. Surely there was some type of grace period where people gave you slack when your parents fell into your lap without so much as a "tag, you're *it*."

I closed my eyes. Better to get the cards on the table. "So, you're sending me to the corner, or you're handing me a pink slip?"

"I'm not sending you anywhere." She crossed the room and stood in my office doorway. "For *godsakes*, I'm trying to help. You can work from home, like you used to do. I just don't want to see you in here until you can make it through a day without tears."

I looked at her eyes for a long moment, wondering exactly when that might be. I dropped my head on my folded arms, trying desperately not to fulfill her prophesy by bursting into tears right then and there.

"I've got to run some errands now," she said, letting me off the hook for the moment. "Go home. Keep in touch by phone and email. I'll tell Aaron to put you on the daily report so you know where we're at."

I lifted my head and sniffed back the onslaught. Barbara called back over her shoulder as she headed down stairs. "And I'll water the plant."

I waited to hear her footsteps on the stairs to the foyer, then punched the red flashing button, knowing I was about to be sucked down the rabbit hole.

"She won't leave me alone. She took away my face." My mother's voice sounded ragged, harsh, fearful. My stomach pulled into a knot I could hardly breathe around.

"Someone at the window, but they're in my head now. Please. Please come and get me away from here."

I stared at the phone. Finally, I erased the latest message and all the other messages collected since yesterday.

My hand poised over the numbers on the phone. No. I would not call. I'd just go. The hour it would take to drive home would not make a difference in what had to be done.

When I arrived at the home, Reba's car was there. I could hear my mother's voice from the kitchen.

"She pinked my hair, *goddammit!* You let her in my room again."

Reba spoke to her in calming tones with a soft English accent. "It's okay, Betty. Look, Evie's here."

Betty looked up, her eyes shiny wild.

"Oh, Eve. I'm glad you're here. Betty's been a little anxious this morning—"

"Not *anxis.* Betty! I'm going home *now.* Good Bye." My mother headed for the front door, struggling more than usual to put one foot in front of the other.

"Wait, Mom. Let's get a sweater or something." I hesitated in the kitchen, looking at Reba. "What's happened?"

Reba stirred milk into a cup of tea and sat down, her fingers quivering. "She woke up this way. Yelling and banging on the doors. Maria called me at four-thirty. She was afraid Betty would hurt herself."

"But her hair, her face—"

"I don't really know. I sent Maria home when I got here, she was so upset."

Their eyes met as they heard Betty at the front door. "Where's Evie? Go home. *Go home!*"

"I'm coming Mom. I'll be right there."

My mother continued to take her fury out on the front door.

"Eve," Reba said. "You know this is beyond what we can handle here. Our license is for clients that can sleep at night, and—"

I pressed my lips together as if holding back the words would somehow prolong the inevitable. It had been good for my mother here, but it was over. We were both in freefall, this time below the level at which Reba was licensed to operate. I had been thinking this all the way from Santa Barbara.

"I know." I squeezed Reba's shoulder. "You've had a tough morning. I'll take care of it."

I didn't know what I would do, but it wasn't Reba's fault and there was the law.

I pried one of my mother's hands off the doorknob and pulled her into my arms until she let go with the other. "Let's go sit down for a few minutes. I need to talk to you."

She sniffed and stiffly let me lead her down the hall to her room where I sat her down on the edge of her bed. The sun shone brightly now through the pink drapery, glaring against the pink carpet. I pulled the drapes closed and sat down beside her, lifted her chin in my fingers and looked into her darkened eyes. I knew this was something we could not run away from. I wanted her to understand, but how could I when I didn't understand myself?

"Take me home." Her words struck hard. We had sold her home. Everything she knew as home was gone, just money in the bank against long-term care.

"We can talk about that," I lied. "But I need to know what happened. I need to know how I can help you right now."

Had she had chest pains? Was there evidence of a stroke? What had set her off?

She pulled her chin out of my fingers and hunched over a ragged sigh.

"Mama, I need to know how much you understand about all this. What can you tell me?"

She covered her mouth, and the best I could tell, she was searching for some level of composure, searching the walls as if the answer might be written there, then slowly turned and refocused on me.

"You've done so much. More than anyone." She looked around again, as if the room had spoken to her. "It's all changed, broken. And you can't fix it."

She was absolutely right. Reality had shifted for both of us, like the pieces of California during a quake. A little pressure here, a little shift there, until two parts once held firmly together slid apart, never to match up again.

I put my arm around her shoulder and pulled her close. One thing was for sure, I couldn't hold down a job, create a business with Robert, take care of myself and take care of my mother and do any of it well. Something had to go. I just wasn't sure what yet.

"I think we'll go see Dr. Bonham."

"P-s-s-s-h-h. Still broken after him."

True enough. She understood plenty. The "miracle drug" had given us two weeks of hope, followed by this horrible letdown. My natural tendency away from drugs had proven right.

"I'm so sorry, Mama. So sorry." There had to be something. *Something.*

ൟ

The doctor positioned pictures of my mother's brain scan on the lighted wall and stood back, looking. "To answer your question, Eve, we can't definitively diagnose Alzheimer's, but what I can see here is a history of TIAs, mini strokes. Compared to her previous scans, this has progressed rather quickly, not like Alzheimer's which usually takes years. And she's had the two angioplasties, so there's heart trouble."

He spoke directly to me as if my mother wasn't in the room.

I stepped closer to the images, a set of abstractions that made as much sense as a Rorschach test. It was hard to equate them in any meaningful way with the woman sitting on the end of the examination table.

"*Angio-pasties,*" she said, swinging her feet.

I laughed out loud. In the middle of this, *angio-pasties?* She looked up at me, her hand over her mouth, her eyes laughing. We're discussing the deterioration of her brain and she's trying to cheer me up.

Angio-pasties, you see? This is all a joke. A joke. We can go home now.

We had missed so much of each other. So much.

"TIAs?" I asked, fighting for composure. Mom was depending on me to do the right thing.

"Transient Ischemic Attacks. Tiny strokes that eventually add up to permanent damage." The doctor used his pen to point out matching areas on each side of the picture. "You can see this gray area is heavily affected, and older damage, here." He moved the pen on the inkblots, pointing out gray areas. "The drug we tried, while effective in Alzheimer's, would not necessarily alleviate the symptoms."

"The gray areas. That's where we all get into trouble." I put my arms across my mother's shoulders.

She ran gnarled fingers through the colored patches in her hair. "Pink," she said, too loud. "Pink areas."

More jokes. Other people reacted as if she were already gone, lost, her voice gruff and out of control, but I knew she was still very much there. She wasn't a piece of meat going bad, she was my mother. And in her way, she must know where this was going. She could grab on when she wanted to. That was something to go on.

I turned back to the doctor. Mom cut her eyes away from us, fidgeting with her rings, as he continued to dole out his bad news.

"So with vascular dementia, we get plateaus. Things go along well for a while, then the damage occurs faster than the body can repair itself—more strokes—and we slip down to the next functional plateau."

Or non-functional.

His pen moved to another gray spot on the film.

"So, what's the treatment?" I asked. My mother worked at her rings more aggressively now, trying to pull them off over enlarged knuckles.

The doctor continued. "We're actually doing what we can at this point." His eyes cut with alarm over to his patient. "Her blood pressure's down—"

"Hold on a minute." I tried to calm her hands. "Mom. You're hurting your fingers, wait."

"These are yours. You have them now." She pulled savagely at the large aquamarine, the filigreed setting gouged into her thin skin, bringing blood.

"Mom. We don't have to do that now." But she kept at them.

"Oh dear," the doctor said. I pumped a blob of soap from a sink dispenser and laved her hands, pulling the rings off smoothly into my own.

Betty huffed angrily, then settled a little, her emotional

pendulum swinging back.

"So—" The doctor waited while I rinsed her hands in the sink, and toweled them off. "—like Alzheimer's, it's progressive…"

I helped her to sit back down on the table. "But the symptoms, she's so agitated—I mean, there must be something…"

The doctor sighed. I felt almost guilty for pressing him, but at last, he pulled a prescription pad from his coat pocket and scribbled on it. "These will help her sleep, but it's only temporary. A couple of days. We need to have her evaluated by a psychiatrist, they may be able to prescribe something more appropriate. And if she's wandering, well—I'm required to write it in my report."

That was the kicker. I would either have to take care of her myself or she would have to move to twenty-four hour, lock-down care.

Betty slid off the examination table and grabbed me roughly by the arm, glaring first at the doctor, then at me, her blue eyes darkening to a steely gray. She pushed me impatiently toward the door. "We're done here, Evie. *Done!*"

17 Shampoo

An anvil cloud towered over Pine Mountain ridge, drenching its eastern slopes with an August rain. Storm wind, warm and sweet with the fragrance of wet purple sage, swept through the valley and flowed over us as I drove, windows down, back through town. I had no plan, except to drive until my mother's eyes, wild and dangerous as the lightning strikes in the high valley, calmed to natural blue. After that, who knew? We were together and she wasn't hollering. It could turn out to be a good day.

As we pulled past the post office on Signal Street, a pair of teenage girls straddled bicycles, waiting at the corner for the light to change. Heads together, they pointed at my mother, giggling, as we drove by. She straightened in her seat, pulled the passenger-side visor down, and looked at herself in the mirror, turning her head this way and that. Shocks of pink hair spiked out next to dark rooted tangles of lackluster blonde. "*Tch*. It's no good, Sweetie."

She put her purse on top of her head and shrank down in the seat.

"You're right. Maybe I can get us a walk-in." It was a very good idea, in fact. Something fun. Something normal. Something like a connection with reality.

I pulled around the block and parked behind the village salon. The shop was little more than a nook at the back of the town's only department store. We navigated to the curb and then across the sidewalk to the entrance. The going was slow. Her shuffle today was by the inch. I told her to take bigger steps, exaggerating my own. She stretched a toe out ahead of each step, searching for solid ground, leaning more heavily on my arm than she had only a week before. One step forward, two steps back. I pushed my fears about where they would take us as far down inside me as I could.

A slim, dark-haired woman wearing a light gray smock over a white silk blouse and black slacks smoked near the doorway. She looked up and apologized when she realized we were heading for her shop. She pushed her cigarette into a sand container next to the door. A pearl button glinted at her wrist.

"Got time for an emergency?" I lifted my gaze to Mom's pink hair disaster.

The woman followed my glance, raised her eyebrows. "Ah, sure. I'm Doris, and Eileen's here, too. One of us'll squeeze you in."

She held the door as we shuffle-stepped in like a pair of Siamese twins.

"It stinks to high Heaven in here," my mother hollered. I was embarrassed for her, and worried. How could she be so refined one moment and yell like a Santa Barbara street bum the next?

"I'm dying of thirst. Get some water," she went on.

I cringed, but Doris didn't seem to mind. She kept her sweet demeanor while she drew a paper cup full of water from the cooler in the corner and offered it to Mom, then helped her into one of the two chairs in the salon.

"That's the tint you smell. Guess I'm used to it. "

She lifted one of my mother's matted, pinked strands. "Wow, what's this? Lipstick?"

My mother sloughed her hand away, shoulders gyrating, some of her earlier fire returning. "Just need a wash, that's all."

Doris pressed her lips together and pulled back. I was afraid she would change her mind, but then she smiled and said, "*Ho-kay*. Let's just turn you around—"

She spun my mother slowly until her back was to the sink, sailed a black drape over her head, and fastened it loosely around her neck with a strip of *Velcro*.

"Agggghh! I'm choking to death!"

Doris showed me with her finger that the drape was quite loose. "Oh dear, I'm sorry. Is this better?"

She unstuck and re-stuck the Velcro.

My mother fought with the drape. "I can't find my hands!"

Would she never calm down? Oh, for those last few moments in the car. "It's okay, Mom. Just let her shampoo your hair. You'll feel better."

Doris leaned my mother's head back against the sink. She winced, puckered her lips, tense and resistant, but finally let Doris run a gentle spray of water over the pinked strands, working up a fine lather with a squeeze from a shampoo bottle.

"Some people pay me to make their hair pink."

My mother would not be joked. "I'm freezing cold," she said, trying to pull away.

"I'm sorry dear, it feels nice to me. I think it will be all right."

Eileen came out from the back, mixing a smelly dish of tint. She leaned over and whispered to me. "Doris works with the women at Crossroads once a week. She's really good with them."

Crossroads. There it was again. But she was right, Doris had a way of getting my mother to cooperate when I couldn't. I would have given up at the first scream.

Give her some space.

I watched, biting my tongue, as my mother griped and squirmed like a two-yearold, fighting every move. Finally, Doris wrapped a towel around her head and helped her sit upright. She checked the strands.

"Looks like we got most of it." She spun her around. "Here, take a look."

My mother refused to look into the mirror to confirm the results. "It stinks like hell in here."

"I don't know, Mom. Maybe we should skip the tint and just go for the blow dry. Mom?"

She ignored me, suddenly intent on activity just outside the shop window.

A Cadillac had pulled up in front and a woman about my age was helping an elderly woman into a wheelchair from the car.

"Oh, that's my ten o'clock," Eileen said. "You know, Betty, that's Mabel Stroud. She's just turned ninety-two years old. *She's* getting a tint."

Betty straightened in her chair, lifted her chin. "What color?"

Doris and I exchanged surprised glances.

I didn't realize until she had backed her grandmother through the doorway that the younger woman was my friend, Lainie. The pleasures of a small town, you know almost everybody.

"Oh, hi, Eve. Is this your mom?"

"Yeah. This is Betty."

My mother paused, one hand close to her mouth. "Good afternoon," she said in her practiced, receptionist voice.

"This is my grandma. I bring her here every other week. It gets her out, you know."

Mabel was a frail woman with thinning hair, twisted hands, and lavender gray eyes peeking out behind neatly folded layers of translucent skin. Lainie got down at her level and smiled at her grandmother. "You just love getting your hair done, don't you, Gram?"

Mabel smiled and locked eyes with my mother.

"Lavender," she said, her voice reedy thin. "To match my eyes."

My mother was silent a moment longer. Finally she straightened in her chair, and lifted her chin. "I'll match with Mabel."

And suddenly, except for pink shocks of hair, faded now but still there, she had become Betty again—soft spoken, elegant, hands folded neatly under the drape, basking in the center of attention.

Give her some space.

I settled into one of the reception chairs, picked up a *Cosmopolitan* magazine and turned the pages absently. Young girls with flawless skin selling Oil of Olay, Fashion Do's and

Don'ts, Ten Ways to Make Him Beg. Nothing about what's coming right around the corner or how to stop it. The part that fades and never comes back.

Lainie's voice pulled me from thought. "You all right, Eve?"

She held a novel in her lap, a place marker sticking out near the end.

I glanced over at my mother, still sitting quietly, nose scrunched tight, letting Doris apply a soap cap tint. I thought if I brought her to Ojai, the little town would welcome her in, heal her, and give her some joy. She would make friends, have a life of her own after Vern. Instead, the artsy-fartsy spiritual vortex that was Ojai had spun her out like a piece of tainted meat.

"I don't know, 'Lain. I've tried to make it good for her, but it's not working. I'm afraid the problem could be that I don't know what's good for her. I only know what's good for me."

Doris wrapped a towel around Mom's head. "Ow! *goddammit*, you're breaking my neck!"

Back to the street bum with Tourette's.

Lainie gave me a sympathetic look. "We're all on our own journey. You can help, but ultimately it's still hers to make."

It doesn't get any more *Ojai* than that. "Thanks. I wish I could let myself off the hook that easily."

The cell phone buzzed in my purse. I recognized the number from Crossroads. "Sorry, 'Lain."

"Eve?" Sharlene's voice came over the phone. "I'm glad I got you."

Adrenaline zipped from my guts out to all my fingers and toes. "Vern! Is he okay? Did he fall?"

"No, no. He's fine," she said, her voice halting, low. "Reba called me."

"Oh." Reba had taken matters into her own hands.

"I'm burning up," My mother yelled at the top of her lungs. Doris was blowing her hair dry, rolling the ends under.

"I was surprised when she told me what happened. You're mother looked so—"

"Together?" She was right, of course. On the outside, my mother had looked together. But on the inside a battle raged and her brain cells were losing.

"We do have a nice room. I can have Ernesto move her

things here from Reba's this afternoon, if you want."

So that was it. Reba was spinning her out too. Just like that. Unplugged and kicked to the curb. I had broken my promise. Twice.

For a moment, I allowed myself to bump along to Eric Clapton's classic *Crossroads* guitar riff, the words suddenly up close and personal.

> *...down to the crossroads,*
> *fell down on my knees.*
> *Asked the lord above for mercy,*
> *save me if you please...*
> *Welcome to Boomerville.*

Crossroads was ready. This afternoon. If *I* wanted. On the day I found her at the hospital, what was it, six months ago? What I wanted was to have her with me, finally. But, realistically, I would have to quit my job to do that. Robert was all for it. He'd wanted me to quit ever since we started our corporation. But was that what I really wanted? And was that what was best for her?

"Don't bring her here. Not again," My mother howled, all eyes on her. Doris was trying to get her to look in the mirror. She covered her eyes. She was the antithesis of the mother in pictures I'd seen. At the reception desk at Cementek, smiling, perfect manicure, poofed hair, three tiers of gold birthday baubles draping the front of a high fashion suit. *Mr. Johnson... Mr. Jenkins... Mr. Edwards... Mr. Salter...*

"Eve?" Sharlene's voice came at me again from the cell phone.

"Yes," I said. I knew Crossroads was the answer, I just couldn't give it. Not yet.

My fingers fiddled with objects at the bottom of my Levi's pocket. I took them out, held them in my palm. The aquamarine caught a glint of light from outside.

"No, I don't want her!" my mother yelled again. She fought to get out from under the drape.

Doris was trying to get Mom to use the hand mirror. "Just look at the back."

"Sharlene, I have to get back to you." I broke our

connection on her goodbye.

My mother gave Doris the stink eye, but once she got turned away from the wall mirror, she shifted the hand mirror this way and that until she found the image of the back of her head. Doris had sculpted her hair to silky perfection—a shining, champagne beige with just a hint of lavender, and a June-Allison pageboy. With a little lipstick—on her lips—she would look like any other seventy-year-old woman in reasonably good shape. Size four, smooth skin, clear eyes, straight teeth. But inside her head, the connections were scrambled or missing entirely.

"That's good," Mom said at last.

"We girls stick together, don't we?" Doris said, winking at me.

"We stick together," Mom repeated. Fresh color, a blow dry, blush on her cheeks, and the first smile I'd seen all day. I would call Sharlene back later, give the go-ahead, but for now, for today, I wanted my mother with me, or at least, a reasonable facsimile of my mother.

We ate a light lunch at Healthberry, a cool quinoa and cucumber salad and focaccia bread. Mom slurped from the spoon, wolfing the salad like a starving dog. The people at the next table fish-eyed over at us. They must have thought I was crazy, taking her out in public. I stared back, dabbing my mother's chin with napkins like it was nothing out of the ordinary.

We spent the afternoon driving down two-lane back roads over-arched with eucalyptus, pepper, oak and sycamore, uniform rows of orange and lemon swept by like years.

"Like old Anaheim," I said, and she smiled. We had done this sometime in our past, in a lifetime lived before this one, Mom and Vern and I, driving through a misty rain, down Katella Avenue, past orange groves that Disneyland and a gaggle of hotels had long since consumed.

I took us to the lake, through the avocado orchards to Carpinteria, then back to Ojai's East End where a new grove of baby avocados left a wide-open view of Topa Topa mountain, a giant wedge of layered rock pushed up by sea floor spreading a thousand miles and thousands of years ago.

We wound our way to Meditation Mount, a high, flat ridge

where you could see across the valley to the far, layered peaks of Matilija Canyon. The dark anvil of cloud that had shrouded the peaks in the morning had moved off west. The late afternoon sun slipped under them to light the mountain top.

I stopped the car and turned off the engine. We watched as the bright pink light of the slanting sun moved across the mountain's face and then faded, the air cooling as it passed, the silence broken only by the scree of a red-tailed hawk tracing circles in the sky.

I covered her hand on the console, and we sat, quiet, until she grew restless. She pulled the mirror down and fussed with her hair, pushing it behind her ears and pulling it out again. "*Tch.*"

I could see that whatever had gone on inside her head this morning was still niggling at her. "So what are we going to do with you, Mom?"

She shrugged and flipped visor back up. "Can't go back."

"I know. I know."

Together we watched the final act of the Pink Moment. A last swath of altocumulus clouds moved out of sight over the setting sun. The layered cliffs flared fire orange, then pink, then purple, then gray…then gone.

18 One Safe Place

When I pulled into our driveway, Robert was on the front porch. He'd been waiting for us, worried, I was sure. He waved the newspaper at us as I helped Mom out of the car. "The Perseid meteor shower," he called out as we came up the front walk. "It's tonight. Three a.m."

I told him I was sure we'd all be asleep at three a.m.. But as it turned out, none of us were. By the time I sautéed up some garden veggies, Mom had fallen asleep in the guestroom without eating or taking her meds. I stood at the kitchen window, waiting for the pasta to cook. A familiar pair of western blue birds took their evening bath in a plate of water on our patio table. The female cocked her head, her shiny black eye flicked in my direction.

Robert came in from washing up, stood behind me, and wrapped his arms across my shoulders. "Remember the day she got under the house?"

I tipped my head into his kiss at the back of my neck. I did remember. It had been late spring. Near our vegetable garden. The male kept pecking at a screen over one of the crawlspace vents at the house's footing. When we came to see what the fuss was about, he flew to the top of a fencepost near the back bedroom and waited, squawking in dissonant notes. Down on all fours, we saw the female, timidly pecking from inside the vent, caught under the house. I speculated that the bird, drawn by water dripping into the cat bowl near the kitchen patio, got in through an opening in the screen there and fluttered along, from vent to vent.

"Either that," Robert had said, "or the cat took her under." If that were the case, she was a lucky bird.

Robert had put on his overalls and gone down, elbowing himself along, through the crawlspace under the kitchen, under the living room, all the way under to the back of the house. There, he captured the bird in his jacket, crawled back out, and released her in the garden where the male bird waited. She stayed on the ground next to the tomato plants, stunned and disoriented a moment until the male flew down, singing madly. We watched, only a few steps away, as they circled one another, spreading their wings low. Around and around they went, performing a joyful reunion dance.

The pair had stayed on through summer. Now the birds fluttered up to the pear tree as I brought our plates to the patio table. And then the phone rang. Robert picked it up.

"It's Reba. She wants to know if Ernesto should bring Betty's things here or to Crossroads." He handed me the phone, one eyebrow up.

I took it in both hands like it was a dead thing. It may as well have weighed a hundred pounds. I knew what my answer had to be, but it didn't make it easier. Would Mom really be better off? Would she feel like I abandoned her? That was the question that twisted my throat into a knot. I shook my head, squeezed my eyes tight against the doubts, but they loomed like specters, accusing. *You are throwing your mother away.*

Robert pulled me into his arms, slipped the phone away with one hand and held my head against his chest with the other. "That will be Crossroads," he said for me.

Crossroads indeed. I held on to him like breath underwater, and then I let the pounding grief roll over me.

He relayed the arrangements. Betty would stay here tonight. We'd meet Reba for coffee at nine in the morning. She'd bring

Betty's jewelry with her. The rest—her dresser, her paintings, a bedroom chair, clothes, a pair of sneakers—Ernesto would take to Crossroads first thing in the morning so the room could be all set up when we got there.

Robert hung up the phone and held me a moment longer. "She'll be all right Eve. And so will you."

He pushed me away just enough to fix me with a look that made me want to believe. I pulled out a smile. For him.

"Better go out to our dinner before the bugs come."

I went to the living room, put Miles Davis' "Sketches of Spain" into the CD player and joined Robert on the patio. The bluebirds had flown off to wherever they stayed at night and Robert and I ate quietly, alone.

"How can you listen to this stuff, it's so sad," he said.

"It's how I feel."

I pushed pasta around on my plate, picking here and there. Since I had been a young child making my way, the only kid in first grade whose parents were divorced, someone always tried to make me feel happier than I felt, smile when I really wanted to cry, make me excited to see my mother the second Tuesday of the month and forget about her the rest of the time. Tonight I had decided to put my mother away, like taking a hopelessly injured dog to the pound. If you can't wallow in that, what can you wallow in?

Miles played his notes into my soul. I put my fork down, folded my hands in my lap, and slipped into the depths of the haunting music.

"Did you think she would somehow recover and rewind back to the fifties for you?" Robert's voice pulled me out of the void. Even he had a limit to how much pity he could witness. He picked up the plates and left me alone in the backyard. I closed my eyes; castanets and mournful notes pulled me into thin, exquisitely painful threads. I let the CD play over and over until the moon, swollen orange by smoke of wildfires drifting in the atmosphere across from Colorado, rolled low off Topa Topa mountain and disappeared.

My mother was still asleep when I crawled into bed. I lay awake, dressed, on top of the bed covers, worried that she'd get up and I wouldn't hear. That she'd go to the kitchen, turn on the stove, or open the front door and wander off down the street. I fought the onset of a familiar dream. I'm supposed to thread a fine needle, but my fingers are too fat. I wanted the sensation to go away, and then it started.

"Can't stay! Can't Stay!" Her cries pulled me upright.

I glanced at the clock: Three a.m.

She was down the hall, at the front door, pulling at the door handle and banging the window panes.

"Mom!" I went to her, took her hands in mine. "It's too early to get up. Let's go back to bed."

But she would not budge. I feared a repeat of the night before. What if I couldn't handle her?

"No. Not sleepy." She fought me, pushed me away.

"Let's get something to eat then, you didn't have dinner."

"Not hungry. I'm leaving. Now."

Robert came up behind us, wrapped in his robe, a pair of binoculars in his hand. "Let's watch the meteor showers, then."

My mother stopped fighting and gave Robert a curious look.

"Honey, no. It's chilly out there, we can't—"

"It's August, for heaven sakes. It balmy. C'mon Betty." He took her hand, and gave me a beckoning smile as he opened the front door and led her out.

Could I be so lucky as to finally have someone who really cared about me in my life? Who thought beyond his own comfort to soothe and protect someone else? Robert, in the wee hours of the morning, in his bathrobe, had offered both my mother and me a glowing piece of his spirit. How could I say no to that?

I pulled some old quilts from the hall closet, folded them over my arms, and followed them outside. It took some convincing to get my mother to lie down, but finally the three of us lay, side-by-side, sandwiched in quilts on our driveway, waiting, binoculars at the ready.

Robert saw the first meteors come through, burnt orange in the smoke-tinged atmosphere, but still very, very bright.

"There, from behind the mountain!"

And then, it was like someone had released a swarm of flaming bees. Streak after streak, they buzzed across the black dome of the night as we held our breath. Not another person stirred from their homes, we were alone on our backs, with nothing between us and the universe, so close you could almost run your fingers through it.

"Do you see them Mom, the meteors?"

"No," she said, stabbing a gnarled pointer finger toward the spectacle. "Not meteors. Angels."

I'm not sure how long we lay in the driveway, holding hands, watching the night sky. All I know is I didn't want it to end. When the newspaper man drove by and sailed his delivery over our heads, I noticed Robert was snoring.

"I guess we'd better go in."

"Angels," Betty whispered, pointing. But the meteor shower was over.

19 Return to Crossroads

I waited with Mom outside the coffee shop off the main street through town. We sloughed off our sweaters and sipped iced mochas. After the thunderstorm the day before, the temperature was predicted to hit one hundred that day. The metal tabletop was too hot to rest our forearms against.

Across the street, cars gathered in the parking lot next to the town's only funeral home. As many times as I'd sat here, chatting with a friend or reading the Sunday paper with Robert, I'd never paid much attention to the squatty stone building with its high windows and devil-grass lawn.

Black-dressed people got out of freshly-washed cars—some in tight groups, holding hands, talking, some solitary figures— silent and slow—moved reluctantly past an unruly clump of drying bird-of-paradise at the sun-bleached entrance. Near the back door at the other end of the parking lot, two men loaded a long, narrow cardboard box into the back of a green van.

My mother slurped her mocha, her eyebrows bunching in the middle. She cleared her throat. "Are we going there?"

Her question caught me off guard. Of course not. *Not yet.* "No, no. We're here. Meeting Reba. Then we're going to see Vern."

"Why do you care about him?" She slurped again, choked and coughed.

I waited for her to finish, then tried to give her a rational answer. "Because he gave you a good life, Mom." My voice cracked. Muscles bunched at the back of my throat. *You gave me up to be with him and now he's nothing to you?* "Everything you ever wanted," I said, my words barely whispered.

Had she forgotten? The houses, the cars, the travel, the jewelry? "He loved you. Loves you still."

She glared back at me as if I were nuts. "Crazy love," she said, irritated. "Someone else in his skin."

She was right, of course. She had suffered watching him go. Kept his secret, and her own. The last year must have been a nightmare. Maybe even the last five, if I was really honest. How long since they'd shared a true conversation? A sexy look? Free spirits? They had been lovers for nearly fifty years. Lovers until the end of reason.

I didn't recognize Reba coming across the street until she spoke to us. She carried my mother's rosebush and a small Victoria's Secret bag.

"Good morning, Betty," she sang out a little too brightly. The strain of the last few days showed in dark circles under her eyes. She sat with us, set the rosebush on the ground next to my feet, and pushed the bag across the table to me. "Did you have a good night at Evie's?"

"Angels," my mother said. She reached across the table, snagged the bag, and looked in. I knew what was in the bag. Her jewelry. She rolled her eyes back up to mine and pushed it slowly to me, then glared at Reba.

"Not sick!" She patted at her hair and her face. "Not *sick!*"

She jerked her arm, smacking her mocha off the table. Reba jumped away, mopping spills with a fistful of napkins.

Mom shuffled down the sidewalk as fast as her legs would move. I followed, a mother watchfully shadowing her two-year-old. At that very moment the assistants at Crossroads would be moving her furniture from Reba's to her new room there. Her furniture and her clothes and her magazine-cover picture of Frank Sinatra. The last sense of her life in the outside world. And she knew it too. She *knew.*

I panicked. I was hoping we could pull this off. Get her inside Crossroads before she caught on. But she knew. My stomach churned with guilt at the thought of what I was about to do. I had seen the way she ran from the realities at Crossroads. Back then, I swore I would never put her there.

"Mom, wait," I said, staying with her but not grabbing a hold. What if she fought me like she had done last night?

I imagined the headline in the town paper: *Ojai woman charged with elder abuse.*

And then an image of myself as a child savaged my heart— my hands among many little hands, rolling out a long snake of cold, green clay on a plastic table cloth.

"Your mama will be back soon," somebody said. My hands were on the snake, but my eyes were on a blurred image of her as she left me.

I shook off the vision, a cold chill on a hot day. *Grow up, for chrissake.*

I wiped the blur from my eyes and kept close to her as she shuffled into the parking lot driveway. A car waited while I guided her back to me. The driver flicked a sympathetic look my way and navigated slowly past us. I checked my watch. "Come on Mama. We have time to get you another drink."

"Don't *want* it."

"But you like iced mocha." I touched her elbow, and guided her back to the table.

"No!! Not the drink, the *go!*" She refused to sit.

She knows.

I steeled my resolve, remembering comments I'd read in an Alzheimer's chat room. *"They're better off in the closed environment, they calm down,"* the writer had advised. *"It's the right thing to do, believe me."*

But it felt so wrong.

Reba moved in behind me and slipped the handles of the bag of jewelry into my fingers. "I'll see you down there," she whispered, and stepped away from us.

I helped my mother into the car, fastening the seatbelt. Inside, I felt anything but calm, but I tried to calm her. "Vern misses you, Mom. He asks for you every time I go."

"Don't miss him. Don't want it."

She fiddled with the seatbelt, nervously running her hand up the length of it, and patting it down. She gasped and grabbed for the console when we pulled away from the curb.

Another wave of guilt washed over me. I had been so concerned about my losses, I hadn't given a thought to what it might be like for her. The ladies in the chat room were right. I had been trying to fit her into my world. But things in my world were too hot, too cold, too fast—too late. "I'll try not to go too fast, Mom."

I punched a number on the CD player and sped up carefully. Frank Sinatra lit his torch and sang ...

What's new?

How is the world treating you?

Mom turned her face to the window. No, no. We could do without the lonely Frank. I punched another number, replacing Frank with Franklin.

Re, re, re, re

Spect, spect, spect…

...That was more like it...

What you need, baby I got it…

I did my best to remember the words and sang along until we pulled in the driveway at Crossroads.

Betty did not complain until we got there.

"Don't." She folded her arms and set her jaw as if she knew exactly what was coming. Martina, second in command now at Crossroads, emerged from the clinic door and came smiling toward us. I pressed the button to roll down the passenger side window and greeted her. She nodded to me and opened the door for my mother who unfolded her arms cautiously.

"Hi Miss Bet-*tie!*" She reached in and unbuckled my mother's seatbelt as smooth as you please. "I'm so happy to see you."

Martina offered her hand, and magically, lifted my mother out of her fear.

"Good morning." Mom pulled out her best receptionist voice and allowed Martina to guide her in through the clinic to the main room.

"We have a special table for you and your family today. See? Vern's out there waiting for you."

I followed them in, carrying her rosebush on my hip. The square, resistant set of my mother's shoulders melted on Martina's arm.

Right on time, I could see Sharlene talking to Vern at a table out in the shady patio. Boston Ferns and fuschias in moss pots hung from the tree branches. Reba had beaten us there. Feeling my eyes on her, she looked up, smiled, and waved.

Martina was a pro. She slow-waltzed rather than shuffled my mother outside.

Sharlene leaned over and said something to Vern as we walked up to the table. "That's her?" I heard him say. "I thought she would be younger."

"That's her," Sharlene reassured him as she glanced up at me.

"Hum. I must have two Bettys," Vern said, eating a bit of banana from a little paper cup.

When she saw Vern, my mother dropped Martina's arm and shuffled to him on her own, their eyes taking each other in. I sat next to Sharlene and watched as my mother clasped his face in both her hands, then slid one hand under his and covered it gently with her other. "Yes-s-s-s," she said softly.

What's new? How is the world treating you?

Vern squeezed her hands and looked to me. "How'd you know we were here?"

I shrugged my shoulders, tried to smile. "Just a coincidence, I guess."

"Are you going to have lunch with us? We'll have to make reservations." He nodded his head toward the dining room. "They get pretty busy in there this time of day."

My mother slipped into the chair next to him and leaned in. "Don't need reservations here Vern," she said, still holding his hand.

A complete sentence.

Martina returned with a tray of fruit and set it on the table in front of them. Vern took a paper cup from the tray and offered it to his wife. She took the chunk of banana and held it aloft while Vern added the paper cup to a small stack he retrieved from his shirt pocket. "We get first class service here, you know."

Mom looked at the banana chunk, raised an eyebrow. "First class."

"Are you going to sleep with me now?"

My mother's brows drew together. She dropped the banana

chunk on the table and edged out of her chair.

She looked at me, reached out to touch the leaves of her rosebush, then pinned me with her stone blue eyes. I was convicted.

"Not staying here!" Her voice carried over the music piping through to the patio.

"You said she was going to stay with me." Vern's voice was thready, full of pain.

I should have known. Vern said the same thing to me every time I visited. I had planned a more tactful approach, now the spell was broken. My mother threw dagger looks at Reba.

"Not sick," she said, then she shifted all her weight and movement toward the wrought iron gate, moving as fast as her shuffle could carry her.

The color drained from Reba's cheeks. "If looks could kill—"

"Mom! Wait!" I sprang out of my chair to go after her.

Martina touched my arm. "Let me get her," she said, and she sprinted away. "Bet-tie! Wait! I have something for you."

"Why doesn't she like me?" Vern asked, his tone pleading.

"Of course she likes you Vern." Sharlene held both his hands in hers. "She always will. She's just a little confused right now."

"Me too."

Sharlene leaned in and gave him a hug, then got up. "Come on Eve, Reba. We'll take care of this from here."

I looked over my shoulder and saw that Martina had caught up to my mother and turned her in the direction of a shady alcove where another aide was helping a woman repot some orchids. Martina talked and touched the flower petals. Mom squared her shoulders again, stiff and resistant. Sharlene motioned to an aide to sit with Vern, then she grabbed my elbow and turned me away.

"She'll do better if you're not here. Believe me. Give us three days. You'll see."

"Where's Betty" I heard Vern say to the aide as we moved away. Sharlene guided us back through the dining room where a group of the more incapacitated residents were being spoon fed. I tried not to look at them.

My heart was pounding, I could hardly breathe. Sharlene

zipped her key from a gizmo on her belt, opened the clinic door, and hurried us through. I leaned heavily on her arm. Where were my legs? I took in the tiny room with its medicine cabinets, stacks of diapers, TV monitor, and bulletin board of obits, pictures, and thank you cards.

The smell of disinfectant, laundry detergent, and the phone attendant's perfume closed in.

"Here, you better sit down." Sharlene lowered me to the couch, part of the first aide treatment center. She filled a paper cup with water from a dispenser and handed it to me.

I brought it to my lips, and then I saw her.

An image on the tiny TV, blurred and insignificant at first, shifted and spun until it became an image that would haunt me forever. My mother, standing on the wrought iron gate, her feet on the bottom rail, her hands clenching the bars. There was no sound, but I could see the anguish in her features as she violently shook the gate. Her mouth formed the shape of my name, over and over. And then Martina was there, prying my mother's hands loose, pulling her into her arms.

My lips went cold. I saw Sharlene's face through a darkening, narrow tube, and the paper cup slipped from my hand.

20 The Armoire

I've only passed out twice in my life. Both times I'd been in the last trimester of pregnancy, had gone too long without eating, and the incident had me waking to a flurry of panicked activity. This time, there was no panic, only the quiet calm of Katherine's office, a private sanctuary in the center of the storm of lost souls.

Katherine sat next to me on a moss green love seat across from a mahogany desk that anchored the room to some level of reality. Daylight filtered through rose-colored drapes, highlighting the dust motes caught in its glow.

"Welcome back." Her voice was low and comforting as she took my freezing hands into hers.

My body had stopped shaking, but my eyelid twitched incessantly. I tried on a smile. "Sorry. I don't usually do this."

"I do this all the time."

"Guess you saw it coming, then. I sure didn't."

She nodded. "I'll never forget the first time you brought your mom in here. Her pretty jacket, her lovely hair, her perfect makeup, and her jewelry. You did a good job on her. But, yes. The signs were there."

I felt wobbly, almost transparent. I had to keep the words coming so I could feel the carpet under my feet and the air in my lungs. "I thought after Vern was here, she could pull herself together, with the pressure off, you know."

It felt good to talk, but the words clogged at the back of my throat.

"Take a couple of breaths." Katherine rubbed my back a moment and then went to her desk. She waited, holding a folder in her hands. "Take your time."

How much time did I need to accept that my mother was mortal? Twenty minutes? That she could actually be touched by a common thing? Three days? And if she was mortal, then that meant I was too. How much time did I have before the same thing happened to me?

Tentacles of grief and guilt tightened around my chest. The sting returned to my throat. I squeezed my eyes against it.

Enough.

Enough!

I took another deep breath and held it to keep parts of me from flying away. I had never felt so close to losing control.

Katherine busied herself at her desk, giving me time to pull myself together before handing a folder across to me. I put it in my lap and folded my hands on top. I didn't have to open it. I knew what was inside. Contact information, request for medical records, copy of power of attorney, financial, permission for psychiatric evaluation, house rules. The paperwork sealing my mother's fate. Locking her away.

"I noticed she was wearing a necklace today. If it's valuable, maybe you can bring her something else. People here don't always understand the concept that another person's things belong to them. We watch them, but—"

"Okay, yes." I opened the folder, rummaged in my bag for a pen. "I'm sorry, I can't seem to find--"

"You don't have to do that now." She handed me a business card. "I really think it would help if you went to see this woman."

I looked at the card: Psychologist, Family Counseling.

"Thanks, but I'm okay. I don't think I—"

She slipped it into my hand and closed my fingers around it. "Just in case."

My first sense of home was the fragrance of mown grass. I breathed it in deep draughts, a magic elixir of normal, Saturday smells to replace the odor of Lysol and horse manure that had followed me home. Had the leaves on the liquid amber turned yellow while I was gone? A moment ago we were basking in summer and suddenly we were on the cusp of Fall. It had somehow happened without me.

The Victoria's Secret bag sat next to me, a silent passenger that spoke volumes. I made myself breathe again. Where do I pick up the thread of my life from here?

You could start by going inside.

I punched the garage door opener. Robert's van was gone. His wetsuit—usually hanging near the back door, a black rubber stranger lying in wait—was gone as well as his surfboard. At first my heart sank a little. I could do with a hug. On the other hand, I wasn't sure if what I needed wasn't just a little solitude. I didn't know what I needed. I felt like a Mylar balloon of myself, face painted on the outside, leaking air, floating lower.

I pulled into the garage, left it open, snagged my purse and the bag of jewelry and got out of the car. Passing the white board on my way through the kitchen, I saw that Robert had left me a note: *Surfs Up! See you around two.* I checked my watch. It was half past noon.

Good for him. My tide was out, seaweed and debris strewn all around inside my brain. Driven by a vague notion of standing in a hot shower, I ended up in the doorway of our guestroom instead. Mom's jewelry armoire had stood unopened across from the bed since she first came to stay with me, nearly nine months ago. Except for the few rings and a watch she had taken with her to Reba's, her entire collection rested inside, undisturbed.

The armoire was a beautiful thing, like her. Hand painted with chrysanthemums, bamboo shoots, and long-tailed birds created in flowing brush strokes in soft pastels on an ivory lacquered finish.

Inside were her private things, tokens of a life I had never been invited to share. Over the last few weeks, and during bouts of clarity, we had created a trust that gave me permission to manage their financial affairs, to arrange long term care, to authorize...whatever. But standing before her armoire, I felt like an intruder. Who was I to open those doors without her standing next to me?

Her daughter. The one who abandoned her.

The image of her standing on the gate flashed on the screen in my forehead like an item on the evening news. How many times would I have to watch it?

"No. Go away." I slumped on the bed, the bag of jewelry resting on my lap. No daughter should have to see that. It wasn't fair. Not fair at all. I tried to call up an image of her face before she went missing inside. I really tried. A picture of she and Vern on one of their last cruises sat on top of the armoire. In it, she was smiling, but now that I know how it went, I can see that something is already amiss; a little tic at the corner of her smile. A fatal flaw that I had missed in real life.

I took a deep breath, dumped the contents of the bag carefully on top of the armoire and took a hasty inventory— some rings were missing. Then I remembered: Yesterday, at the doctor's office. *Had that been only yesterday?* I went to the bedroom, pulled my Levis from the hamper, and found the rings there. Thousands of dollars' worth of gold and diamonds carelessly tossed into a pile of dirty clothes. Who was I to be in possession of such things? I hadn't one piece of jewelry worth more than a week's groceries.

Hands shaking, I returned to the armoire, slid the little brass cylinder from the door handles, and slowly opened the cupboards. Behind the doors were four shallow drawers stacked over two deeper ones. I opened the top drawer on the right, the brass handle tinkling to rest as I let it go. Inside this red-velvet-lined drawer there were several ring boxes—black velvet, blue, brown plastic with gold trim, and a blue satin— and more at the back. I had no idea which of the boxes went with which piece of jewelry. My only intention was to return the jewelry from the Victoria Secret bag to its rightful place.

I opened a satin box. Inside the inscription read: Sausalito Jewelry. The slot was empty. I remembered her telling me they had had the aquamarine designed on a trip to San Francisco. I found the ring in the pile and slipped it on my right ring finger, too big. I moved it to the middle finger. The gold warmed to my skin like a living thing. I closed the little box, empty, and picked up the solitaire. A diamond the size and shape of an olive pit. I slipped it on my left middle finger, tall and awkward on my hands, smaller than hers, but dazzling all the same. I opened another box, the black velvet. In it was a ring I had never seen, ribbons of gold spiraled around a sprinkling of seven diamonds, a quarter carat each, at least. I slipped it on my right pointer finger, turning it in the light. A worthy bauble.

In another box, a heavy gold rose with a huge diamond at its center blared out at me, big and gaudy and bold. Was it real or a Zirconia? I knew women who could tell at a glance, but I was clueless. In all there were ten rings, strands of pearls, flashy cocktail rings of varying size and value, a black pearl pinky ring, and the swirled gold and platinum band I'd remembered as a child. I slipped this on my right ring finger.

In the next drawer, the boxes were long and flat. Watches. The first was empty. It must be for the diamond studded gold my mother had been wearing. I took it from my pile and fastened it on my wrist, the gold warming instantly to my skin. Inside the other boxes were three more watches. Two gold, one antique with velvet bands.

The next little drawer contained more boxes, each with its own treasure—freshwater pearls, a diamond and emerald linked bracelet, a long string of black pearls with a pendant of rose jade in a bed of gold, a delicate bracelet of Japanese characters, a pin of elegant gold leaves each bearing a perfect pearl, a serpentine chain with a Tiffany heart, matching earrings—a lifetime of birthday and anniversary gifts, enough to start a jewelry store.

One by one, I fastened each piece on, layering by size: bracelets, watches, a pair of diamond stud earrings. The next drawer held more of the same and an interesting silk pouch. I slipped the contents out into my hand: a delicate pendant of aquamarine, a diamond at the yoke of its slide, and earrings to match. Aquamarine, our birthstone.

I put them on.

Under the cupboard doors were another five larger drawers, each hand painted with a different scene: an island pagoda, two small boats at sail, ferns and bamboo around a pond, a pine bough, and finally, a willow tree weeping over a pair of cranes. The Island Pagoda held clutch purses; beads on satin—gold, silver and black. Clutches I had seen in pictures at captain's tables on cruises to Europe, to Scandinavia, and to the

Bahamas. I slipped them over my arm and up to my shoulders. In the drawer of fern and bamboo I found a nest of silk scarves. I couldn't resist sliding my hand in, then I hit something hard. Beneath the scarves was a lacquered box. I pulled it out and sat back on the bed, holding it in my lap. My heartbeat raced. I pushed the corners of the box up with my thumbs and tipped the lid open.

Inside was a faded, bound book: the *Log o' Life*. Presented to me at my (my mother's) baby shower. Her cousin had copied a quote from Hamlet inside:

> *This above all—to thine own self be true,*
> *And it must follow, as the night the day,*
> *Thou canst not then be false to any man.*
> *—Shakespeare*

Inside the bulging warped pages were pictures I had never seen, inky footprints, a lock of hair, a pair of flattened leather baby shoes, a family tree filled in to three generations, and, decreasingly faithful entries from there: first word, first tooth, first streetcar ride; a collection of first valentines, first birthday cards, and then, at the end of the second year, nothing. A little bundle tied with a folded and dog-eared satin bow fell in my lap as I closed the book.

Someone, I'm assuming my mother, had wrapped a plastic baggie of broken candy inside two small photographs. One was my mother at the window of a shotgun cabin in what must have been Cottage Grove, Oregon where my grandparents had made a go at farm living. Mom's face was in shadow but I recognized the profile—pin-curled pompadour, haughty nose, full lips—her hand rested on the urgent bulge of a baby about a month away. The other was of me in front of her on a horse, our hair catching the same strawberry blonde halo of light. Inside the baggie, a tiny paper figure of Peter Rabbit floated in a jumble of white sugar chunks and bits of purple frosting. Not for me. Not then, but now. My young history in a box.

This, above all....

But no, there had been something else. Even then. And it had nothing to do with me.

With the *Log o' Life* next to me on the bed, I placed the

lacquered box back in the drawer. I would look at it later when I had more time.

The last drawer, the one with the willow and cranes, was empty, except for a pillow-slip sized piece of silk. Jade green medallions in alternating rows of boxing lions and fire breathing dragons, woven into a rich red field. A table runner perhaps? I had no idea, but the tag sewn on to the back side of the pattern said Pure Silk, Tatsumura.

"What'd you find?"

I nearly jumped out of my skin. "Robert! I didn't hear you come in."

Had I really been there at the armoire for more than an hour? Robert looked me up and down, his eyebrows raised as he took in the display of diamonds, jade and gold. Heat rose up my neck all the way to my ears, like a child caught playing dress-up in her mother's forbidden closet. I refolded the silk, dropped the little book on top of it and slid the drawer closed.

He gave me a hand up, clutch bags dangling off my shoulders. "So, how'd it go?"

I put my truest face forward, but kept the fainting spell, the breakdown, and the pain inside, tucked away. "They said, *'give her three days'*."

The Goddess of Undo

21 Three Days

Day One

Shoo-shoo, shoo-shoo. Shoo-shoo, shoo-shoo.

Betty pushed the bedcovers down and looked around the room. There was her own dresser against the wall at the end of the bed, her pictures of Vern, Evie, and her grandchildren. Next to her bed was another, a twin, empty, with a bedcover that matched her own–the ones she'd used at Reba's. Beyond that, a closet, and a doorway leading to…where?

Shoo-shoo. Shoo-shoo.

She took a mental inventory: her dresser, her pictures, her bedcovers…her dresser, her pictures, her bedcovers…but a different room. And then she remembered Martina. That sweet Martina had helped her into bed in this room last night. Helped her forget the gate.

"Oh, look at your cute pajamas," she had said. Betty knew Martina was deliberately distracting her. But she was grateful. She needed to be distracted. Her mind had sailed away someplace and Martina had helped her get it back.

Betty slipped her legs out of the covers and stood looking

at her sleeves, her pajama bottoms. Her Scottie dog pajamas. She felt warm, safe, nothing crowding in where she didn't want it. But she had to pee.

Outside she saw tree branches through high windows across the top of the room, lit pale yellow by the porchlight against a sky still the darkest blue-black.

Don't get up yet. Not yet. Betty slipped back under the covers and waited, but urge overtook reason.

"A person has to pee, Goddammit," she hollered. She lowered the covers again, swung her legs to the floor, and pushed herself up.

A tiny red light blinked near the ceiling, and just then the door under the high windows opened and a woman with a familiar face stuck her head in.

"Hello, Miss Betty." She stepped through the doorway and closed it behind her, breathing hard like she'd come at a run.

Somewhere along the line, somewhere between now and when everything had changed, Betty had been transformed from Mrs. Salter, wife of Vern, to simply, Miss Betty, like some Southern Belle at the heart of a romance novel. She liked it, Miss Betty. A new person.

"It's Sharlene, remember me?" The woman came over to the bed and helped her up.

"I can't wait."

"You don't have to. I'll help. And then if you want, you can come out into the morning room with me."

Betty saw herself walking past the other bed and around the corner to the bathroom, but her legs must have seen something different. They only wanted to move an inch at a time. It made no sense. One day, everything works, and the next, nothing.

"Step out, Betty." Sharlene demonstrated.

Betty leaned forward and pushed one foot along the floor and then the other. With Sharlene's help, they made it to the bathroom.

A cubbyhole on a shelf above the sink had a name on it: B-E-T-T-Y. She giggled. "Someone else has my name."

She reached into the shelf and pulled out a hairbrush, and a toothbrush and toothpaste in a plastic pouch. "...and these."

Her robe hung from a hook on the back of the bathroom door, and her tiger pictures, the ones she'd made a long time ago, decorated the bathroom wall. "So. I'm here now."

Sharlene took the bag and the brush and helped her get on the pot. "Yes. These are yours, and you see, there's Una's and Charlotte's here as well."

She pointed out the other women's names on their cubbyholes. "It will be okay, dear. You'll see."

Betty pushed down threads of thought. They only got tangled. She concentrated on letting go, until she heard the sound again: *Shoo-shoo, shoo-shoo.* Louder: *Shoo-shoo, shoo-shoo.* And then, there was a woman behind Sharlene, standing at the bathroom door. She wore nothing but thin, yellowed panties, the elastic frayed at one hip, and a pair of bright pink slippers. Her breasts hung like teardrops down the front of her pale chest. She smiled at Betty and raised her hand to her lips as if to keep a secret.

Shoo-shoo.

"Oh, Una, could you wait a minute hon? Get your robe dear, can you get your robe?"

Sharlene pulled a box off her belt and talked to it. "Two up in 202."

"Got it," said the box .

The woman shuffled away again and the *shoo-shoo* sound faded. Betty unfurled a handful of tissue from the roll and—oh, that felt good—wiping, wiping, wiping—the glowing warm teased her mind with unformed visions, her breath quickening, the room dropping away. Then there was Sharlene, helping her up, sluicing warm water over her hands.

"Shall we go to the morning room and see what's to eat?"

In her pajamas? Her face flushed. She turned to the mirror out of habit, pulled her hair over her ears. That woman was still there. That one who would not smile at her. "Tch."

She worked the corners of her mouth, but the face only pruned and folded. She sighed and turned away.

Where did that other woman go? The one with the secret smile? She wanted to see her again. She tried to tell Sharlene, but all she could get out was "*Shoo-shoo.*"

Sharlene gave her a puzzled look. "What do you want, dear?"

"Shoo-shoo," Betty insisted, working her feet across the bathroom and into the hall after the secret woman.

"Not there, Betty. That's Una's room." She gently guided her back to her own. The one with the door to outside.

Again the door opened and a young, dark-haired woman in a pastel pink smock and white pants like Sharlene's hustled into the room.

"Good morning." She grinned at them, passing through to the hallway. "Where's my *Oooh-naaa*?" she asked as she went into a room on the other side of the bathroom.

Sharlene wrapped Betty in her robe, warm and soft and white, and helped her into her slippers. Together, they went outside.

Betty shivered as the cool air touched her face. The courtyard was well lit, but it was still quite dark outside. They shuffled down a covered walkway, near the main gate. Betty turned her head to see cars in the parking lot past the tinkling fountain.

Sharlene urged her on. "Come on, only a few more steps."

Betty hesitated, and she reached for the gate. Her life was out there, not in here. But Sharlene pulled gently at her elbow. "Come on, dear. Let's get you something to eat."

"Something to eat," Betty repeated. "Yes-s-s-s."

Inside the morning room a few residents sipped coffee and nibbled biscuits. Some snoozed in their pajamas. Sharlene helped her find a seat near a white-haired gentleman who perked up when he saw her.

"Johnathan, this is Betty, maybe you could get her some coffee."

"I can do that," he said and pantomimed tipping his hat as he turned and walked confidently to the galley counter.

Sharlene patted Betty's hand and leaned in. "He'll be sound asleep in his chair in an hour, but for now, you two can chat. I'll be back to check on you in a few minutes. You okay?"

Betty pressed her hands together between her thighs. It could be an adventure, or a bad dream, she wasn't sure which. She straightened her back and turned her head to see if Vern was sitting in his usual place. He wasn't.

Well, okay. She could wait a few minutes for Sharlene. If okay meant she was awake and the *zhumm zhumm* wasn't pulling her into a spin, then, yes. She was okay. For now she was okay.

There were fresh flowers on the tables and someone had

stapled a large American flag on a bulletin board at the back of the room. Betty stared at the red and white stripes until they shifted and overlapped, then something bumped her shoulder. The man with the white hair, sitting beside her, held out a Styrofoam cup.

"You have lovely eyes," he said. Betty lifted her chin, and looked him up and down. He was wearing silky maroon pajamas and a robe, like her. He grinned and pushed the cup at her again. "I can get us some cream, if you want. They have lots of it over there."

She rose slowly out of her seat, pushed her feet hard into the floor, and turned her back to him.

"I'm a pilot, you know," she heard him say as she struggled to start her feet going. "I can take us away from here."

Oh. That just doesn't make any sense. A pilot? Fly them out of here?

"Psh-h-h-h," was all she could manage, and she willed her feet to take a few steps away. Nothing she'd like better than to get away, but he was nothing but a white-haired man in pajamas. She tried to move again, but her legs wouldn't work. Wouldn't do what she wanted. The room felt suddenly foreign and threatening. Where was Evie? Why wasn't she here? This is not what she'd planned. Not at all. Tears welled in her eyes.

From deep inside her, an animal began to wail. Louder and louder, it bellowed through, like water from a broken fire hydrant, or vomiting, or giving birth; the sound erupted from her throat and she threw her head back and let it go. A gusher of anger and frustration, hot and hollow, and no way to turn it off.

"E-e-e-y-a-a-a-h-h-h-h-h-h!"

Sharlene and another woman came running. She flung her arms at them. "Not sick," she cried. "No, no. no."

A man in a blue suit exploded from a door marked "Clinic," raced across the room, and enveloped her in a warm, pink blanket.

"No-o-o-o-o-o!" She hollered until she crumbled under the weight of it, all her strength spilled out onto the floor.

"Betty, I've got you." A woman cooed into her ear, gentle and sweet and calm. She held her arms still inside the warm blanket. "I've got you now."

"Not sick," Betty pleaded, but she knew she was wrong. All

wrong. Ladies don't bellow and stumble and go out in their pajamas. Ladies fold their hands in their laps and cross their ankles. *Seen and not heard. Never tell. Hide.*

"Get us some tea," said Sharlene, gesturing to the man in the blue suit. "It's okay, Betty. I've got you. I've got you, honey."

Betty folded into herself, like a plastic blow-up doll losing air. She closed her eyes and let herself sway in the arms that held her tight, tucked her in, and took her down into a warm quiet place. She sipped the tea when it came, and with a glow like rum sliding down her throat, the jagged thoughts smoothed out into a pleasant, quiet, emptiness.

Day 2

Betty awoke to *Shoo-shoo* perched on the twin bed across from her, stark naked this time, holding a brown teddy bear in her lap. A two-year-old in an old woman's body with pale, haunting eyes. Betty pulled the covers up to her chin. *Am I that pale?*

It was still dark outside, but around here, she guessed, morning was whenever you wanted it to be. Just like yesterday, no sooner had Betty realized Shoo-shoo was there, than the tiny red light began to blink. In a moment, someone—probably Sharlene—would be at their door. Betty hauled herself up, swung her legs over the side of her bed, and straightened her nightie. Yesterday had ended in a blur, but today would be different. She would try to behave.

Their knees almost touching, *Shoo-shoo* pushed the teddy bear toward her, reached to touch her face. Betty liked her, a friend here. But the gesture caught on a jagged memory.

From somewhere deep inside her muddled thoughts sprang a vision of her childhood bedroom in Cottage Grove.

Sun tops the pine trees surrounding their clapboard house, her brother is curled against the cold in the twin bed next to hers, her baby sister cries in a crib at the end of her bed. How she wishes someone else would get the baby; but they never do.

"Betty." Her mother's voice comes from the other side of the wall. "Get your sister."

Betty drags herself out of bed, barefoot across the cold wooden floor, pulls little Carol into her arms, and takes her to her own bed to wait for dawn. Most mornings it is she who bathes and dresses her sister, before she gets herself ready for school. And there is her mother in jodhpurs, sipping coffee, ready to ride out across the farm as if she is some hoity-toity socialite instead of a dirt farmer with a few pigs and cows.

"Tch." Betty pushed the bear back. "*Not* that!"

Shoo-shos's smile dissolved to confusion.

Betty was sorry, but harrumphed anyway. She was nobody's babysitter.

At that moment, the door to the outside corridor opened. Sharlene, with her tray of pills and Josephina, Shoo-Shoo's helper.

"Good morning, ladies." Sharlene handed Betty two paper cups: one with pills, one with water. Betty eyed Sharlene, eyed the pills. She took them one by one, held them in her cheek, drank, and coughed. Yesterday she fell asleep after the pills. The doctor had said, give them a chance. She couldn't tell if they did anything or not. Threads of thought that seemed to make sense to her at the beginning of the day, fell apart before she got to the end. She floated, unable to anchor down, and then, she slept, and woke with a start to find she was in a different chair or back in her bed. Her legs still had a mind of their own, a mind that was shot, apparently. And the gate still taunted her.

When Sharlene turned her back, she spit the pills into her hand and wiped them under the bed covers.

Susanne and Josephina helped them bathe, brush, and dress, then escorted them across the courtyard to the morning room where the other *Earlies* sipped coffee, nibbled biscuits, and waited for the sun to come up. Betty saw the white-haired man sitting across the room. She angled away from him.

She took a seat next to the window where she could see the sun when it touched the tops of the mountains. She could hold onto herself. She could. As soon as it was warm outside, she would go out and find the gate.

Vern came in, long after everyone else, assisted by a bearded man in green pants. Vern had put on weight, mostly in the belly, and his nose though healed was missing a little half-moon piece of its left nostril. She saw him as he should be though, not as he was, the old handsome Vern, nails buffed smooth, and wearing a Hong Kong suit. He gave her a little wave, patted the seat next to him.

The stinging began just at the back of her throat. She looked away. That they could both end up here was the hardest pill of all to swallow. If only she had known, maybe they could have done something different. She saw them jumping off their favorite cliff at Pismo, holding hands until they could see the grains of sand in the green moss in the salt wet crevices of rock, then swooping up and away, intact. Or maybe like the movie she'd watched with Evie. On their last cruise, to Alaska. She saw them jump off the back of the ship—he in his tuxedo, cheeks rosied from a last highball, she in a beaded silk dress. A last kiss and—

Shoo-shoo shuffled to the seat next to Betty and sat. She didn't say anything, didn't have to. Just patted Betty's hand and smiled. Betty gulped back on the sting and lifted her chin. "Tch."

She felt it coming again, this time like a rushing piston of water, raging through her body. She held her chin higher against it but it was no use. She gulped air through her nose and let it go.

"E-e-e-y-a-a-a-h-h-h-h-h-h!"

When she woke, the tables were set for dinner. Had she slept all day? Vern sat next to her, holding her hand too tight. She was too sleepy to pull her hand away. "I'm worried about you, Bett," he said, leaning in, his voice lowered so no one else could hear. "If you don't get better soon, we might have to put you in a home."

Betty stared at him, her thoughts drifting to a dream where she saw their champagne-beige golf cart upended in a ditch at Pebble Beach.

22 Resurrection

Day 3

I waited for my computer to boot up, warming my hands on a steaming cup of coffee. Robert had gone out for *dawn surf patrol*. Thank goodness the Surf God had come through, leaving me alone to concentrate. If things went well, I could have our new display booth ready to ship to Tennessee later in the week for our first trade show.

Who was I kidding? Things were not going well.

Despite the coffee and bright sunlight already slicing under the eaves on the porch, I shivered. The circling dialogs inside my head had taken on lives of their own, crowding me into a very cold, small corner. I had exhausted my strength for fending them off.

How could you leave your mother there like a dog waiting to be put to sleep? This one, the Guilt Monster, whispering a whisker away from my ear, was easy to slap down. I had spent the better part of a year focused on their dilemma—selling their house, moving them, managing their finances, their taxes, their medical care, even jeopardizing my job—I had nothing to feel

165

guilty about.

What do you care, she never took care of you. She deserves this. The voice of my father, still resentful after fifty years. Again easy. In all fairness, I could say the same of him.

And then there were the *what ifs. What if she was still angry with me? What if she had slipped to another plateau because I took her there? What if there was something I'd missed? Something that would bring her back? What if, what if, what if...*

But the one that stabbed me to the core—the one that made it impossible to drive, to read, to eat—was the voice of a small child. She had only to call "Mommie" through those old, empty spaces to make me pull over to the side of the road, blinded by tears, put down even my favorite novel, not remembering what I had just read, or choke on a bite of dinner. The one that sent me crouching in the corner with my hands up over my head. Even as I tried to sleep, she was there, keening, rendering me helpless against the flood of emotion.

The demons harassed me from one end of the house to the other until I found myself in front of the coffeepot again. Now I wished Robert was home. At least having him there made me feel real. Without reality, what was the point?

The chills came again. My thoughts had never taken me to such a place. There was always a point, wasn't there? I stared at the cup of coffee I had just blindly poured, until I realized the phone was ringing.

"Robert!" I clung to his voice like a lifeline.

"Hi, do you miss me?" His usual greeting.

"Yes." I crawled into his words, gasping. "How was the surf?"

"Small, but perfect conditions. Glassy here, but you can feel the Santa Ana building. S'posed to kick up overnight."

"Hum." Wouldn't be September without warm wind dropping the humidity and clearing the sky.

"How 'bout breakfast at The Nest? I'm starved."

"Not hungry, but I'll go with."

"See you in a few minutes then."

Robert remained uncharacteristically silent as I told him about my slow progress on the booth. Now he sat back in his chair, his eggs Benedict only half consumed. "You know, Eve, this show is a big commitment, not just in the bucks we've got wrapped up in it, but it's a commitment to our future in this business."

My heart took a dive. The business? Did he not get it? "I'm barely able to keep my head on straight and it's all about the business?"

How could he miss the all-out panic? It must be leaking from my ears.

"This show was your idea, remember? I can't pull it off by myself."

"I'm sorry. I just can't concentrate. It's like there's a big argument going on inside my head and I can't make it shut up."

"Argument?"

"I mean, one minute they say I'm guilty and the next, they're angry, and—"

"They?" Robert closed his eyes and huffed out a deep breath. When he looked up, it was not Robert whose eyes pierced mine, but a person not my soulmate. A person I'd never seen before, serious and doubting. Closed off. I felt my gut pull up into a tight, cold knot.

"Eve, you know I've been trying to carry you along, boost you up through this. I thought having Betty in twenty-four hour care would give you some relief. Get our lives back. But this—this is way beyond me." He scraped his fork off the table and dropped it noisily on his plate. "I can do sad, worried, upset, stressed out, lots of things. But I'm just not equipped for crazy."

I stopped breathing. This couldn't be happening. I willed the crouching Evie out of her corner.

"No, I didn't mean…Just today, you know. I couldn't—" I felt like a person whose reason for living was being dragged away by mistake.

His face softened back into the Robert I knew. He leaned forward, keeping his words as private as he could, and reached across the table to hold both my hands. "I married a smart, sexy, exciting woman whom I can't live without. Where is she? I need *her*. Not just for the business, for *me*."

I dared a shallow breath and looked around. I knew that at any second I could melt into the floor unless we got somewhere alone.

Reading my mind, he said, "Let's go." He steered me by the elbow, dumping way too much money at the cashier's stand as he hurried us out to the car.

"Do you still have that card Katherine gave you at Crossroads?"

"It's in my purse, why?"

He pulled his cell phone off the visor as he slipped into the driver's seat. "I want you to call."

I buckled myself in and pulled the door shut. "She's a therapist, Robert. I don't need a therapist. I'll be okay, if you'll just—"

"I can't Eve. I just told you." He slapped the cell phone into my hand. "Call. Right now. For both of us."

❧

Denise's office turned out to be a covered, bamboo platform in a secluded corner of her generous backyard. A welcome surprise. The short drive to Carpinteria from Ojai might have been pleasant if my stomach hadn't churned all the way there. The wind was already picking up as I came over the pass, the atmosphere fairly crackled with clarity. I wished I could say the same for my mind.

I hadn't been to a therapist since one at the Veteran's Administration had tried to convince me my ex-husband's alcoholism was not his fault. I half expected vinyl tile floors and fluorescent lighting and men in striped pajamas shuffling in the hall. Instead, I was treated to a shaded meditation garden, gentle incense floating in the air, and two comfortable silk pillows facing each other on top of a cushy Indonesian rug. Avocado branches laden with green fruit draped over the length of the fence, creating an intimate enclosure.

Denise, a small woman who sort of reminded me of myself, but with dark hair, invited me to take off my shoes and sit on one of the pillows. She lit a candle on the floor between us.

"So, Eve. Tell me why you're here." Her voice was soft and compelling at the same time. Make no mistake, it said. It may be nice here, but we're going to get some work done.

I bit my bottom lip. Where should I start? My eyes shifted

from my bare toes, in just as much need of a manicure as my fingers, to the candle, to her calm, cat-green eyes. "I'm sorry. This was my husband's idea. I'm not used to—"

She smiled, and rescued me a little. "Just go for the quickest most immediate reason, for starters."

The quickest, most immediate. My throat constricted. That was about as immediate as it gets. "I can't concentrate, my mind is all jumbled up, and I just can't stop crying."

And then, as if saying the words opened the faucet, the tears came gushing out. "I'm sorry." I blew my nose and tried to pull myself together. "It's like a major handicap," I spluttered.

I felt so foolish, blubbering in front of a complete stranger. "I can't even think. It just comes, and then…oh…just give me a minute."

Denise reached behind her, grabbed a box of Kleenex off a low, black-lacquered table, and put it in front of me. "I'll give you as long as it takes. In fact, I put some tea on just before you came. You just go ahead and let this all flow and I'll get us some."

By the time I had blown my nose again and dried my eyes, she had returned with a Chinese teapot and two small cups on a bamboo tray. She placed it next to us on the floor and sat down cross-legged on her pillow.

"Katherine told me you might be calling. Your mom and dad are both at Crossroads?" She poured tea into the cups, holding the lid carefully in place as she did. Then her eyes glanced up to mine. My cue to start talking again.

My eyes stung again and spilled over. The choke came around a garbled answer. "See? I'm completely useless."

"I doubt that." She held one of the cups out to me and I took it in both hands. Her voice soothed like a lifelong friend. "You've just got something stuck in there and we're going to get it out so you can get past it."

I lifted the tea to my lips and was greeted with the fragrant essence of jasmine.

"So here's what I want you to do. I want you to tell me about your mother and anytime you feel like crying, just let her rip. I mean, big time. Don't hold back. And then when it calms down, start talking again."

I took a jagged breath. "I'm afraid that would go back to

when I was born."

The last words squeezed off into a sting.

"Usually does." She smiled, and handed me the Kleenex box.

So I started. I told her everything. From Betty hanging on the gate to getting the first phone call, to picking my parents up at the hospitals, to selling their house. From waiting for my mom to come visit on weekends, to waiting at the preschool, to napping on the back porch with the dog. Told her of how I wished I knew if she was there, behind all the confusion. Of how I wished I could have just one more normal conversation with her.

One more chance.

And I told her how I'd worn out the ears of my friends and the patience of my husband. And in between I bawled. I howled and wallowed while she fed me tea. I used up the entire box of Kleenex and she gave me another and I bawled and wallowed some more.

I'm not sure how long I had been quiet when her hand squeezed my shoulder. I hadn't noticed her getting up. The September afternoon light slanted across her yard, picking out only the tips of the highest blooms of a hibiscus and then lighting the avocado-covered hills behind her house.

My eyes were finally dry.

Denise returned with pear slices on a Blue Willow plate. "Most of us only lose our mothers once." She offered the pears. "You've lost yours twice."

Still silent, I took a slice of pear. It tasted of clarity and peace, if there could be such a thing. I felt a calm I had not felt in what seemed like years. I wasn't going to spoil it by trying to speak.

"Only the first time, you were afraid to cry. Always the peacemaker, you held it in." She folded herself back onto her cushion and looked in my eyes. "It's grief as sure as though she had died all those years ago, yet you were never allowed to grieve, were you?"

I shook my head, still afraid to break the peaceful spell by talking.

"So today, we let the little girl grieve."

"Yeah. A lifetime worth."

"Two boxes of Kleenex worth."

"Yeah."

"Now here comes the clincher." Denise reached for a slice of pear, keeping her tender eyes on me. "You're going to lose her again."

I took this in. Not that I hadn't known it. But like the grieving child, I had pushed it away, hoping. My mother was not going to be one of those amazing women who live to be ninety-two, still playing bridge and volunteering to build homes for abandoned children in Croatia. There would be no mother-daughter cruises. She would never see her great-grandchildren.

At seventy-one, her trembling feet were on the slippery slope to her end times, and there was no turning back.

No undo button.

I had seen my grandmother go, and my grandfather. It seemed fitting for them, at eighty-five, their lives had been long and full. But seventy-one? Wasn't that too young? Then I remembered her parents had died in their fifties. She would beat them by at least fifteen years. And one day, I would step up into line. I swallowed hard on that thought, perhaps the one that scared me the most. But my eyes were still dry. I pointed this fact out to Denise.

She patted me on the hand. "So, I want you to save some time out every day to let little Evie cry if she needs to. But adult Evie must determine where and when."

"Now that's what's been hard. It just comes on by itself."

"Tap into your goddess power. Put *clear-eyed* Evie in charge. Your mother needs her now more than ever. And you need her too."

The image made me smile. The goddess Athena was compassionate, but also cunning and smart and protective of the ones she loved. "I think I can do that."

"You must do that, or you won't survive this intact."

Denise got up and offered me her hand. "Little Evie's been in the driver's seat too long. She had no control over what happened to her. But *you* do."

I knew she was right. I felt a little foolish that I hadn't come to the realization on my own. I had to lead the way and get out of the way all at the same time. A neat trick if I could do it. I started by putting clear-eyed Evie behind the wheel and drove, dry-eyed all the way home.

❧

Betty awoke to Shoo-Shoo snoring in her ear, annoyed to be disturbed from a pleasant dream, though she couldn't remember what it was. She rolled over as best she could with Shoo-Shoo curled against her side, pulled the covers off her shoulders, and waved her arms at the blinking red light.

Where were they, Goddammit?

At last, she heard someone at the door. Sharlene came in, holding a can of apple juice in a plastic cup. She balanced two muffins in a napkin on her forearm as she pulled the door closed after a quick backward glance.

"Oh for Heaven's sake," Sharlene said, smiling over at Una snuggled into Betty's bed. "I'm sorry that took so long, Miss Betty. We had a little trouble, ah, over in the men's wing."

Betty shrugged her shoulders. It was odd having a strange woman slip into her bed, but in a way, it was comforting. Shoo-Shoo was no trouble. Betty climbed out of bed and sat on the empty twin.

Sharlene pished open the juice and poured a little into the cup, swirling the liquid like thick brandy. "I thought I'd bring you early girls some eats in here this morning, 'till things settle down."

She slipped the juice cup into Betty's hand and spread the napkin on the nightstand. Betty shifted her eyes up to the high windows.

What things?

The porchlight was still on, but the sky was polished with a tinge of pink. She heard voices outside—a sharp command, a quick reply. Betty sipped the juice, sweet and…something. She flicked a glance to Sharlene, whose eyes were on her.

"Have a little muffin with it, Miss Betty." She broke off half a muffin and nested it in a napkin.

Betty sipped, coughed, nibbled, coughed, her swallower acting up on her again. But she was hungry. Shoo-Shoo still snored in her bed. Sharlene refilled her cup. It tasted better this time. She gulped it down, coughed, and cleared her throat.

Sharlene opened Betty's closet and tidied the hangers. "My, you certainly have some pretty things here, Miss Betty."

Betty nodded. Sharlene pulled a velvet blazer from one side of the closet and hung it on the other, as well as Betty's wool slacks.

Betty munched, coughed.

"We'll have to ask Evie to take these home for you. They won't go through our laundry."

"All clear," the box squawked on her hip.

Sharlene pressed a button on the side of the box. "Thanks."

By the time Shoo-Shoo awoke and they were dressed and brushed, the sun had ridden halfway up the sky and though Betty could see a tinge of red on the leaves in the courtyard, the air felt warm and dry. Most of the residents were in the dining room, having breakfast. Sharlene helped her to a group of seats where a black woman in a flowered smock led some residents in a sit-down exercise routine. Frank Sinatra's voice blared out of a portable CD player on a TV tray, singing something about ants and high hopes.

The ladies kicked out first one foot and then the other, clapping to the music, and singing off key. Betty didn't feel like singing. Instead, she shuffled a few seats away, and nested her arms over her chest. She looked for Vern in his usual place, but he wasn't there. In the dining hall, she saw the white-haired man lean in and say something to another gentleman that made him smile, then they both looked over at her, then they got up and made their way over.

Oh, for Heaven sakes.

The white-haired man, Jonathan, was as surefooted as she remembered him from the other day, and the other man, nearly as round as he was tall, shifted heavily from one leg to the other.

Jonathan spoke first. "This is my friend, Brownie. Says he remembers you from high school."

Betty was sure she'd never seen him before in her life. "Tch."

Martina and two other helpers came to Betty's rescue. "Wanna walk outside, guys? We're going down by the stables. We can look at the horses."

Outside? Betty stood. Her legs were wobbly, but she needed to get outside.

With Jonathan on one arm and Brownie on the other, they followed a group of residents led by Martina and her friends, out a side door, across the street, and down a bend that ended at a barbed wire fence. The horse pasture was more of a stable, smelled like one too, and not too pretty to look at, but from there, she could see across the valley. She stopped and shifted her weight. Large homes perched atop green hills reminded her of a lifetime lived before this one. The others moved on, but Jonathan hung back. "Come on, we have a new foal, Mom."

Mom? How curious. His energy was contagious. Betty reached out her hand and took his. They moved along the roadside and indeed, a mare had just foaled, the wobbly creature pronked and nudged against its mother. Betty's heart lit up. She wished Shoo-Shoo had come with them.

Later, at the lunch table, Betty sat between Jonathan and Brownie, pushing food around her plate. Enchiladas and beans, should be easy to swallow, but lately, nothing was. She chewed, coughed, drank, and coughed. Cleared her throat. And then she saw him.

Sitting in his usual place at the banquette, Vern nodded, snoozing, chin on chest. A large bandage covered the back of his head, a Band Aid strip on each hand.

23 Sundowner

The morning had dawned clear and Santa-Ana warm. I'd sent Robert off to an early meeting with our corporate lawyer and our business partner, and I headed out early to be at the mall when it opened. Betty needed more washable clothes, nothing that pulled tight over the head, with plenty of room for the Depends she would wear from now on. Not Betty's usual wardrobe, but what could I do? I threw in a cuddly, Velour jogging suit and a pair of fancy sneakers to match. What woman wouldn't smile for a new pair of shoes? And why not a mini-box of Sees candy, while I was at it? Sure. Always a hit. And a cute Beanie Baby bear. Something was bound to tickle her fancy.

I checked my watch as I pulled into the parking space outside Crossroads. I was fifteen minutes early. Good. I had a few moments to stuff the goodies I'd bought at the mall into a large, bright pink tote. From now on, this would be my Betty Bag. I checked my watch again. *Okay. Okay. You can do this.* I stepped out of the car, determined to be strong for her.

The tote slung heavy over my shoulder, I entered through the clinic, as instructed. A woman at the phone console turned as I came in. "Well, hello, Miss Evie."

Her nametag read *Jonelle*. "Let me just call Martina and tell her you're here. We've been expecting you."

"Thanks, Jonelle." I took a seat on the upholstered bench I remembered from the other day, deliberately angling myself away from the TV monitor in the corner.

After a moment, the inside door swung open and Martina greeted me. "Come on in. Betty's ready for you. Well, actually, she's been ready since six a.m."

"I've been anxious to see her too." We hadn't gotten half way across the 'living room' before I heard someone yell, then realized it was her.

"That's my daughter!" Her voice a hoarse croak; she shuffled toward me as hard as she could go, arms outstretched.

We trembled through an awkward hug. Martina led us to the alcove where Vern had taken up residence. He gave me a little wave as we sat. "Hi! How'd you know we were here?"

"Oh, I'm just funny that way."

As I sat next to him and Martina helped Betty to sit, I noticed the bandage on the back of his head. "What happened to you?"

"What do you mean?"

"Your head! Does it hurt? Martina, why didn't anyone call me?"

Vern felt the back of his head and pulled on the bandage.

"Hum." His brows tightened. "Didn't know about that."

Betty scowled at him. "Hard head," she said with intensity, then she re-channeled her attention to the bright pink tote.

Martina smiled and patted Vern's knee. "He fell last night."

Vern tugged at the bandage and winced. "I did?"

"It was, you know, around three in the morning," Martina said, gently pulling his hands away. "We sent him to emergency for a few stitches. We didn't want to disturb you at that hour, so—"

My stomach churned. While I slept, comfortable in my bed, one of my parents was in the emergency room? I wanted to explode but I tried to keep my voice level. "I want you to call me *every* time there's any kind of problem. I don't care about the hour. If one of them goes to emergency, I want to be there."

I couldn't bear the thought of him being hustled off in an ambulance in the middle of the night with no one there for support.

Betty pulled one tote strap off my shoulder and pawed inside. "My shoes," she cried, kicking at the heels of her slippers.

"Yes, those are your shoes, Mom." I helped her pull them from the bag. She held them aloft, tracing the day-glow orange Nike swish with her gnarled fingers. I fended the shoes off from banging me in the head and tried to smile. Anyone watching might have thought the scene comical, but I felt all prickly. This wasn't happening the way I'd planned it.

Martina rescued me from the shoes and sat them on the banquette next to Betty. "I'm sorry, Miss Evie. So many of our residents have no relatives nearby, we just do what's necessary."

"I understand. What's necessary for Betty and Vern is that you call me no matter what." Betty tugged the bag completely off my shoulder.

"I'll tell Katherine to make a note on their charts." What else could she say? "He's okay now, though, aren't you, Vern?"

Vern looked nervously from Martina to me. "I hope so."

Betty worked a pair of lavender sweats out of the tote. "*You* would go shopping," she said with a hint of exasperation. Her way of telling me she would never have picked those? Hard to say. But she was definitely prickly too. Maybe it was contagious.

I tried to correct my tone. "I had to, Mom. You needed these things, and—"

"Tch." Betty pushed my helping hands away and pulled the rest of the items out of the bag as if she expected to find some missing treasure at the bottom.

"I'll leave you guys to visit, then," Martina said, sidling away.

Vern wanted a drink of water now, the tangled pile of clothes slid to the floor, Betty found the chocolates and opened them, and stuffed two into her mouth. A lady across from us, pale and fragile as a baby bird, patted her chest and told me she couldn't breathe.

I felt like a mother on a bus with two brats pulling in opposite directions while a third headed for the exit doors. I called Martina back, catching a chocolate Bordeaux before it hit the floor.

"That lady says she can't breathe." I corralled my mother's busy hands. "Just a minute, Mom, wait, *wait!*"

Martina sat down next to the little bird woman, circled her arm around her shoulder. "How are you doing, Maria Anne?" she asked, cooing softly. She smoothed stray hairs off the woman's forehead.

"She gets a little nervous around too much activity," Martina said to me, and then to the woman, she said "Let's go into the clinic, okay?"

I sighed, relieved, and turned my attention back to my mother who had just used her new shoe to wipe chocolate off her lips and chin. She got up, shoved the rest of the Bordeaux into her mouth, shuffled a few seats away, and sat down. I moved to sit next to her. "Mom, what's the matter?"

"Don't see me," she said, and shuffled away again, this time taking a position next to the window. She looked out over the patio as if I wasn't there, shoulders hunched up around her ears, hands plunged in to the pockets of a sloppy, cable-knit sweater I didn't recognize.

Again, I went to her and took her hand. "Mom," I said quietly, and saw the track of a tear down her cheek before she turned her face away.

"Don't see." Her voice was tired, weak, full of anguish.

Little Evie threatened to choke up my throat. *Later. You can cry later, but right now we're going to act like grownups.* I pulled my mother into my arms again and held her tight.

She squeezed tight for a moment, then pushed me away, her mouth working. "Tch."

It was obvious to me she was fighting to find the words. "Are you cold?"

"No."

"Hungry?"

"*No!*"

This was ridiculous. We could play twenty questions all day. "Mom, can you just say any words you are thinking?"

"Ugly. Stupid. Nothing works." Her face reddened and she shuffled a few steps away again, stopping in the middle of the floor, lost.

Yes. A person in her situation would feel that way if she were aware—oh. Oh. She was embarrassed and angry and didn't want me to have to see it. I stayed where I was, giving her some space, as Robert would say. "It's okay for me, Mom. Really. It's been hard, but I can do it now."

She shuffled a few more steps and stopped. I moved a little closer, but not too close. "I know you're frustrated and frightened. I am too. But I'm going to be here, see you every day, no matter how ugly and stupid things get."

"Get out of here," she whispered, and cut her eyes to the clinic door. She took my hand and started to lead me toward it. I couldn't believe she wanted me to go. And then she stopped, cocked her head as if she could read my mind. "I want *us* out."

I looked over her shoulder to see Vern getting a handful of grapes from the aide along with a little paper cup of water. I hadn't really had a chance to visit with him, but I could see he had already forgotten I was there.

"I suppose we could go out for a little drive, if you feel up to it. Would you like that?"

She pulled up her half smile. "Feel up to it. Yes-s-s-s."

Martina helped me slip Betty into the car and fasten the seatbelt. She told me she would gather the new clothes, mark them with Betty's name, and put them in her room. I thanked her and we pulled away; Betty's hand slid up to the door sill next to her window as she looked out, and her shoulders relaxed into a more natural position.

It was less than a mile over to the lake, a pretty drive on a crystal clear day to give us both some pleasure. But as we entered the marina area, it was clear the wind was a challenge for the other visitors. I pulled up as close to the shore as I could, intending to get out and at least feed the ducks. But the Santa Ana wind whipped the lake's surface like sugar frosting. We sat, comfortable with the windows rolled up, watching a line of ducks head for cover under a stand of willow. Everyone at the lake was packing up to leave. We watched a couple pull a small sailboat out of the water and onto their boat trailer. The wind slashed at their jackets and their hair as they called out to each other, trying to coordinate their efforts.

My mother pushed against the dashboard with both hands and pressed herself into the seat, jaw clamped tight. "Let's get out," she grumbled. Not the effect I was going for.

The couple struggled and fought with the boat in the capricious wind until finally they had her cranked up onto the trailer and themselves inside the cab of the truck. We watched them hit up a high five, and then a low and then the man revved up the engine and pulled away from the ramp.

"Maybe we should try this again on a nicer day."

"On a nicer day," she mimicked, and relaxed a little. "Just get back."

I took my time driving around the curves, pointing out a new winery near the earthen dam, and a group of geese escaping the wind in a straggly Vee formation. By the time we got out of the car at Crossroads again, Betty seemed at peace, ready to go inside. Martina met us at the clinic door.

"Shoo-Shoo," Betty said, and craned to see around Martina's plump body. Just like that, she was going inside? No goodbye? No hollering?

"Well, I guess I'll see you tomorrow, then," I said, reaching out to her. She turned and without a word, gave my hand an awkward, mismatched slap, then gave me her silly half smile.

I remembered the people and the boat. Five high and five low. She smiled again when I gave her hand a little slap, then she turned and shuffled into the living room without looking back.

Three days. Just like Katherine said. My mother had found some kind of balance.

Warm wind chased oak leaves around my feet, sending them under the car and across the parking area in a clattery swirl. The air carried a faint odor of smoke, unwelcome on a California Santa Ana day.

❧

"The fire's northeast of the Sespe, not much out there. They'll let it burn for now." Robert got home in time to help me load the last of our show materials into the shipping containers and roll them out onto the driveway. "Did you call Yellow

Freight?"

"They'll be here by four," I said. And in less than ten days we would meet up with them in Tennessee. For the first time since I'd started the project, I felt that I might actually be able to fly off into my own life again without worrying that I was abandoning my parents. Clear-eyed Evie was in the house.

I looked up at the sky thinking about the Sespe wildlife preserve. "I hope the condors'll be okay."

I had to worry about something. I marked the containers one of two and two of two. We stood back, arms around each other's waists, smiling, like we were about to send our eldest off to college.

Robert gathered up the marking pens and shipping label debris and clomped his foot on a piece of leftover bubble wrap before it blew down the street in the whipping wind. "I don't think they'll find any condors standing on their rooftops with hoses."

"No." His words dragged a giggle out of me. "It's Friday. Let's go down to the club for happy hour and celebrate."

"Now you're talking."

I felt the lightest I'd felt in months. Mom seemed relatively settled, our product show was launched—well, almost—and Robert had *segued* back to his old self. Maybe it would be more accurate to say that I had segued, or at least I had my head leaning in that direction. I had talked to my boss. They were still in a holding pattern on their product release. I could stay home until at least after our trip. Without pay, of course. But Robert had assured me we would do all right. He was getting used to having me home. Campaigning actually, for me to give up my outside job and focus on our own company. A leap of faith, he told me, but with a safety net. The software industry moves fast. If I pulled out, would I ever be able to get back in? But there I went, worrying about something before it happened. Something I was going to have to change.

My first priority was going to be getting myself back in shape. With at least ten more days off work, our project "in the mail," and the good fortune to live in California, still warm in September, I had no excuses. Tomorrow, I would resume my morning run.

The Goddess of Undo

24 Out of the Frying Pan...

Shoo-Shoo never spoke. She didn't have to. Betty and she understood each other just fine. It was the first time since leaving home, what was it, a year? Betty didn't know, but being with Shoo-Shoo was the first time since leaving home that she felt she had a real friend. She was no longer alone in a landscape she didn't recognize. A look or a gesture, and they fell into sync. Like her cousin, Jeri, back in high school, they were joined at the hip.

They sat together now after breakfast, shoulder to shoulder, in the little alcove where Vern would eventually sit for the day. Shoo-Shoo wore one of Betty's coats, covered in flowers woven in golds and burgundies. Though it was washed and faded, it was festive, Betty thought, and nicer than anything Shoo-Shoo had. It made Betty feel happy to have her wear it.

Martina had helped Betty dress that morning in one of the new sweat outfits Evie had brought. Lavender velour bottoms with a hooded, zipped jacket to match, and the new shoes. She wiggled them now, fancy soles and a bright slash of color on the sides. Shoo-Shoo's hair was a little frazzled, but Betty thought hers probably didn't look much better. Anyway, they were ready.

"Let's get out," she said in a whisper at Shoo-Shoo's ear, the old urge to leave returning. Whatever they'd been giving her in the apple juice made her feel good inside her head.

Shoo-Shoo smiled and they helped each other up, then the two of them headed for the door to the courtyard, arm-in-arm. Betty was happy to move before they brought Vern in. As much as she missed him, her old Vern, the new one made her nervous, pressed her with the same questions over and over. How the hell did she know where his car was? He obviously wasn't going to get to drive it.

They pushed through the door and stepped outside. The air was warm, but there was something. Betty sniffed. "Smoke."

Shoo-Shoo sniffed and ducked as if the odor could fall on their heads. She tried to steer them back inside, but Betty held her ground, bringing Shoo-Shoo full circle. She wanted to see what was behind the rooms across from hers. *Where smoke is fire*, words sing-songed through her head using the voice of her father. She smiled to herself as the image of his face drifted through her mind.

Martina waved at them as they shuffled across the patio. They were all sitting at a table in the courtyard—Katherine, Martina, Sharlene, and the rest—having coffee and looking at papers. They look important and serious, Betty thought. She waved back at them, nodding and smiling.

Just going for a little stroll.

Betty leaned a little on Shoo-Shoo's arm, bending her toward a walkway that led to the back of the buildings across from their own rooms. The walkway was hidden by a huge bush. Maybe there was a way out back there. She fingered a rouge-pink flower. Its fading petals fluttered to the ground as she cut a glance at her caretakers. No one noticed Betty and Shoo-Shoo as they slipped past the bush and rounded the corner.

What she saw was interesting, if not a little disappointing. The walkway continued along the back of the building. Deep green, wide-leafed plants pushed flowered heads up against the back wall of the rooms on one side, and a bare, chain link fence bounded the other. After a few steps, Shoo-Shoo dropped

Betty's arm and shuffled toward a little pergola hung with potted fern, fuchsia, ceramic birds, and wooden whirligigs.

Shoo-Shoo dipped her fingers into the bowl of a stone birdbath and patted her face and hair with droplets of water. Betty shuffled through the pergola and out the other side. As far as she could see, the little walkway led back to the courtyard. No gate, nothing. The fence was high and pointy on top, and on the other side, someone's rusty washing machine had been upended, a stand of drying thistle pushing out from beneath.

At the corner, just above her head, Betty saw one of those cameras. "Tch."

She glanced back at Shoo-Shoo who squeezed a fuchsia blossom in one hand and twirled the wings of a woodpecker whirligig in the other. She looked like she was enjoying herself. Betty sniffed, moved on, back toward the courtyard, back along past the men's wing, past the table where Martina and the others still sat.

A big man in a yellow jacket was sitting with them now. He must have been very important because they were all looking at him and he didn't so much as bat an eye in her direction as she shuffled by. A brief image of the yellow-jacketed men wheeling Vern down the shiny hall made the back of her throat sting. She shook the feeling away. Vern was right there, somewhere. Safe.

She moved on toward the front of the complex.

Behind the dining room wall stood a row of machines. Martina always had coins in her pocket that could get you a soda or chocolate milk. Betty sat down on the bench across from the machines to give her legs a rest. A loud hiss and then a bang sent her to her feet, startled, until she reconciled the sound with a truck pulling up outside the wall. She sat again, her heart pounding, her fingers gripping the neck of her jacket. Why did everything have to be so loud? She startled and settled again as she watched what had been a solid wall only a moment before slide over enough to allow a man through, pushing a load of soda cans on a cart. She took a deep breath, willing her heart to slow down, and watched him wheel the cans over to the machines. He zipped a key out to the end of a cord from a silver bell on his belt, then opened the front of one of the machines. The man had broad shoulders and big muscles sticking out from the sleeves of his brown work shirt.

"I like that," she said, and got up to take a closer look.

"What? Oh." The man turned around as her hand circled his bicep.

"Here. Is this what you want?" He *pished* a green can open and handed it to her.

Betty smiled into his eyes. "Thank you."

She stepped back a little, giving him room to maneuver the cart into position. Then he busied himself loading the cans into little slots inside the machine. Betty took a sip of soda, coughed, and sipped again. And then she saw it. The opening in the wall. Was it really there? She shuffled over, glanced at the man. He was still working. She reached out with trembling fingers and touched the edges of the wall.

"Yes-s-s-s."

She stood a moment, watching a plastic bag ride a gust of wind down to the end of the street, through the horse corral, and then up into the oaks. She took another sip of the soda, coughed, and set the can on an overturned clay pot just inside the wall.

25 ... and Into the Fire

I woke up at four a.m., my hands asleep, the smell of smoke strong and thick in the bedroom. Shaking the life back into my fingers, I went to the open window. It was still dark, but the odor was too strong to ignore. I went to the dresser, rummaged for a pair of sweats and pulled them on.

Robert stirred. "What'er you doing?"

"Smells like smoke. I'm going out."

"Hmmm." He attempted to roll over, but one of the cats was holding ground between his legs.

So much for feline heroism.

I stepped through the French doors onto the patio outside our bedroom. The sky, crystal clear last night, was starless now, mountains to the east just the faintest silhouette against a pale blue halo of dawn. No roofs afire, no sparks flying. Closing the doors, I went to the front of the house and out onto the porch. Up and down our street, all was quiet, no smoke plumes or fire, but when I stepped back into our kitchen, I saw that after only a few moments outside, I looked like a powdered doughnut, speckled with a fine, white ash.

Wide awake now, I took a few moments to start some coffee, then snuck back down the hall. Robert snored.

"It's okay. You can go back to sleep," I said, mostly to myself. Grabbing my jogging shoes, a pair of socks, and my bedside read, I headed back to the kitchen. By six a.m., I had drunk more than my share of the coffee, had two pieces of peanut butter toast, and finished the last of a Nora Roberts trilogy.

I had promised myself a daily run, starting today, but I was worried about the smoke. I poked my head outside again. The halo of blue to the east had grown to an orange, oval glow and an eerie brown pall draped the rest of the morning sky. My stomach gave a little lurch, a gut reaction to the smell of smoke, even from a barbecue. I pushed it down to my mental garbage bin where it belonged. Common sense told me to take it easy.

I scrawled "out walking" across the white board next to our back door, grabbed my ball cap and sunglasses, and slipped outside.

My route took me down an oak-shrouded lane that skirted town, winding toward the River Preserve trailhead. My eyes smarted and burned and I wasn't at all sure it was safe to breathe, but the bizarre landscape pulled me along. I gave up running but I couldn't make myself turn away from the surreal landscape. White ash, blown to the road sides by passing cars, swirled around my feet with every step. It powdered the tops of street-side mailboxes, crotch rockets parked in driveways, ceramic yard ducks, and split-rail fences along private drives. The horses in the stables next to the Preserve entrance stood, morning still, flicking their ears as the ash collected on their blankets and blinders. Some, nervous and edgy, snorted and tossed their heads as I tramped by.

I looked straight into the sun, now up above the mountains at the east end of town, a pale orange disk in a dark brown sky, glowing like the beam of a flashlight in the hand of a giant, peering through the murk. To the north, darker clouds towered over the brown haze, boiling up from below. Ash fell through the heated air like Ivory Snow, thick and dry and light.

Up ahead, a truck with a Land Conservancy logo on its door had parked on the shoulder in front of the Preserve. The driver had unrolled a length of black and yellow caution tape across the entrance.

The old fear peeked out from its garbage bin, gripping the edges of reason. Again I pushed it down. There was no immediate danger, but there could be. I crossed the street to see what was happening.

"River trail is closed, miss." The man played out a heavy chain across the dirt entrance.

"Oh, no. I'm stopping right here." I moved past him to the railing outside the gate. "You part of the Preserve?"

"Preserve Manager," he said with a nod. "Don't want anyone down there today. At least until we see where the fire goes. Wouldn't want to have to go looking for someone down there if this thing turns ugly."

"Looks pretty ugly right now."

I gazed out across the river bottom, a wide expanse at this end of the valley; the remains of an old vineyard marched in splintery crosses across a patch of dry grass and scrub. A blast of warm air blew dust into my eyes.

"You here in eighty-three?"

I turned around, interested. That was in my previous life, a lifetime before Ojai. "No. I wasn't."

The Preserve manager's forehead was smeared now, sweat and ash blending together in streaks. "Sky looked just like it does now. Fire came roaring down that river bottom like a flaming tsunami."

He took off his ball cap and wiped his forehead in the crook of his arm. "At least it cleared all the bums out of the river bottom."

Robert had been here. He had told me about how they packed up and left for a few days just to get away from the smoke. I could see why. Dark clouds of it mushroomed behind Chief's Peak and now behind Topa Topa ridge. "Should we be packing up our stuff?"

"We're not in danger yet, but the fire department has teams out notifying schools and nursing homes in the area."

The Preserve Manager dusted his hands off on his thighs and got back into his truck. "Doesn't hurt to be prepared."

Nursing homes? Of course. They would need extra time and help to evacuate. My God! Crossroads was right along the river bottom, just over the crossing at Santa Ana road. My mother and I had used that road only yesterday on our drive to the lake.

It got suddenly harder to breathe. That road was only a couple of miles from here. How stupid could I be? A fire threatened the valley and I was out jogging?

"Crap! I gotta get home." I started off in a trot.

By the time I got to our driveway, my throat burned and my eyes watered. Robert had the garage door open, folding his wet suit into the back of his van. "Hey. You okay?"

"Fire's getting closer." I bent over, hands on my knees, out of breath. "Maybe we should think about—"

Robert caught me up in his arms. "Now don't get your buns in an uproar. The fire's still way to the east of here."

"I know…but they just blocked off the Preserve…I just, I just…I gotta pee." I made for the back door. "…I'll be right back."

Robert called after me. "Hey, check your phone messages, sounded like Crossroads, something about a head count."

When I called her back, Martina rambled, breathless in her Hispanic accent. "—so we did a fire drill, you know, to get prepared, you know, in case of fire, and then we see, Miss Betty, she isn't here. We call the Sheriff and they're on their way, but—"

I couldn't believe my ears. My mother was missing? It was a locked-down facility for *chrissake*.

"How could that happen?" A blast of panic lit up my brain with unspoken fears. *What if? What if? What if?*

Martina kept on blubbering "—Una, you know, her roommate, well she was acting fidgety, I think she was trying to tell us, but, you know, she doesn't really talk, and—"

"Oh, never mind. I'm on my way." I slammed down the phone.

Grabbing my purse and keys, I ran through the house to the back door. "Robert! She got out! She's not there! She's—"

He closed the distance between us in two long strides, grabbed me by my shoulders, and forced me to look at him.

"Evie. Slow down."

"Mom. She's not there." *Mommieeeeeah!*

I pushed against him to get to my car door, but he grabbed the keys out of my hands.

"I'll drive."

When we pulled into the parking lot, a sheriff's car was already there. Sharlene let us into Katherine's office where an officer the size of the Incredible Hulk was asking her questions. He had been jotting notes on a small clipboard.

"How long has she been missing?"

"We're not sure. We think maybe only an hour or so. We were meeting with the guys from the Fire Department, about possible evacuations." She paced the room, ticking off the details. "We decided to drill, did a head count, and that's when we realized we had one missing— "

She looked over at me, the apology swelling liquid in her eyes. "Betty."

Oh my God. I covered my mouth with my hand against a rush of nausea.

Robert pulled me to him, slipping his hand into mine, and then he addressed the sheriff. "So now what? Helicopters? Search dogs? What?"

"Well now," the sheriff shoved his haunch up on the edge of Katherine's desk. It creaked under his weight. "She can't have gotten far in an hour. She's what, seventy, not very agile…"

The fear was up in my throat now, strangling my words. "Officer, my mother has dementia or she wouldn't be here. It's dangerous for her outside alone under any conditions. And, in case you haven't noticed, there's a fire—"

Robert squeezed my hand hard. "He's right Eve, she can't have gotten far."

I struggled to keep my anxiety from exploding out onto everyone around me. It seemed that the cop was taking his time. "So exactly what are you doing, so far, I mean?"

"We'll have her back safe in no time," he said, officially. Unofficially, I could tell he was running the routine. My mother was just another event in his log.

Katherine handed me a flyer with a photo in the center. "We made this up. Some of our staff are circulating it now."

There was Betty, looking like a deer caught in the

headlights, the "mug shot" the day she arrived, and a description below.

MISSING
70-year old Female
5'4", grey/blonde hair, blue eyes
Last seen September 18, 8:30 a.m.
Crossroads Senior Care
Wearing a lavender jogging suit
Call 555-7272 or 911 with any information.

My lips turned cold. This wasn't a dream. It was real. A set of chills wracked my body. Robert, felt it. His eyes met mine.

Katherine handed the officer a copy of the flyer.

Robert slipped a business card out of his wallet and gave it to the sheriff. "Both our home and cell numbers are there."

The officer added the card and the flyer to his clipboard and stepped toward the office door. "We'll be in touch."

I watched as he stepped through the clinic and Joleen buzzed him out.

"That's it? We'll be in touch?" I couldn't believe that was all there was to it. "My mother is missing and they take a flyer and—"

Robert circled his arm around my shoulders. "We'll look for her ourselves. Right now."

Katherine pulled open the bottom drawer of her desk and grabbed a pair of sneakers. "I'm coming with you."

Outside, a huge red and white helicopter roared overhead. I shaded my eyes as I followed its progress across our field of view. "Do you think they're already looking for her?"

Robert reached into my car and grabbed his cell phone, then looked up at the plowing machine. "It's a tanker. For the fire."

"Oh."

He clicked out a text message. "I cancelled my meetings."

My hero was stepping up to the plate.

I sat next to Katherine on the edge of a stone planter as she changed her shoes. She swiped at her eyes with her sleeve, her face red. I put my hand on her shoulder.

She looked up; a tear streaked down her cheek. "I let you down, Eve. I'm so sorry."

I nodded and squeezed her shoulder. What could I say? She

was right. She had let me down. They all had. My new life was beginning to feel just like the old one. Little Evie crouched in the tightest corner of my heart, her eyes bugging wide, swallowing tears.

I heard the text message chime on Robert's phone.

"James and Carolyn are on their way to help." *Our business partners. That was nice.* He stepped to the back of the car and scanned the short side road in each direction.

Katherine finished tying her shoes and stood. "My staff have already gone to the homes down that way," she said, and pointed out to the main road. "They spread the word and handed out the flyer to every house. Miguel and Luiz went on up Beach Road looking for her that way.

We walked to the edge of the parking lot. "That little dog leg leads past a horse pasture and down to the Santa Ana road river crossing," she said, shielding her eyes.

My mind raced to the worst case scenario. "What about the river bottom? I mean, there's so many trees and brush and…" *Oh God.* "…the fire."

Katherine sighed. "We walk them that direction sometimes, to look at the horses. She might head that way."

"It's still early, Eve," Robert said. "The officer was right about one thing. If she went that way, she couldn't have gotten far, it's rocky and—"

"Let's just get started then," I said as another helicopter roared up the valley, a long hose hanging from its belly. Behind us, brown smoke tumbled over the highest peaks and spread like a stifling blanket over our tinder-dry valley.

26 Cocktail Hour

Betty leaned in to her new gait. It wasn't efficient, it wasn't pretty, but it had gotten her this far, *goddammit*. She twisted her body to see back over her shoulder. The fountain in front of Crossroads and the locked gate at the entrance were no longer in sight. Good. She was done with that old lady in the mirror and the bent people with vacant stares. She wanted to go home.

Turning toward the horse corral, she kept moving, taking the big steps like Martina had showed her. As she pushed herself down a dirt driveway that dead ended at a pipe rail fence, her mind reeled back through half formed visions of the homes she'd had... *elegant draperies, marble floors, oriental grandfather clocks, maple sofas in nubby fabric with little flared skirts and milk glass lamps, oversized dressers with big round mirrors, and finally a room with twin beds, faded chintz curtains, a hand-hooked rug on the floor, ice glazed on the inside of the kitchen window...*

Out in the dirt, she marveled at a two-headed creature, a brown thing with a horse's head on both ends, or... Betty tried to make the creature conform to some reasonable model, but finally gave up. Beyond the creature, outside the fence, there was a tall eucalyptus, and then it was wide open, like the fields beyond their fences when she was a young girl.

She could get out there. She could just.

Bending her stiff body low, she held on to the bottom fence rail and wrestled one reluctant leg through, then rested. It did remind her of home. Not home with Vern, but home, in Cottage Grove, where there were no loud noises, and the sky was clear blue, not smoky and brown, and the trees were tall pine, and there was never anyone around but her family. She bent her head down and grunted through the narrow space between the pipes. Her foot pushed into a pile of horse droppings.

One of the horse's heads looked around at her, shifted its weight, and stepped aside, revealing its true nature to her.

"Ha!" Her mind playing tricks on her again. She stopped moving. Horses could be stupid, she remembered. They would step on you if you weren't careful. She kept her eye on them as she slowly pulled her other leg across the rail and through the fence.

Betty had loved their old horses, but never quite got used to the smell. "It stinks like hell, you know," she told them.

They ignored her.

The ground was bumpy and her legs were wobbly, but she stood at last. The outside fence, the tree, and the wide open were only a few steps away. She straightened her back, lifted her chin and went for it. When at last she was free of the corral, she was out of breath, but she felt good. She was alone for the first time in…in…*gawd*, she couldn't even remember, but it felt good.

Tubes of curly red bark draped the arms of the eucalyptus tree like the sleeves of a kimono. They clattered and clunked in a gust of wind, calling her closer. She picked her way through twigs and piles of fallen bark, at last reaching the base of the tree, where she slid her arms around its great bulk and she pressed her cheek against the skin where the bark had fallen away. She ran her hands over the surface, new and pink and smooth like a baby's bottom, its fragrance so pungent, it nearly masked the smell of horse manure and smoke.

She lingered there, in the arms of the tree until her legs began to wilt. Then she turned her back to the giant trunk and slid down until her knees bent and her bottom rested on the ground. Leaning into the giant trunk, Betty felt its heart beat run through her to its hidden roots deep in the earth. She could not move.

Breathing slowly, she gazed through sleepy eyes out across the big open, the rocky dry, trees flickering yellow and brown, the mountains in their gray-straw blanket, and the muddy water sky. *This is the way it goes.*

A big blue bird swooped down, chasing a squirrel.

"We have those at home," she said out loud, thinking to point, but she could not move a muscle. She remembered seeing those big blue birds with the little pointy hats on outside her bedroom window in the faded white wooden house where she grew up. The cold bedroom, the dirt, the pigs, the sway-backed horses, and the smell of smoke in the old white house in Oregon, miles and miles back in her lifetime.

Home to daddy with a tiny baby. Home alone, waiting. A bottle of sweet brandy and a cigarette. The baby sleeping, warm in her lap. The brandy warm in her throat. The smell of smoke. The stinking smell of smoke in her nose. Hard to breathe. Flames shooting up dusty curtains, crawling across the wooden slats of the ceiling, filling the air with the choking smoke. The baby's shrieks, the running and running. Her father's sad, defeated eyes. No place to hide. Her fault. She was to blame, she was irresponsible, no good.

The old pain awakened in her chest, squeezed, and crushed her down. *Now isn't this just peachy?* Maybe this time she would leave her old skin behind, her old body. Nothing was working right anyway. Good riddance. She closed her eyes, feeling small against the towering tree, the brown sky crushing down on her.

She lay quietly, waiting for the pain to pass—or not. When she opened her eyes, she breathed easier and the sun had moved higher in the sky. In the distance, strange birds struggled across the brown hills. Noisy birds—no, those, those, *coppers. Choppers!* Their whirly tops beat the air and pounded her eardrums. She crushed her hands over her ears and clamped her eyes shut against the blowing dust until the noise faded. When she opened her eyes again the choppers were small and quiet.

Betty snickered out loud. They looked like guppies swimming in muddy water, long hoses dangling under their bellies like trails of poop. Off in the distance, another, dragging a bundle behind it on a rope, passed in front of the flat, orange circle of the sun. She had better keep going. Wait a minute. Which way? Where was the fountain? And the road? The smoke was in her nose again, strong and thick. Oh, this had been a mistake, coming out here. She was all alone.

She shielded her eyes and looked across the field in front of her. A patch of blue in the trees caught her attention. Was that someone crouched there, just under the trees, under the blue, just at the edge of the dry, the rocks? What was he doing? She pushed herself up from the ground, using the tree for support, then rested, catching her breath. The blue was not that far away, not that far. Step by step, she pushed herself. She didn't like being out here alone.

The man looked up as she came near, his beard an old gray rag hanging off his chin; a dirt brown cap pulled too far down over his head hid his eyebrows. He squatted over a bumpy sleeping bag, rummaging.

"Get out." Betty pointed back the way she came. She wanted to go home. Somewhere. She wasn't sure. The way she had come looked different now. Not at all what she remembered.

The man scowled at her, fishing a bottle out of his sleeping bag, and took a long pull. She watched his neck bobble and stretch until he put it down. "Hell if I will. This is my place. *You* get out."

"Yes-s-s-s. Get out." Another fish machine thundered over. Betty pressed her hands to her ears and crouched down, her knees bending awkwardly under her.

The man looked at her closely. "Whatcha' doin' out here?"

He took another pull at the bottle, throwing glances the way she had come.

"That's my wine." She reached out toward the bottle. He held it close to his chest, looking her up and down. She crawled closer, grunting, reached out again, and then touched her lips. "That's my wine."

"Well, all right." He grumbled to himself as he rummaged in his lumpy bag again. "I got a cup in here someplace."

He pulled out socks and bits of string, chunks of metal on a beaded chain, a blackened pan, and finally, a stained coffee cup. He poured some wine into it. "Here."

Betty sipped, coughed, and sipped again.

"I like that." What she meant to say was that it was bitter and burned her throat, that it wasn't a proper glass, that it tasted like piss, that he was dirty and scraggly and should get a shave, but none of those words made their way through her mouth. She sipped again and felt warm. His metal necklace caught her eye and held it. She reached over and grabbed it, holding it up in the dappled shade. *Vern had something like this once.*

"What'er you doin' lady?" The man pulled away from her, but before he could snatch it back, she slipped the chain off over his head and transferred it to her neck. Next she went for the picture frame. She turned it over in her hands. A pair of boys in cowboy hats on the back of a pony.

"Tch." She wagged her finger at him.

"Oh, don't you look down at me lady." He slapped the picture out of her hands and stuffed it down inside his sleeping bag. "They're off some'eres, all grown up. Busy."

Betty just blinked at him. She remembered sitting on a pony for the camera once. She and her brother. Looked like the same pony.

Again the thundering pounded her ears, but his time she could only see the blue tarp overhead. She covered her ears, tried to stand up, but her foot tangled in the rope tie on the blue plastic and she went down hard.

"Oof." She wrestled and turned, trying to get comfortable on the bumpy weeds and dirt.

"You okay lady?" She heard him say it, but she didn't move. It was nice inside, under the tarp. Cool and not so smoky. Too bad the poor man didn't have a pillow. She could really use a pillow. She felt sleepy. She would just rest. Just rest awhile. Not think. Not think. Just dream. She glanced over at the man. He squatted on a makeshift stool and fidgeted with his raggedy boots and faded, raggedy shirt.

ॐ

The sun had crossed most of the sky and was setting down to

the west when Evie and Robert saw him. They had made another pass at the neighborhood, walked along under the river crossing and come back up the dogleg toward Crossroads. He was sitting at the base of a large eucalyptus at the back of the horse corrals. When he saw them, he ducked behind it.

"Hey!" Robert yelled out and jogged down the dirt driveway. "Hey. I just want to talk to you."

Evie was exhausted and stood at the end of the drive. The man, a bum, Evie saw, crouched and waited. Robert showed him the flyer. The man backed away shaking his head. He looked scared, confused. Robert lunged at him, grabbed him by the front of his dirty shirt. The man flailed, then pointed, down into the ravine.

"Oh my God!" Evie took off at a run, edged the corrals and caught up with Robert at the tree. The man scrambled away.

"Come on." Robert grabbed her hand and they hustled down the easy slope toward a stand of live oak about a hundred yards away. "He said he gave her some wine, she got sleepy and fell on the tarp cord. She was still there when he left."

Evie rushed along beside Robert, her fatigue gone now, driven out by adrenaline. They hobbled over some rocks and came up on a low hill. Just below them, the oaks made a little hollow where Evie could see someone had camped, their rumpled clothing and sleeping bag strewn inside. And then she saw, at the back of the hollow, a blue tarp, one corner still tied in the tree and the rest folded like a rumpled blue burrito.

Robert dropped her hand and moved forward. "Betty?"

No answer.

Evie froze, her hands over her mouth. There, at the corner of the tarp, she saw a new jogging shoe, the day-glow Nike swish, and the dry skin of an ankle. She could scarcely manage a whisper. "Robert."

She pointed, Robert saw and knelt, met her eyes, then pulled back the blue tarp.

"*Goddammit*, I'm freezing cold." Betty held fiercely to the tarp with her gnarled fingers, her eyes wild and dark, steel blue.

Evie fell down beside her mother.

"Oh God, Mama." She grabbed her into her arms. "We were so worried."

She checked her head and then her legs. "Can you walk?"

Her mother peered into her eyes. Evie wondered if she knew who she was. Then she touched Evie's face, her hand lingering in a tentative caress.

"Hi Sweetie." She heaved a shuddering sigh. "I got lost."

Robert leaned in and steadied them as Evie helped her up. "Let's get you back, Mom."

"Yeah. Get back." She looked around at the bum's camp. "Don't drink the wine," she said. "It tastes like piss."

The Goddess of Undo

27 The Old Man's Friend

We stayed on at the home to see my mother through a change of clothing and a bristly reunion with Vern. By then an SUV from the local media had shown up. The stringer shouted at us as he bailed out of his door, his cameraman only a step behind. "Mister, uh, Salter is it? You thinking lawsuit?"

Robert guided me past them and on to our car. "I'm thinking get the hell out of my face."

A more characteristic Robert might have pushed quietly past, even grinned at the camera, but Robert had been operating out of character now for quite some time. The set of his jaw and his clipped tone were new to me, but not all that unwelcome under the circumstances. I drew a measure of strength from his stiff arm at my back and resisted the urge to look over my shoulder. I was sorry that Crossroads would be under scrutiny because of my mother, but there had been an escape and that was news.

Bad news.

The kind that follows you around long after anyone remembers the *who* and *when*. We stuck around until the paramedics had checked my mother over and determined she was a little dirty, but uninjured.

The shipping containers were gone from the driveway when Robert and I finally arrived home, relieved, but exhausted. I flopped down next to him on the sofa and clicked on the TV, hoping for some mind-numbing diversion. Instead *we* were the topic of the day.

> *...The Ojai fire was turned back at the far end of the pass this afternoon as crews secured the highway...In other news, a happy ending to a story that could just as easily have turned into a family tragedy... we'll have that story and more, after the break.*

Robert popped up. "Gettin' a beer. Want one?" He headed for the kitchen.

"No, I think I'll skip it." I wasn't so sure getting a buzz would calm the knot in my stomach.

Was that a car rumbling in the driveway? "Robert, I think someone's—"

The doorbell rang. I heard a beer bottle top pish in the kitchen, then Robert's footsteps going to the door. Thank goodness. I was too tired to think, let alone talk coherently.

I could hear one side of the conversation at the door. Robert's. *No, my wife isn't available for comment—yes, my mother-in-law is all right—no, we aren't planning to sue the home—No, you can't call her later—I'm sorry, you'll have to leave!*

Just as he sat next to me, the phone rang. "My turn."

"No, no. You stay put. Let me handle this." He answered the kitchen remote. *Look, there's no story here...Nothing happened...No. We're not planning to... I've got another call coming in...Yes? Look. It's over, everyone's safe. End of story.*

He rejoined me in the den, the remote ringing again in his hand. "No fucking comment!" he crabbed at the phone without answering it. Then he drained his beer and headed for the kitchen.

I followed him in. "Maybe I'll have that beer after all."

We stood staring at each other, mouths agape as the doorbell and telephone jangled and beeped in syncopated rhythm like the beginning of that Pink Floyd *Money* song.

Robert grabbed two Pacificos from the refrigerator and stuck one under his armpit while he twisted the cap off the other and handed it to me. "Let's go out back."

"Good idea." I swigged a big gulp as we slipped outside. The beer, cold and bubbly at the back of my throat, worked a simple magic on my nerves after all. The smoky smell had all but disappeared from the air and only a thin trace of brown veiled the late September sky.

Robert slid our Adirondack chairs onto the grass where we would be out of sight to anyone looking over the fence and we slipped into them. "What was it I started out to do today? I swear I can't remember."

"I think we were planning to get our lives back on track."

"Yeah. That must have been it." He took a slow pull on the long neck bottle. Outside he was calm, but inside he had to be thinking: *Ten days 'till Tennessee* and *what next?* We drank our beers quietly in the backyard until the ringing and the beeping died away. I leaned my head against the tall chair back and closed my eyes. His hand came to rest over mine on the arm of the chair. "Better?"

"Much." In spite of it all, I had managed to stay in charge, my connection to clear-eyed Evie intact. "How 'bout if I go make us something to eat?"

His hand trailed across my backside as he followed me through the kitchen and headed on to the den.

I set the phone console to answer after one ring. Alone in my kitchen, feet firmly on the floor, I braced myself against the sink, took a deep breath, and focused on the image of my mother as I'd left her, safe and sound. A little flushed, but smiling, she fiddled with a pair of military dog tags on a chain around her neck, her eyes gazing off at some vision the rest of us couldn't see.

I smiled now too as I set my grilling pan on a burner and drizzled olive oil into it. My mother, cast into the loony bin with crazy legs, an unstable mind, and her beautiful face folded like a Chinese fan, had managed to take herself on one more adventure. I pulled a pork tenderloin out of the fridge, slit the wrapper, and tonged half of it into the pan.

How could someone in twenty-four hour care still manage to control our life? How long would this go on? A pang of guilt swept over me as I pondered the answer to that question, then I heard the TV volume come up.

"Eve, you gotta see this."

"Coming!" I rushed to the den, half a tenderloin flopping in the tongs.

Robert busted up.

"What?"

"Don't point that thing at me unless you're willing to use it." His eyes sparkled with mischief as he pushed the raw tenderloin out of his face. My heart sighed free for the first time that day, as the news anchor's voice segued in.

...Ojai woman returned to 24-hour-care home by Vietnam Vet after spending the day in the river bottom...

A wide shot of Crossroads' fountain gave way to a headshot of Sheriff Mitchell Decker.

...Could have been a lot worse...

Then the shot faded to the gate. I half expected to see Betty hanging there, shaking her fist.

...the family was unavailable for comment...

"No shit," Robert said, and then, there she was, in the dining room, Vern on one side and the bum who'd found her on the other, a plate of fried chicken in front of him. Aides and fellow Crossroadies cheered in the background as Katherine helped Betty drape the dog tags back over the bum's raggedy neck. Then Betty *tootled* her fingers at the camera, chin up, her lopsided smile triumphant.

"Twenty people out looking for her all day long and she's giving a cameo on the evening news." I shook my head in disbelief.

"So," Robert said, pointing his bottle at me. "That's what I'm in for when you're fifty?"

"Fifty! I'm fifty now." I tried to smack him with the pork, but he was too quick for me. Before I could get him a good one, he swiped it from the tongs and stuck it in my ear. We play wrestled until we slid off the sofa and into uncontrollable, tear-streaking, soul-purging laughter. Spent, we lay on the floor while the TV droned on about the upcoming elections, and some pending financial debacle of corporate greed.

"Think we should eat that thing?"

"Eew, no." I wiped tears off his cheek. He was my hero.

"At least not before I cook it." Struggling to catch my breath, I wiped tears from my own cheeks and with them some of the pain I'd been feeling inside. My mother was still a person after all. I realized then how little credit I'd given her for being an individual. Her inner strength and capacity for fun and adventure were still there. Who was I to think she could only be happy if I was in charge? She had gone through an ordeal and come out laughing. And if she could laugh, so could I.

On cue, the calls came rolling in again, this time friendly voices: *Eve, was that your mom...I hope she wasn't hurt...She's quite a character.* And from my closest friend. *Now I know where you get it.*

That's what lifelong friends are for. To remind you who you are and where you came from. I was my mother's daughter—not my grandma's and not my stepmother's—my mother's. Through and through. There was baggage and shame and loss and regret, but there was also beauty and grace and laughter. And I could choose.

We finished our tenderloin with little more drama than usual. So much so that we retired early, slipping easily into each other's arms, and afterward, into easy sleep.

As it turned out, we were lucky we'd started early, because the bliss ended at three-twenty-three a.m. Sharlene had hung up by the time I roused myself, awakened first by the ringing and then sobered by her words on the machine, "...so we sent her down to the emergency."

I replayed the message as I yanked on my sweats. "Hi Eve, I just wanted you to know we sent your mom over the hospital, just to be safe. She was coughing and had a hundred and four temp so we sent her down to the emergency."

Back on the roller coaster.

I scrawled a note and left it on my pillow, grabbed my shoes and purse and ran out to the car.

The doors of the emergency room slid open with a swoosh as I arrived in the reception area, one shoe still in my hand.

"That's my daughter," my mother hollered out as they trundled her through the doors, her gnarly finger jabbing in my direction.

That's my mother.

She gave the paramedics her best glamour-girl wave as they handed her off to the emergency crew inside. I slipped on my shoe and tied it while they ensconced her in a stall in the treatment room. When at last they let me in, I had to squeeze in between her bed and a heart monitor while they tried to insert an IV.

"Ow-w-w-w! *Goddammit.*" She squirmed like a two-year-old until the nurse gave up.

"I'll come back in a few minutes," the nurse said, wagging the IV kit in our faces.

Betty patted my hand. "Tired?"

Her blue eyes shone steely and bright, her cheeks on fire. I sighed. "Not really. How're you doin'?"

She responded with a rattled cough.

The nurse came back, as promised, this time with an ear thermometer. "Just a little tap in here, Betty, then we'll take a look at your chest."

My mother scowled and pulled the bedsheet up to her shoulders. The nurse made a note in her chart, then asked me to step out of the way as she rolled the bed back out of the stall and parked it in the hallway. Betty propped herself up on one elbow like Cleopatra on her litter.

"The hall?" she asked, offended.

I moved past a cartload of thin blankets and bedsheets and took her hand. I had to agree with the patient. "You're leaving her in the hall?"

The nurse had one of those smiles that somehow turns down at the corners instead of up. "X-ray's busy right now. Might be a while."

"Be a while, *Goddammit,*" Betty said, her voice chalky and liquid at the same time. "It's freezing cold."

The nurse, who had already started to leave, looked up and then came back to us. She leaned in and whispered to me. "Didn't I see her on TV earlier tonight?"

I nodded. *My mother, the celebrity.*

"I'll try to squeeze her in next."

"Thanks, and how about one of those blankets."

"Sure. Okay." Just then, the outside doors to the emergency

room slid open. The nurse pushed a blanket into my arms and rushed away through the reception area. When I turned to Mom, she was pulling at the plastic strap on her wrist with her teeth.

By the time we got the results of the X-ray it was nearly five a.m. The night nurse had managed an IV insertion while Betty half dozed, and rolled her into a semi-private room. "The X-ray looked cloudy. We're starting an antibiotic."

"Cloudy?" *What does that mean? Rain?* I dumped my purse on the wide windowsill next to the bed, set my cell phone to buzz, and slipped it into my back pocket.

"Dr. Bartlett makes his rounds about eight, so you'll get the details then."

My mother startled awake at every noise in the hallway, then drifted back to sleep just as quickly. Her breathing rattled like a percolator sucking the last drops of brew through its innards. I snuck out to the lobby for some coffee and a magazine and settled again in the room in a garish orange chair that looked like a leftover from a fifties motel. At some point I must have dozed off because I awoke to discover someone had tucked a blanket over me in the chair, and a new nurse was checking my mother's IV. It was ten after eight. Mom snored softly, her mouth hanging slack.

I heard some rattling outside the door that turned out to be our doctor coming in. "I understand your mom had quite a day yesterday."

He held a large yellow envelope under his arm as he slipped one of the X-rays in front of a lighted frame on the wall.

"There's infection, here, and here." He pointed at rain clouds on the film. "The antibiotics will clear that up for now."

"She sounds better already." I got up and stood near the bed.

The doctor checked her chart. "Temperature's down too."

Mom snorked, batted her eyes, and came full awake.

"Hello Betty. Nice to see you," the doctor said to her in a quiet voice.

She put on her best smile for him and perked up a little, then rolled her eyes to me.

"Hi Sweetie."

I patted her free hand.

"We're going to keep you here today." The doctor looked pointedly at me over the top of his glasses. "If you can't stay, you need to arrange someone to be here, or—"

The image of Vern tied down to a hospital bed flashed in my mind.

"I'll stay."

A nurse's aide brought in a tray with a bowl of oatmeal and some juice for Mom. I slipped out the door behind the doctor. "You know, Dr. Bartlett, I have a question."

He turned back sharply, eyebrows raised at me. "Hum?"

"The pneumonia? This is the second time in six months. Can't we do something? You know, they have insurance. Lots of it. I mean, it *is* the twenty-first century—"

Dr. Bartlett closed his eyes for a moment, then looked away down the long, polished hallway, as if the answer might lay down there somewhere. Panic nibbled at my toes and worked its way up to my stomach. He steered me toward two chairs near the nurse's station and we sat.

"You know, Eve. We doctors focus on curing disease. We tend not to do a very good job with the end times."

My throat tightened. "End times? You said her temp was down. I don't understand—"

He pressed his lips together, slow blinked and breathed in deeply through his nose. "Forgive me if I haven't explained enough to you. I assumed you had already discussed this with her doctors in San Diego."

"I never met them."

"Her body is failing. On a number of levels. In her case, deterioration in her brain has compromised her ability to swallow. It's common in dementia cases. We can slow it down a little, but we can't stop it."

"How do we slow it down?"

The doctor stood. I could see that he was anxious to get away. "We can insert a tube for feeding. This will keep particles out of her lungs that tend to cause infection."

"A tube? She wouldn't stand for it. She'd fight it, I know."

He gave my shoulder a squeeze. "Pneumonia is the old woman's friend, Eve."

He turned and continued down the hall. I heard him greet his next patient brightly, his words to me still numbing my brain.

End times. Now that was an interesting, but somehow vague concept. In my grandmother's house, death was a lower case word, therefore entirely unreal because Life (with capitol ell) was real and we can't have both at the same time, can we? A young mind never questions, just believes. (And that smashed cat on the roadway? It was just taking a nap.)

But *end times*. Now that concept seems to float death into a nebulous category. End times as in *process. A process that can be slowed, but not stopped*. A sort of pre-death flirtation. But for how long? *How long…*

I don't know how long I sat like a mannequin in the hallway, an empty plastic shell, eyes painted on, seeing nothing, mind grabbing for any foothold on the slippery slope—a back arrow, a delete key, an undo button—something, because I'd seen the lifeless hulks in the rest home, curled into fetal position, living on feeding tubes and nothing else. That was not what my mother would choose and I knew it.

The cell phone buzzed in my pocket. Robert was on his way to Oxnard, bringing me a bagel and some good coffee. Bringing me out of my funk. Again. I ended the call at his goodbye and stood on wobbly legs.

While I was out of the room, my mother had patted blobs of oatmeal across her tray. She pushed one of them into her mouth now as I walked up to her bed. Chunks of oatmeal fell onto the sheet as she worked her jaw in tight, mechanical bites.

"*Ine* not done yet." She squeezed the words out between her teeth.

"I know, my sweet mama." I smoothed the hair back away from her mouth and picked up the pieces of oatmeal as they fell. "There's no hurry. Take your time."

28 Between the Cracks

Betty picked bitter blobs of something out of her teeth. Her mouth was full of them. She chewed again, but didn't like the feel. What crawled into her mouth? Her thoughts jumped around. Meat? Pieces of herself? She couldn't tell the difference. She stopped chewing and let the blobs fall out onto the sheet. "G-r-r-a-a-ah!"

She struck out at the tray, her hands scrubbing through the mess. With a mind of its own, the tray bounced up, out of control and flipped onto the floor with a tooth-rattling clatter. Betty gasped, slipped sideways, and grabbed at the air.

"What! What happens?" she asked the empty room.

"Wait, Mom, stop!"

Someone grabbed Betty's hands, pinned them back against the bed and held them tight. And there was Sweetie, her head bent over at a funny angle, her hair caught along with Betty's hand.

"Out! Get out!" Betty hollered, trying to free herself. She fought with every ounce of her strength.

"Mom, you've got to calm down. Please!"

Betty's heart raced. A ghost monster had a hold of her. She couldn't get away from it. They were trapped. *Trapped!* It held them in its grip. Betty could feel her nails digging into its skin, but it wouldn't let go. Sweetie's face twisted, her eyes squeezed shut.

"Help her!" Betty bellowed, then bit into the monster's flesh.

Sweetie cried out.

Betty struggled. At last, her hands went free. She grabbed at Sweetie's shirt.

"Wait, Mom, wait," she was saying. "You've got my hair."

Betty allowed Sweetie to pry her fingers open and untangle the strands. She strained to see beyond her daughter's face. The terrible fighting thing had gone.

She let go. At least she was still good for something. The monster was gone and they were safe. But her jaws worked hard against her teeth and her hands were still ready for a fight.

Sweetie held her in her arms, rocking, as she caught her breath. One of the aides cleaned the mess off the floor. Sweetie helped her lay back and pulled the sheets up to her chest. Betty watched the light play on the bottle suspended next to her bed.

A nurse fiddled with it. "You'll feel better in a minute, honey. Just relax."

Sweetie got up to meet a man who walked into the room. That handsome one, Betty thought as she melted more deeply into the bedcovers. She watched him from beneath half-closed lids, her jaw relaxing. He squeezed Sweetie's shoulder as he handed her a little paper sack.

Sweetie's man.

Betty closed her eyes and felt herself flatten slowly on the bed like warm honey.

Sweetie and her man look tired today. They work too hard. Busy, busy, busy. They are the reason. The reason I haven't fallen between the cracks. They treat me like I'm me when no one else does. They work and juggle stuff, and smile at me. What wonderful creatures they are when they smile at me. Who is me, anyway that they treat me that way?

Sweetie and her man talked quietly together. Betty couldn't get their words. The nurse cranked the back of her bed down. "No," she said, but the nurse ignored her and hurried out of the room.

Won't somebody look over and say my name? Am I not me still, looking out at the world?

She rolled her head toward the window. The tips of tall trees outside jostled in a breeze. She knew those trees with their pink, sickle leaves, yellow puff blossoms, and crisscross buttons. She could almost smell them. The thoughts made her feel warm inside.

Happy again.

She closed her eyes and allowed herself to play her little game, the one that helped her fill the gaps. Something she could still do all by herself ... *Thinking back. Back when Sweetie was only a glint in Jimmy's blue, blue eyes...under the apple trees...bareback ponies tied to the split-rail fence, hands sticky with the juice of half eaten fruit...when life was close up, not just out of reach.* She closed her eyes and invited the memory to fill the empty spaces in her mind.

"Betty," she hears him whisper just behind her ear, his breath teasing fine hairs at the back of her cheek. She turns her head. "Betty," he whispers again and lifts her chin to touch her lips with his...

She is breathing so deeply now she can almost pull inside herself and disappear completely.

Betty startled awake as Martina squatted in front of her. *What happened to the trees? The ponies? Her cut off shorts?*

She realized then that she was wearing the cute little shift she and Evie had picked out of a catalog. She and Evie at Crossroads. Images of the events of the day came jumbling back—the trip home from the hospital, a shower, a change of clothes—all in a fog, until now. She squeezed her eyes shut tight and pulled away from Martina, folding back into herself.

Not here. Not here again.

"It's time to wake up, Miss Betty." Martina sat next to her on the banquette, propping her into an upright position with a pillow. "The singers will be here soon."

"Singers?"

"Singers, Betty. You know, music. You'll see. Here's some juice." Martina gave her a paper cup half filled with golden liquid.

"They're going to sing for you." Martina had a way of making an ordinary thing seem special. Betty had heard people sing here before. Some of them were good. Some not so.

"We have Manhattans every day," Vern said, touching the arm of one of the aides handing out juice cups on a tray. He sat across from Betty in the alcove, in his same old shirt, eating ice cream from a paper cup with a little wooden paddle.

Betty took a tentative sip of the juice and tipped her head back. "S'apple juice," she said in a low grumble, and drank it down, suddenly very thirsty. Apple juice with a hint of sour.

"Thank you," she said to Martina, handing her the cup. It wasn't Martina's fault.

Paper and plastic and wood and apple juice. That's what they had come to.

Vern patted the seat next to him, but Betty didn't feel like moving. She let her hands rest limp on her thighs, palms up, like the little jade Buddha statue on her dresser. She closed her eyes. *Go back,* she told herself. *Back into the dream…*She waited expectantly, but nothing came, nothing at all.

And then a flooding of warmth swept through her stiffened limbs. Her awareness expanded. Eyes still closed, she took in the sounds of chairs moving in the dining room. She heard the door from the courtyard thump, clack, and swish open, and then she heard her, at first far away and then closer.

Shoo-shoo, shoo-shoo,
Shoo-shoo, shoo-shoo.

Betty opened her eyes and there she was standing in front of her. Shoo-Shoo touched her cheek and smiled, and dropped a wadded Chrysanthemum blossom in one of her hands. Its pale yellow petals fell into her lap and spilled over onto the floor like tears.

Betty and Shoo-Shoo sat next to each other holding hands as the musicians set up their equipment and the helpers moved more chairs into the living room. Betty felt better than she could remember feeling in a long time. In fact, by the time the band had started their music, she felt almost perky. What was that song they were playing? She knew that one…

> *Gonna take a sentimental journey,*
> *Going to set my heart at ease…*

She tapped her fingers on her knees and let her head nod to the beat.

> *Gonna make a sentimental journey,*

216

To renew old memories.

My goodness that man singing was tall. Betty dropped Shoo-Shoo's hand and scooted to the edge of her seat. She felt light, almost giddy as they stepped up the tempo and went into the next number.

> *You make me feel so young,*
> *You make me feel like spring has sprung...*

Betty stood. She couldn't help herself. The music got into her hips and arms and everything started to move like magic.

> *I want to go and bounce the moon,*
> *Just like a toy balloon.*

She pinched the front of her shift at each side and swished it back and forth, stepping toward the tall singer with each downbeat.

The man with the white hair and his chubby friend were up now, gyrating with Martina. Betty bopped forward, the words bouncing in her head.

> *...you and I, just like a couple of tots...*

She was close to him now. She had to crick her neck back just to look at him. He smiled a smile full of white teeth and started another song.

> *I've got the world on a string,*
> *Sitting on a rainbow, Got the string around my finger...*

He gestured a circle with his finger as he sang on.

Ohhh. She felt so-o-o warm. She swished her shift to the beat. She hadn't felt these feelings since, since—she didn't know since when but—it felt like just the two of them, alone.

"Ohhh," she sighed and swished her shift up over her waist and let her hips swing out.

"Betty!" Martina called out.

> *What a world, what a life—I'm in love.*

Betty loved the sound of his voice, his eyes, the way his arms reached out to her. She wanted him to touch her, hold her, fill her. She dropped the shift and pressed forward, ignoring Martina's calls.

"In love," she echoed, and before she could stop herself, she reached out, slipped her hand up between his legs, and grabbed something warm.

The music stuttered to a stop. The singer pulled away and covered his smile, eyebrows raised.

Martina grabbed Betty around the waist and gently turned her back to her seat. "Sorry, Miss Betty, you have to sit down now."

Betty smiled inside and out. "I *like* that."

"Sleeping," she heard someone say over the stillness. "Why is she sleeping at two in the afternoon?" Now that sounded like Evie. Betty wanted to open her eyes, see her daughter, but she didn't feel like moving. She was floating, peaceful, serene. Didn't care that she drooled on the pillow.

"I'm sorry, Evie." She heard Martina say. "I didn't know you were coming. We, ah, had to adjust her meds."

Betty could feel Evie's breath close to her ear now. "You rest. I'll be back tomorrow, Mom."

She smiled inside. Evie was a good girl. Betty breathed deeply and let herself slip back into the song words...

> *...got the world on a string,*
> *I can make the rain go...*

29 Angel's Flight

I pushed through the dining room doors with my back and swung around, the pink Betty Bag full of goodies in the seat of her wheelchair. I first glanced over where Vern usually sat and saw that he wasn't out among the residents yet, and then I heard her. "Dog *man!*" she hollered from across the room, waving her arms.

Martina gave me a funny look as I approached. "Dog man?"

"She wants to go to the beach, don't you, Mom?" Betty ignored both of us, her eyes now fixed on the Betty Bag. As I rolled the chair up to her knees, she leaned over to paw through it. I was happy to see her energetic and focused. There was color on her cheeks and a little glint in her eye, a fair notch up from the last time I'd seen her awake, oatmeal stuck to her chin. She had really lost it that day, I had teeth marks on my arm to prove it.

She may have slipped to a new plateau that day, but from where I stood, it looked very wide and inviting. Anyway, I had no choice but to step out onto it.

First to spill out of her hands was the straw-colored scrapbook I'd put together from bits and pieces I'd recovered from her things and from my own. Some of the photos I knew well. Others I'd never seen. I'd arranged it in chronological order, beginning with pictures of my mother as a child, her parents, her brother and sister, and finally my father and me.

I rescued the binder in half fall and resettled it into her lap.

One of the items fell out onto the floor. A dog-eared photo of my maternal grandmother in a knee-length bathing suit, a tight hat pulled down over her ears, the twin rails of the Long Beach roller coaster in the background.

Martina picked it up. "Who's this, Miss Betty?"

I sat down next to my mother on the banquette, hoping the scrapbook would make her day. When Martina gave her the picture, she pruned her lips and worked them up and down, turning it this way and that. Finally, she flipped it back onto the floor with a scowl. "Tch."

Martina bit her bottom lip.

"Her mother," I said and shrugged my shoulders. "Maybe she doesn't remember."

Martina smiled and shook her head. "*Orrrr* maybe, she no like *herrr*," she said, reverting to her clipped English. Betty glanced up at Martina. "Psh-s-s-h!"

An alarm bell went off at the central board. Martina scooted the wheelchair out of the aisle. "I have to go," she said, and trotted away toward the patios.

Betty refocused her attention on the scrapbook and worked at the corners until I helped her turn the page. Clumsily, she flitted her fingers over the images, clicking her tongue. She stopped on a picture of her father sitting aboard a tractor hooked up to a large pine log with a chain. Someone had scrawled the date across the back of the photo, 1932. She looked over at me and tapped the photo, then closed her eyes and patted her neck just under the dip between her collar bones. I had one just like it. I waited a moment, not sure if I should interrupt her, then slipped my hand across her lap and turned the page again. "Shall we look at some more?"

"Yes-s-s-s," she whispered, her eyes coated in a bright sheen. On the next page, I had arranged some pictures of her and her dad, and her and her sister around two memorial pamphlets, one for each. Her dad had gone at fifty, her sister at twenty-five. She hesitated a moment over the flowered pamphlets announcing the events of two Episcopalian services, that I realized for the first time were dated within a few months of each other.

Episcopalian. We'd never talked about religion, except to acknowledge that my grandma was in charge of my indoctrination. As far as I knew, she and Vern religiously attended the church of the eighteen holes every Sunday without fail, and that was it.

Betty tapped the face of her baby sister and smiled.

"Angels," she said, finishing in a whisper. She hesitated another moment, then slipped her fingers under the page and turned it on her own.

On the next page, I realized, I'd entertained a selfish fantasy. There must be hundreds of pictures of Betty and Vern, enough to fill three more albums full. Happy pages, rich with wonderful memories of a successful couple. But this page I reserved to indulge myself. I'd dedicated it to my parents, Betty and Jimmy. The two of them riding bareback in an apple orchard, who knew where, the two of them picking apples from high in the tree while standing on a split-rail fence. I'd included locks of their hair I'd found, braided together and tied with a shriveled satin bow. And in the center of the page, a picture of her reclining on a plaid blanket, her hand resting on her flat stomach.

I reached my hand out to turn the page, a little embarrassed. How thoughtless of me, how cruel. But as I slipped my fingers under the corner, my mother stopped me. She flitted her hands over the pictures one at a time, coming to rest on the one of herself looking into the camera through the eyes of a woman in love with life. Betty lifted her fingertips to her lips and kissed them, then tapped them the her stomach in the photo.

"That's my Sweetie," she whispered. She leaned her head into mine, her soft hair feathered against my forehead. "My secret Sweetie."

At that moment, in that picture, my mother had a secret and hadn't told a soul. At that moment, in that picture, we were the closest we had ever been. Until now. Right now. I had waited a lifetime to feel it and there it was, seared into my heart.

I slipped my fingers over hers and she laced her fingers through mine and held them tight. My chest expanded, taking my words away.

Just then Martina ambled up and leaned over my shoulder. "Mr. Vern just fell down. *Heet's* not bad, just a *leettle* bump, but if you two are going out, maybe you should go now, before we bring *heem* into the clinic."

Betty looked up as if waking from a dream.

"Want to go for a little drive?" I gently closed the book. "We can look at this again later."

Betty waved her arms in the air, feeling the sea breeze rush between her fingers. The crashing water and the calling birds and the kids screaming and running in front of them blotted out the *zhumm zhumm* that had started up again in her head. She had come to recognize the annoying pulse as the last thing that happened before something got lost. But today, she felt like singing. If she could just remember the words.

Evie had parked them near the bend in the trail where the river runs into the ocean. This was one of their favorite places. There was always something to look at. Evie sat beside her on a low rock and took a book out of her bag.

Betty watched seagulls bobbing in the river current, through a little narrows, and out into the salt water. One in particular had a wing that jutted up in the back like a broken tail. He was broken, like her, and like her, still here. Still riding the river, like the others, *bobbity bop.* They reminded her of a game at the carnival, *bobbity bop, bobbity bop, ding!*

"Oh, no."

"What Mom?" Sweetie looked up from her book.

Here came the broken one again, *bobbity bop, bobbity bop.*

Betty scooted to the front of her chair and let Sweetie help her up.

"Broken, see!" she said, pointing to the gulls bouncing in the river jetty. "She's backwards."

She came to the end of the current, flew up, floating backwards, back to the beginning again. Sweetie looked where she pointed, following the bird along.

"Oh, my gosh! You're right. They're riding the current just for fun."

Betty sat down, transfixed by the sight. Each bird in turn rode through the narrows, pitching and bumping, for the sheer joy of it, then took flight like little angels, back to the beginning. Each time, the broken one, taking her turn.

"She's dancin' up river," Sweetie said, and Betty giggled at the thought.

She could have watched for hours, but the *zhumm zhumm* had started up again. She covered her ears with her hands. "Better get out."

"Yep. I'm getting cold too. Let's get you back home."

30 Gamma Normids

I had my first brush with mortality in the summer of 1957. A boy my age fell from a brick wall on the dry side of the dam that held back Lodi Lake, crushing his skull and the hopes and dreams of his parents. This in itself did not impress me. Ten-year-olds don't think about their parents' hopes and dreams. Instead they occupy a state of egocentric bliss, in which the real world is laced with fantasies and secret roles, near-life experiences shared between best friends. What I remember was the electric arc that passed between my cousin and me when we heard the news. We had been there that day. It could just as well have been one of us.

Most summers I spent in Lodi, whiling away the dry, hot days with my cousins while Aunt Eileen and Uncle Herb worked at the unemployment office. My cousin Nicky was six months older than I. We'd lived next door to each other from the time we were in kindergarten until the fifth grade. We had the same teachers, the same friends, and the same tolerance level for each other's shenanigans. The minute I got home from school, I'd change out of my dress and into an outing flannel shirt and corduroy pants, just like Nicky. We'd conspire on the front porch, heads together—how we would pick the tomato worms from the leaves and burn them in a paper sack—how we would gather the neighbors' evening newspaper before the dads got home and make paper maché—how we would dig a foxhole in the backyard and fight off the Japs—and how we'd escape by running the tops of the brick walls that honeycombed between our little tract houses. (How our fannies would burn when my uncle got through with us if we got caught.)

I felt my Siamese twin had been ripped away when the family was transferred to Lodi, but I'm sure my grandma was relieved. "What do you think your mama would say if she saw that dirt under your fingernails?"

I didn't know, or care. My mama was the furthest thing from my mind when I was out playing with Nicky.

Lodi was eight hours up the interstate, as the old Pontiac drones. The summer never started for me until I packed my suitcase for Lodi and we topped the first hill out of LA over the pass they called the *Grapevine*. From the moment my grandparents dropped me off, Nicky and I were rejoined at the hip. I would have followed him anywhere.

Raised in the knowledge that we were, in fact, spiritual beings incapable of sin, sickness, or death, we put ourselves out there, fearless conquerors of the material world. We snuck out at midnight and rode our bikes to stick our arms into holes in the crumbling corners of crypts in the Lodi Cemetery to see what was inside. We crawled through wet trenches in Tokay vineyards in the early morning, the huge leaves dripping dew on our backs, while the farmers shot rock-salt over our heads. We waded, Indians escaping capture, waist deep in the slow-moving, poison-oak edged waters of the Mokolumne River which emptied from the swimming hole below the dam at Lodi Municipal Lake, and we "tight-roped" from the three-foot base of the dam to its thirty-foot spillway, on the cinder-block wall, arms out, tipping, balancing.

"It's just like in the backyard, Evie," I remember him yelling ahead to me, "only higher. Don't look back, and don't look down." But I was too scared. About ten feet from the wooden spillway, I got down and straddled, scooting the rest of the way, a ten-year-old butt's width at a time.

The reward was feeling the weight of the water press our bodies against the spillway and watching it sheet like liquid glass over our shoulders as we looked down. We shinnied all the way across, escaping *our enemies* in the nick of time.

The punishment came the next day. We were grounded for breaking down my aunt's camellia bushes in front of Nicky's bedroom window. He was sprawled in agony on the family room floor, painted waist down with Calamine lotion and losing miserably a fifth game of Chinese checkers when the phone call came.

"See! That's why you guys aren't allowed at the lake without us!" Aunt Eileen yelled, punctuating each word with a stab of the phone receiver.

Nicky's chin quivered, something I'd rarely seen. "I'm sorry, Mama."

I think he really was.

My mother was in Japan, I thought. Or China? How long would it take to find her, if something happened to me? Would anybody try to find her?

It doesn't surprise me that no one knows where my cousin Nick is today. If his New York-Italian ex-wife and mother of his three children can't find him, I figure nobody can.

The second time I got the sense of my mortal self being governed by certain irrefutable material laws was the spring of 1969. Life came knocking in a little fist, (foot? elbow?) through my belly and then wrenching my back, two and half months too soon.

I had shed my hip huggers for loose fitting dresses only recently. It was great at first, feeling the little one grow inside me, even though my stomach couldn't hold anything but Fudgesicles. But suddenly here it was, a baby, ready to come out. That wasn't right, was it? It was too early, too small, and too big all at the same time.

The process had started and I didn't know how it went. I drove myself to the hospital. They put me in a room all by myself. No one to coach me through, share a story, hold my hand. My mind first skipped a generation, automatically, reaching back to my mentor, my grandmother. Hadn't she done this five times and lived? Okay, and yes, my own mother, obviously, beautiful pinup girl, apparently survived it without so much as smeared mascara or a hair out of place. But it just didn't feel possible. Something must be wrong because it just…didn't…feel…possible! The force pushing against my pelvis was greater than any power I had ever felt before. And much, much bigger than any part of my natural anatomy could resist. I was about to make my contribution to the next wave of humanity, physical limitations notwithstanding. I wanted to push, they told me to wait—wait—*wait!*

My mind lost itself into the distinct sensation that I was straining at the bottom row of a wide pyramid of clothespin dolls, each ejecting another clothespin, and another, and another, one on top of the other, all the way back to Eve. All screaming. I had seen it in a painting somewhere—and now I was on the bottom row with all of female humanity pushing down on top of me.

And suddenly there was only one scream. The voice of my small, way-too-early son. A red-faced, screaming angel come down to earth through the most amazing and incomprehensible route. Suddenly I had sympathy for my mother, no matter what mistakes she had made along the way. And, once again, I wished she was there with me.

The third time—

The third time is a charm they say, whoever *they* are. And I suppose, they're right. The third time is when you finally get it. That accidents can happen for no reason at all, that death is as close as the back side of our embossed dream of life, that there are things not meant to be undone, that we cannot live inside another's skin.

The third time I experienced a brush with mortality, it was less like a brush and more like an invitation. I was at my mother's bedside, on the sixth day of her hospice care. I had read the manual the hospice volunteer had given me and there she was, my mother, manifesting all the signs.

End times, with a capitol E.

That period before death when everyone knows there is no going back. Shallow breathing, blue feet and hands, cool cheeks…

I never expected on the days following my mother's passing that I would want to relive the events over and over. That I would welcome the memory back in to my heart each time it returned. But welcome it I did, as if by reliving it over and over, she wasn't really gone. Not yet. Not forever.

&

When the phone call came at three a.m. on March fifth I was blissfully asleep curled into Robert's back. With my mother at Crossroads, our lives had segued into a more natural routine. Our business had taken off and with Mom settled, we could now jet away secure in the knowledge that Sharlene and Katherine and Martina and whomever else it took would make sure my mother did not escape, or lay lonely and afraid in her room, or suffer any spike in temperature without someone taking action. I could visit her any time, knowing she would be there, waiting with a "Hi Sweetie," even if she couldn't utter any other words.

But that morning, despite my comfort, spooned against a warm back, I knew, before the second ring of the phone, that this was *the* call.

The call in the middle of night that everyone is secretly expecting and no one wants to get. Another round of pneumonia had filled her lungs, shot her temperature over the top, and sent her precariously to the brink.

After the incident with the homeless man, Betty had managed a new life within the confines of Crossroads. She had become everyone's sweetheart, the movie star of the afternoon social hour. She had started up a "romance" with the old pilot who informed me that they were to be married in the spring. Vern still invited her to breakfast at the captain's table and she still rebuffed him every time.

But after a midnight incident that ended with Betty and her elderly pilot stark naked in the courtyard and, I'm told, had set off every alarm in the place, Betty had slipped to a new plateau. She freaked out when I took her in the car, reacting to even the slightest change of speed.

She still hollered "That's my daughter," each time I arrived to visit, but after that, not much in the way of words. It was common for us to start by looking at the photo albums I brought and end with her snoozing against my shoulder.

And then she slipped into anger, refused to look at me,

fought anyone who tried to feed her. I suppose it was the only power she had left. She did not voice it, could not find her own words, but I knew in my heart that my mother would not want this for herself. Nor would anyone, if they could choose. I secretly prayed to that old trickster God to steal her away in the night.

I waited, watching the emergency room door until the ambulance pulled silently into view. She lifted her hand in acknowledgement of my presence as they gurneyed her in.

Ignoring the flurry of activity around her—nurses poking at her ears to take her temperature, pumping a blood pressure cuff on her arm—my mother just stared at her feet. No jokes, no fury. Just calm as you please, waiting for them to leave her alone.

Dr. Bartlett, who was coincidentally on duty that night, raised his brows at me from the end of her bed. The conversation we'd had the last time we met still burned in my heart. I knew what he was going to say. Politely he addressed his patient, but I knew his words were for me.

"We can insert a feeding tube for you Betty. That way you get the nourishment you need and reduce the risk of infection." He gripped the end of the bed. "It has to stay there, Betty. Do you understand? You can't take it out yourself."

My mother gazed at him a moment, her cheeks blushed with fever, her eyes flat blue stones, and then she turned her face away.

I slipped my hand into hers. "What are you thinking, Mama?"

When she turned back, her eyes burned with the same intensity as her cheeks.

"Angels," she said, the words sending her into a coughing spell. When it was over, she squeezed my hand with all her might. "Angels."

The next day I moved her to Hospice care.

We spent our last days together knowing she wanted to go. Each morning she called out "Hi Sweetie," when I came in, as if she had waited up all night, and let me pull her up in bed and straighten her pillows. Each morning I played her music, Frank

Sinatra and Tony Bennett. I massaged her legs with lavender scented oils, washed her face with rosewater. I asked if there was anything else I could get her.

"Rose," she whispered, patting her breast. Clearing her throat, she said it again, "Rose," and I understood and moved her rosebush from the dresser across the room to the table next to her bed. I pinched a pink bud from one of the branches and laid in on the pillow next to her head.

On Tuesday morning, March tenth, eleven days before her seventy second birthday, and eighteen months since I'd rescued her from the hospital in San Diego, she greeted me with a cheery "Hi Sweetie," and a beautiful, relaxed smile. I straightened her covers and oiled her legs as I had done for the last five days, this time finding to my surprise (and an almost guilty feeling of relief), that her feet had turned a translucent, alabaster blue.

When the hospice nurse made her rounds, she flicked her gaze to mine as she noted the same thing. Because I had not allowed the feeding tube, my mother's body had slipped to the last plateau. My heart squeezed itself into a tiny fist of guilt. But my mother smiled at me.

❧

Betty felt the warmth of Evie's cheek upon hers like the last glow of a sunset in late summer. The visions came now, clearer than she had seen in a long, long time. There was the golf course at Pismo, and then the fantail of a great ocean liner at Glacier Bay.

She was cold.

The visions came faster, rushing by like movies played on a screen somewhere in her head. There were geishas laughing and drinking sake, there was Vern stepping up to meet her at the back of a giant pipe machine. There was Jimmy, with his irresistible smile, bare-chested, his thumb hooked in his Levi's pocket, his foot on the running board of his old Terraplane, and that naughty bulge behind his zipper.

"I'm right here, I'm right here," someone was saying, but the visions rolled on. She stood at the front window of her mother's clapboard house in Oregon, her hand resting on the rise of her big, pregnant belly. Something moved inside her, bumped at her fingertips. Outside the window, a spotted fawn drank from a horse trough next to a split-rail fence, then looked up and met her gaze before it bounded away to join its mother in the pines.

Betty tipped her face toward the warm sun until the window dissolved into clean, fresh air. It pulled her along like a sigh. Thin and thready in the fragrant light, she drifted over the trees and the visions dissolved into heat, wicked as sex, warm as sake, and fragrant as a rose.

She felt as though she could fly forever, but something pulled her back.

"I'm right here," the voice whispered.

Betty opened her eyes.

❧

"Sweetie," my mother said. "I luff you, Sweetie."

She looked at me for a moment, then her gaze shifted upward and her breathing fell into a soft, measured cadence, like scales issuing from a flute.

I had dreaded this moment all week long, maybe longer if I were honest, but now that it had come, it wasn't like I'd imagined. I pressed my cheek against hers. Her breath was sweet, like Mocha Polka lipstick on a crinkled hanky.

"I love you too, Mama. I'm right here with you." We moved closer. Closer to the light. I could almost see it, expanding, gentle, serene. Her breathing slowed, and then it was only me breathing.

The sadness lasted only a moment before magical thinking kicked in. She hadn't left at all. She was hovering somewhere off my shoulder, whispering in my ear, words clear and distinct.

Let's get out of here.

I slipped her twisted hand from mine and lay it on her breast.

Someone tapped my shoulder. I turned, expecting to see my mother's face with a whole smile and a bright eye and eyebrows perfectly drawn. Instead, it was Martina. Her cheek bones pink, her eyes shiny with tears. "Do you want to be alone for a while?"

I turned for a last look. This wasn't the mother I wanted to remember. With fingertips steadier than I felt, I eased her eyelids gently closed.

Good. Now that's enough, Sweetie. We're finished here.

I looked up at the ceiling, fully prepared to see my mother's face.

"No." I rested my hand on Martina's forearm a moment, as much to thank her for being there as to steady my liquid knees. "I think Betty's ready for us to get out of here."

They don't tell you how you relive it, again and again. Welcome it, even, like the memory of the death itself is your life preserver pulling you from the brink back to the living. The soft cheek, the sweet fragrance, the open door, the white light—the soft cheek, the sweet fragrance, the open door, the white light—as long as I could embrace those moments she would still be with me.

It wasn't until I stood before her jewelry armoire holding her ashes in a plastic box that I felt the empty space where my mother used to be.

Until that moment, I'd allowed myself to believe she was nearby, somewhere, just over my shoulder, riding down the bike trail squealing with delight or bumping along the freshwater current out of the river mouth at the Point. I had allowed myself to believe that whether it was my mother close by, encouraging me, or whether it was me encouraging me, pretending to be my mother, I was still encouraged, buoyed up on an expanding bubble of non-belief. *Time will make it better* those around me whispered. I doubted there would be enough of it.

All I knew was that my mother had left me.

Again.

I heard Robert's footsteps coming down the hall like an echo in a dream, and then he was standing beside me. "You going to stay in here all evening?"

I held the box to my chest, unwilling to put it down.

"You know, the Gamma Normids will be visible tonight."

"Gamma Normids?"

Robert circled his arms around my shoulders from behind the way he always did. "Meteor shower. Won't be too bright from here, but I thought we'd drive up to Rose Valley and park up on the ridge."

"Sounds nice. Just give me a couple of minutes."

Robert slipped away silently and let me be.

The box of ashes grew heavier the longer I held on to it, crushing my spirit, challenging my beliefs, pulling me off balance. I could believe that she was free, but I could not believe that she was gone. On one side of the scale were the ashes. On the other, a lifetime lived. And there I stood, fixed like a statue in front of the armoire, afraid to take my first breath in the reality.

At last, my thoughts quieted somewhere near a balance point, clear-eyed Evie in charge. At last, and without any particular plan, my arms began to move.

I slid open the third drawer down.

I took the photo album out of the drawer and put it on the bed.

I opened the folded Tatsumura silk inside the drawer.

I placed the box inside the silk, inside the drawer.

I folded the silk over the box, first one side, and then the other.

I slid the drawer closed.

I breathed.

Epilogue

The year and a half since my mother died weighs heavy on our hearts. The loss of Robert's father on September 4th and Vern on September 5th of the same year was somehow overshadowed by the thousands lost on September Eleventh.

We keep our remembrance—for all of them—in March, on the top of Nordhoff Ridge. Holding hands we lie on a plaid car blanket as the stars appear one by one, waiting for the Gamma Normids.

I scoot closer to Robert, and think about the blue birds in our backyard, and the way my mother's ashes curled around Vern's when we spread them behind a lazy catamaran in Santa Barbara harbor.

The first of the meteors streaks across the sky.

Robert leans in, his breath warm feathers against my ear. "There she goes," he says and pulls me tight against him.

As we lie quiet in the night, wave after wave of heavenly bodies burn themselves out in the atmosphere, angels streaking away from Earth on their way to stardust.

An owl hoots into the silence and, barely audible, its mate answers. I squeeze Robert's hand as the sound of wings beat the air over our heads and softly fades away.

❧

I hope The Goddess of Undo touched you in some way. I would love it if you would find it on Amazon or Goodreads and leave an honest review..

Losing a loved one is never easy; losing them to dementia can be excruciatingly painful. But "the long goodbye" does give us an opportunity to dig deep into what it means to be human and find ways to be generous and kind, both with the person slowly losing touch with reality, and with ourselves.

If you or someone you love is experiencing the disruptive affects of dementia, you may want to contact a mental health care provider, or reach out to www.act.alz.org to find a source for help in your community.

ABOUT THE AUTHOR

Kat Drennan is an alumni of the Squaw Valley Community of Writer's, where this novel first took shape. She has been a member of Romance Writers of America, served as secretary of the Contemporary Romance Writers of America. In addition to literary fiction, she also writes romantic suspense, historical time travel, and epic fantasy fiction.

She lives in Ojai, California with her husband, a sweet dog, and two rowdy cats.

More Books by Kat Drennan

A Classic Car Romance - Romantic Suspense
Book One - Mint Condition
Book Two - One of a Kind
Book Three – Hotrod Lincoln
Book Four – Five Window Pickup Coming Soon

Love on the Faultline Collection
Book 1 in Love on the Faultline Series: Borrego Moon
Love on the Faultline Historical:
Lies In White Satin
Love on the Faultline Standalone novel:
High Tide

Serpent's Coil Historical Time-Travel
The Cloisonné Brooch
Lesidi's Coin
The Serpent's Coil

Speculative Women's Fiction - Fantasy
MONARCH – FIRST MIGRATION

Award-Winning Women's Fiction
The Goddess of Undo